"I'm only her
bottoms."

D1040308

"How about we make a bet?" Doug backed her up against the credenza, stopping only when his body was pressed completely to hers. He moved one hand to her waist, slipping it beneath her crop top.

"What sort of bet?" Kinsey couldn't think. His hand cupped her rib cage, sliding upward until the heel of his palm brushed the full curve of her breast.

"This weekend's football game." He wedged her legs apart with one knee. "The Texans win, I keep your bottoms. They lose, you model them for me."

"How fair is any of that?" she asked, then gasped when he touched her.

"I like winning." His hand made quick work with the hooks of her bra. "And getting my way."

"So I can tell."

Doug growled and ground his body against her until she whimpered. "Why the hell are you wearing pants?"

"I like pants." She moaned.

"Learn to like dresses."

Blaze™

Dear Reader,

A favorite story theme of mine is best friends who fall in love. We've all seen these couples in real life and in television, but reading about them in books gives us a deeper look into their thoughts as the magic happens.

What's a girl to do when her decision to pursue a man comes too late—after he announces that he's packing up and moving on? Why, she plays *Wicked Games,* of course! When Kinsey Gray and Doug Storey finally realize that the magic is greater than their determination to keep things simple, that's when the fun begins. After all, personal complications and seemingly impossible odds are no match for love that is meant to be.

(And for those of you who've written to ask about the couple on the veranda in *Bound To Happen?* Here's the book that reveals all!)

In January look for the final book in my gIRL-gEAR series— *Indiscreet*—in which outspoken Annabel "Poe" Lee meets her match in a hero who deserves every bit of grief she gives him!

Enjoy, and let the games begin!

Alison Kent

P.S. Don't forget to visit www.girl-gear.com for the latest on the series, and then stop by to see me at www.alisonkent.com for excerpts and contests and all sorts of fun.

Books by Alison Kent

HARLEQUIN BLAZE
24—ALL TIED UP*
32—NO STRINGS ATTACHED*
40—BOUND TO HAPPEN*
68—THE SWEETEST TABOO**
99—STRIPTEASE*

*www.girl-gear...
**Men To Do!

WICKED GAMES

Alison Kent

HARLEQUIN®

TORONTO • NEW YORK • LONDON
AMSTERDAM • PARIS • SYDNEY • HAMBURG
STOCKHOLM • ATHENS • TOKYO • MILAN • MADRID
PRAGUE • WARSAW • BUDAPEST • AUCKLAND

ISBN 0-373-79111-9

WICKED GAMES

I owe a huge debt of gratitude to Mauri Stott
for stepping in at the last minute to rescue me from myself,
to Tamara Collins for helping me bring Izzy and Baron to life,
and to Jan Freed for making me see what I couldn't.

Also, a belated thank-you to Rob for the technical assistance
regarding Webcams and capture software.
In fact, a big shout-out to the entire ninth floor
for putting up with my writing flurries
and my lack of participation in waffle making.

gIRL-gEAR
urban fashions for gIRLS who gET it!

SYDNEY FORD
Chief Executive Officer

CHLOE ZUNIGA
Executive Coordinator
gUIDANCE gIRL

MACY WEBB
Content Editor
www.gIRL-gEAR.com

LAUREN NEVILLE
Design Editor
www.gIRL-gEAR.com

ANNABEL "POE" LEE
Vice President

gRAFFITI gIRL   gADGET gIRL
the cosmetics line   the accessories line

MELANIE CRAINE
Vice President

gIZMO gIRL   gOODY gIRL
the technology line   the gifts line

KINSEY GRAY
Vice President

gROWL gIRL   gO gIRL
the party wear   the active wear

The gIRLS behind gIRL-gEAR
by Samantha Venus for *Urban Attitude Magazine*

Welcome back, loyal readers, to another deliciously dishy and voyeuristic peep into the world of gIRL-gEAR…a place where the women have brains and the men don't stand a chance.

This month we catch up with two of our long-time bachelorettes whom we last saw on that luscious island vacation off the coast of Belize. And our number one bachelorette of the month is none other than that Scandinavian beauty, Kinsey Gray.

Those of you male readers who might like to get to know Kinsey better will have a chance later this month. *Urban Attitude* is pleased as punch to bring you the scoopage on the Halloween night bachelorette auction.

During said auction, Kinsey will be put on the block and made available to the man among you whose pockets run deepest. Get out those checkbooks! Don't be cheap! The cause—and Miss Gray—are worth every penny.

Until next time, this is Samantha Venus for *Urban Attitude Magazine*. Ta-ta for now!

1

"DID YOU HEAR THAT Doug Storey is moving to Colorado?"

Holding a forkful of spring greens halfway between her plate and her mouth, Kinsey Gray stared across the gIRL-gEAR conference room table at one of her lunch dates and business partners, Lauren Neville.

Doug? Moving to Colorado? Impossible. Unbelievable. "Run that one by me again?"

Lauren nodded, cutting off a chunk of spinach-and-feta cheese pizza and stabbing it with her fork. "Anton told me last month. Doug got an offer from a firm in Denver. An offer so amazing that he's considering selling his half of Neville and Storey."

"Selling out to Anton?" A curious frown creasing her brow, Annabel "Poe" Lee, the newest gIRL-gEAR partner, squeezed a lemon wedge into her steaming cup of tea.

Lauren shook her head, took a sip of her soda before answering. "No. One of the junior execs wants to buy into the firm. Nothing's been settled."

Maybe not in the world of the architectural firm Doug owned along with Anton Neville, but one thing had certainly been *un*settled—Kinsey's stomach.

Slowly, she lowered her fork to her plate and twisted her fingers into the linen napkin on her lap.

The thought of parting with even a pittance of her

stake in gIRL-gEAR, the fashion empire she and her five girlfriends from college had launched the year after graduation, was absolutely unfathomable. Equally unfathomable was the idea of Doug selling his half of the company he'd been a part of building from the ground up.

But the thing she had the most trouble understanding was how he could even think of leaving her when she was still undecided about her feelings for him.

What did that song say about not knowing what you've got till it's gone? Something like that, anyway. She took a deep breath and looked back at Lauren. "When is he leaving?"

Lauren shrugged, sawing again at her pizza. "The date's still up in the air. Nothing's been finalized. I thought he might've already said something to you."

"No, he hasn't." And why hadn't he? *Why hadn't he?* The dog! Friends shared the goings-on in their lives. Especially friends with the history she and Doug had. In fact, if their history wasn't so…scandalous and her feelings for him so personal, she'd think of him as family. He was that much a part of her life.

Still, Kinsey was not going to panic yet. "And, anyway. If nothing's been finalized, then you should've said that Doug *might* be moving to Colorado."

"No," Lauren answered, shaking her head. "He's definitely going. The timing and whether or not he sells his share of the firm are the only things not yet decided."

Now Kinsey was going to panic.

"He's flying back from Denver today, in fact, and flies out again on Monday." Lauren took another sip of soda, then transferred another slice of pizza from the raised serving pan in the center of the table to her now empty plate.

She dived right back in. "But I can guarantee you the man will be in the office all weekend long. One day his work habits will be part of a case study on burnout, I swear."

Watching Lauren attack her food, gIRL-gEAR CEO Sydney Ford frowned. "Uh, Lauren? You're not eating for two, are you?"

Lauren rolled her eyes, but barely looked up from her plate to do so. "Ha. No. I'm not pregnant. I'm starving. Anton and I argued over bedroom furniture until the store closed at ten. I wasn't in any mood to eat when we got home, so I went straight to bed."

"And this morning?" Sydney blotted her lips with her white linen napkin. "Don't tell me you were still arguing at breakfast."

"Actually, no. We were making up." Lauren didn't even stop eating to blush. "I hardly had time to get to work, much less eat."

"I think I'm going to be sick," Kinsey said. Her stomach rolled; her face felt clammy, as did the palms of her hands. This true love stuff was disgusting.

And now Doug was leaving Houston for parts unknown. Okay. For Denver.

Arching one dark brow, Poe studied Kinsey's plate. "You don't like your salad?"

"I don't think it's her salad." Sydney ran a finger around the rim of her iced tea glass, a far too intuitive smile lighting up her face. "I think it's Lauren's news."

"What?" Lauren finally stopped eating long enough to glower at her tablemates. "My fighting and making up with Anton is sickening?"

It was, but that was the least of Kinsey's trouble.

She glanced from Lauren to Sydney to Poe, all the while feeling as if she'd left her body and was looking down at herself and the other three gIRL-gEAR partners. The four of them sat around one end of the conference room table.

The three remaining original partners—Poe having joined the firm only last year—had taken the afternoon off to spend a long Columbus Day weekend with their respective significant others.

Macy Webb and Leo Redding were busy moving the rest of her furniture out of the loft she'd once shared with Lauren in preparation for Poe to move in, while Chloe Zuniga and Eric Haydon were off for a weekend trip with Melanie Craine and Jacob Faulkner.

Kinsey almost needed a scorecard, so much had happened this last year: Sydney, Macy, Chloe and Mel finding their soul mates. Lauren finally marrying hers. Poe coming into the company as a full partner, taking over Chloe's product lines, while she and Rennie Faulkner, Jacob's sister and soon to be Melanie's sister-in-law, launched the gUIDANCE gIRL mentoring program.

And what had Kinsey done? Waste the sixteen months since last year's trip to an island paradise—a vacation during which she'd gotten to know Doug Storey intimately—twiddling her thumbs.

She and Doug had dated off and on. Nothing serious. Dinners and movies and ball games and concerts. Neville and Storey functions; gIRL-gEAR soirees. She'd thought he would always be around. She'd never imagined he'd move out of town.

Or leave her.

Now what was she supposed to do?

Poe offered her clearly expert opinion on Kinsey's sudden illness. "No, Lauren. Not the fighting-and-making-up news. The news of Doug's abandonment. Kinsey just realized she's about to lose a friend with convenient and sizable options."

"*Pfft*. Doug and I are friends, yes," Kinsey said. "But I don't know a thing about the size of his, uh, options."

Poe returned her teacup to her saucer and laced her fingers together along the table's edge. "Wait a minute. You're saying you haven't slept with him?"

"Not that it's any of your business, but no. I have not *slept* with him." Emphasizing the word *slept* saved her from telling a lie.

"Even last year on Coconut Caye?" Sydney asked. "Like maybe late one night on the first-floor veranda?"

Kinsey shook her head. She wouldn't call what she and Doug had done on the veranda that night sleeping. No bed had been involved. No postcoital cuddling. Besides, they'd been drunk and that meant it didn't count.

Or so she'd been telling herself for sixteen months.

Neither of them had spoken of the incident again. And as much as she enjoyed her girlfriends' kiss-and-tell bonding, she couldn't bring herself to reveal the things that had happened that night.

Or how she felt about Doug.

Especially since she wasn't quite sure what that was. "Doug and I are friends. That's all. I haven't even kissed him but once or twice since last summer."

Three women turned their full attention on Kinsey. Two sets of blue eyes and one of brown prodded and probed and drilled. Brows up, brows down, brows level.

"What? What? What do you expect me to do? I'm not a first-move kinda girl. Besides, he's always got work on the brain." Kinsey was not going to put in any serious pursuit time only to end up an afterthought—after work, after business, after meetings, after deals.

No sirree bub. Once she settled down, it was home and hearth all the way. Dinner on the table at six. Kids' homework done by seven. Bedtime no later than eight. Cuddled up to the hubby by ten. Hmm. Okay. She was getting a bit ahead of herself here.

"So, give him something else to think about." Lauren waved her fork, then stabbed again at her pizza.

"Yes," Poe added. "Change his mind."

"About moving? How am I supposed to do that?" And did she even want to do that?

"Tell him how you feel." This advice from Sydney.

Good advice if Kinsey hàd a clue as to how she did feel—besides panicked and sick.

"No." With a vigorous shake of her head, Lauren shared a kernel of her wisdom. "*Show* him how you feel."

Kinsey moved her gaze from one woman to the other to the next. "You're talking about sex."

Poe folded her used napkin into a precise square and placed it in the center of her plate. "Aren't we always talking about sex?"

Feeling suddenly bullied, Kinsey crossed her arms. "*You're* only talking about it because you're not getting any."

"Is that so?" Poe replied, her dark eyes giving nothing away.

Calm. Calm and collected. Deep breath. In and out. *Ohhmmm.* Kinsey slumped back in her chair. Her usual ability to relax and blow off stress wasn't working. She had a feeling nothing was going to work this time.

She hadn't been looking where she was going and had stepped off into a big pile of emotional poo. Ask her a month ago, and she'd never have believed it possible that what she'd thought was friendship was actually more.

But with the specter of Doug's departure hanging over her head...

She blew out a frustrated breath. "So, what do I do?"

Sydney looked to Lauren, Lauren to Poe, Poe back to Sydney, then all three turned their attention on Kinsey. Sydney was the one who finally spoke. "I think we need to put a few of the Web site's gIRL gUIDE tips into play."

Kinsey closed her eyes, shook her head. This was exactly the reason she kept her private life private. Glancing around at her girlfriends, she said, "I'd really rather not become a gIRL-gEAR project."

Puffing up her cheeks so she looked like Dizzy Gillespie, Lauren pushed away her plate and scooted her chair back from the table. "Get over it, Kinsey. The rest of us have had to put in time as test cases. It's what keeps us honest and makes the site's advice columns such a success. We know of what we speak."

"Besides," Sydney said, a teasing smile blossoming as she glanced from Kinsey to Poe. "It's time for you two holdouts to take the relationship plunge so those of us who have can return the grief you've given us now for months."

"That's what I'm talking about. I don't need six hovering fairy godmothers when Doug comes running should I decide to crook my finger.'' Now if only her bite lived up to her bark, Kinsey ruefully mused.

Sydney laughed. ''C'mon, Kinsey. You know I'm kidding.''

Lauren butted in promptly. ''Ha! You'd better be only partially kidding, because I am quite in the mood to return the relationship harassment Kinsey has been so generous in doling out.''

''And what about Poe?'' Kinsey was not going to suffer the payback alone. ''Ms. Cool-As-An-Asian-Cucumber over there is hardly the picture of innocence.''

Poe's chin and nose went up. ''I certainly hope not. I work hard at my cosmopolitan image.''

''You just wait.'' Lauren pointed a finger. ''Some guy is going to come along and take you down so hard and fast you won't have a clue what happened.''

''I welcome the challenge,'' Poe said, keeping a straight face as she added, ''Many have tried. All have failed. Most have begged for another chance.'' Even the hand holding the china cup remained steady, as if serenity were the woman's middle name.

Kinsey, on the other hand, sputtered the tea she'd been drinking. ''Poe, you crack me up. Truly. And manage to make me envious at the same time.'' She pressed her lips together in a grimace of sorts. ''If I had even a smidge of your confidence, I'd go after Doug in a heartbeat.''

''It's not about confidence,'' Poe said, her fingers now drumming thoughtfully on the arms of her chair. ''It's all about the game. You have to know your opponent's weaknesses. And then you dig in.''

Pondering that, Kinsey shook her head. ''I'm not

sure Doug has any weaknesses. But I've never thought of him as an opponent.''

"Then you need to change your way of thinking. If he's standing in the way of something you want, then he's an adversary. And you have a decision to make.'' Poe waited. One heartbeat, two. "How badly do you want it?''

"That's the thing. I don't know if a relationship with Doug *is* what I want.'' Kinsey gave a slight shrug. "Maybe I'm overreacting, and once the shock of his moving wears off I'll be first in line to throw him a bon voyage bash.''

Lauren leaned forward. "Do you want to find out?''

That seemed to be the question of the day, didn't it? No matter the denial that leaped to the tip of Kinsey's tongue, her first flustered response to the news of Doug's move had been too strong to discount as meaningless.

What would it hurt to explore the chemistry they'd largely ignored this past year? As long as she kept her eyes wide open and did nothing as stupid as putting her heart on the line, no harm, no foul, right?

It wasn't as though she was going to set a trap, then watch him gnaw off his leg trying to escape. If he decided to stay, she didn't want it to be because she'd crippled him.

"I don't know. I just don't know. I like him a lot.'' She toyed with the cherry tomato on her plate, stabbing at it with the tines of her fork. "We have loads of fun, and I don't want to screw that up. I don't want to lose a good friend because I was desperate and stupid.''

"Then don't be desperate and stupid,'' Lauren said with a shrug, reaching for her diet soda. "Promise yourself you won't do anything you'll regret.''

"That sounds all well and good in theory, but in practice?" Kinsey shook her head. "It's more like I'll seduce Doug, we'll get married and have three children, then we'll turn forty or so and realize we have nothing in common. That's when the regrets will set in. And divorce and child support. I just can't deal with it all," she said, and with one last stab, her tomato went flying.

While Poe rolled her eyes and poured herself another cup of tea from the white ceramic pot she kept at the office, Sydney took the fork out of Kinsey's hand. "Kinsey? While you're not being desperate or stupid, why don't you try not borrowing trouble? You have no idea where you'll be five years from now, much less fifteen."

"Where she won't be is running a five-star kitchen," Poe said, eyeing the tomato on the floor.

"See?" Kinsey slumped in her chair. "I can't even manage something as simple as testing the theory that the way to a man's heart is through his stomach."

"Let me tell you a little secret." Lauren pulled her chair back up to the table, braced her elbows on the edge and leaned forward. "A man has only one organ he wants taken care of. And it's neither his heart nor his stomach."

Sydney nodded. "For the most part, Lauren's right."

"I never had any doubt," Poe added sagely.

"So?" Lauren asked. "Yes or no? Do you want to explore the untapped possibilities between you and Doug?"

With an enthusiasm that continued to grow the longer she considered the question, Kinsey glanced from one woman's inquiring gaze to the next. "Yeah, I think I do."

Lauren rubbed her hands together gleefully. "I love the chance to put a plan in motion."

COLLAPSING ONTO the leather sofa in Anton Neville's office, Doug Storey stretched out his legs, laced his hands behind his head and gave in to exhaustion.

Who knew flying between Houston and Denver three times in one week could take so much out of a guy?

Either he was getting old or he needed to find more time to work out. Sleep wouldn't hurt. Whatever. Something had to give before he collapsed like a bad knee.

He had decisions and deals stacked one on top of the next, and needed a working body and a fully functional mind. Right now he felt as if the only thing working was his ability to sit still and not move.

Anton finished his phone call and cradled the receiver, his hand lingering on the phone, his eyes lingering on Doug as if something vital hovered on the tip of his tongue.

Finally, with a shake of his head, Anton walked around to the front of his desk. He dropped into one of the office's visitor chairs and waited—the way he always waited, sitting and thinking and driving Doug crazy.

Doug had to be on the go all the time, which he was rapidly coming to learn was not as easy to manage when his going was spread from the Gulf Coast to the Rocky Mountains several times a week. He'd be glad to get settled in Denver at last.

"Man, I can't take much more of this," he said, shaking his head and stifling another yawn. "If this is what it feels like to be eighty, I'd rather go out in a blaze of glory at thirty-one."

Anton snorted. "If you're what blazing looks like, remind me not to light a match."

Doug rolled his eyes. "What? You'd rather sit behind your desk than burn up the street?"

"No, dude." Anton leaned back and squared an ankle over the opposite knee. "I'd rather get out of here by seven and take my butt home to Lauren."

Dragging both hands down his face, Doug grunted. "Damn marital bliss. I remember when I wasn't the only one around here ordering in pizza and chicken teriyaki. We got a hell of a lot of work done afterhours back then."

"I still do. It's just business I don't want to be taking care of up here. Especially with you for an audience."

"Your discretion is much appreciated." Ah, but it felt good to be able to smirk. "I don't think I could take it, seeing you snowed under by a honey-do list."

"Oh, yeah. Funny," Anton said, flipping him off.

"Hey," Doug said with a slow-rolling shrug and a grin. "I just call 'em like I see 'em."

"Then you need to clean the dollar signs out of your eyes, because work is making you blind."

"And here I thought it was all that stroking I've been doing on the road."

"Man, you need help. Hell, you need a woman, at the very least."

Doug scooted forward to sit on the sofa's edge, knees spread wide, elbows braced on his thighs. "No woman. Women. Plural. One woman means complications, expectations. And honey-do lists."

This time it was Anton who smirked. "One woman also makes for a much warmer bed."

"Except when you're sleeping on the couch."

"Whoever's giving you advice about women is

charging way too much." Anton grunted. "You don't know jack about what you're saying."

"Maybe not. But I know more than jack about what I'm seeing. Especially on the soccer field. You guys who've shacked up or gotten your butts married? You suck. Leo can't defend a goal worth a crap anymore." Doug liked his life fine just the way it was. He had no plans to put his nuts on the line to be snipped.

Anton didn't even bother with a comeback. "Speaking of soccer, are you planning to make the scrimmage Sunday night? What with you being eighty and all?"

"Nah. I'm having dinner with Kinsey." Slumping into the cushions again, Doug grinned and waggled both brows. "She's cooking."

Anton did that waiting thing again. Then that smirking thing. "You know Lauren will kick your butt back to the Rockies if you hurt that girl."

"Screw you, Neville. It's just dinner." Though Doug almost had trouble convincing himself that Kinsey didn't have more on her mind. When he'd picked up his voice mail on the way to the airport earlier today, he'd been surprised to hear her message.

And even more surprised at the invitation.

Her tone and the words she'd chosen made him think she wasn't just wanting to put food in his stomach. He couldn't help but remember that breakfast-time kiss they'd shared while vacationing last year on Coconut Caye.

Not to mention the tabletop pole dance he'd watched a very tipsy Kinsey perform, her head thrown back, her blond hair swinging down to the red thong bikini bottom that bared her fantastic ass.

Then there was that night on the veranda when they'd both had too much to drink. A night neither of them had spoken of again. A night he wished he could better recall because he had a feeling he'd forgotten a hell of a lot he needed to know—though the most important part he did remember.

Oh, yeah. He remembered.

He cleared his throat, slumped lower where he sat. "It's just dinner."

"You said that already."

"Well, I'm just making sure you heard me."

Anton leaned to the side, shifting his weight onto one elbow. "You sure you're not trying to convince yourself instead?"

"Of what? The fact that Kinsey and I are only friends?" Doug snorted and picked a loose string off the knee of his khaki Dockers. "She knows I don't want a relationship."

"Just dinner and…dessert?"

"Dinner." He shrugged. "Dessert's up to her."

"Right. It's not like you're on a Kinsey-free diet or anything."

Doug didn't say anything because he didn't know what to say. He liked Kinsey a lot. If he'd been the type to settle down with one woman, she'd be there at the top of his list. Correction. She'd *be* his list. But he just didn't see himself ever giving up the freedom that let him live his life without baggage or…honey-do lists.

"Does she know about Denver?" Anton asked.

Doug shook his head. "Dunno. I plan to tell her Sunday night."

"And then what?"

"What do you mean, and then what? Then I go home and sleep for six hours or so, get up and pack."

That was the routine he'd settled into of late. "I'm flying out again first thing Monday morning."

Anton narrowed his eyes. "You're going to have to decide about Reuben buying you out, you know. Especially considering how he bailed you out with Media West this afternoon. We can't afford to screw up this remodeling job."

"Yeah, yeah." Doug hated that his late flight had cost him the Media West meeting, hated even more that he would've been on time if he hadn't rescheduled to make one more contact in Denver. A contact that had been a big waste of time.

"Hey. Don't blow this off," Anton barked. "You're lucky Reuben runs with Marcus West's boys or you'd be eating crow for a very long time to come."

"As a matter of fact, Reuben and I have tickets to tomorrow night's Rockets game. A few beers and it'll all be good." This decision was the hardest one Doug faced. Not the beer or the basketball, but the firm. He was no closer to making a decision tonight than he had been a month ago.

He and Anton had made their original Neville and Storey plans while at the University of Houston's College of Architecture, nearly ten years back. The move to Denver felt like an upward move on the career ladder. Doug had been wooed by the biggest boys on the block, and that was something that came along only once in a lifetime.

It was just that selling his share of their architectural firm made him feel as if he were giving up on a dream, as well as selling out and betraying his very best friend. He'd thought the change would bring a sense of calm to his restlessness of late. He'd been wrong.

And that was what was keeping him from signing on the Denver group's bottom line.

"You've got time," Anton said, pensively studying the leather arm of his chair. "And I'd rather you take it than do the wrong thing." He pushed to his feet then, shaking off what seemed to be a remnant melancholy. "Now, me? My time's up. Lauren's waiting."

Doug slapped his palms to his thighs and forced himself to follow. "Yeah, I've got to get going. I've got a lot of work ahead of me."

"And all I've got is a honey to do."

"POE, I THINK you're the only one here who doesn't know Isabel Leighton, a friend from further back than I care to admit. Izzy, this is Annabel Lee, known fondly around the office as Poe." Sydney made the only introduction necessary, then turned and gave Kinsey a grin of devious proportions. "Kinsey, who everyone knows, is the reason we're here."

Where they were was in the kitchen of the suburban home Sydney shared with Ray Coffey. Sydney, Lauren, Izzy and Poe had all come to help Kinsey put together a meal guaranteed to make Doug weep. And weep in a good way, not because her cooking sucked. Since her woefully understocked kitchen sucked, as well, Sydney's state-of-the-art setup made for a much better classroom.

It was definitely good to see Izzy again. Though Kinsey had lost touch with the other woman once both were busy in school, the two of them had been fast friends as young girls. They'd spent hours running wild at Kinsey's parents' home where, for almost twenty years now, Izzy's uncle Leonard had worked magic with the Grays' lawn and tropical garden.

"You know this is hopeless, don't you?" Kinsey really wanted to smack whoever had started the rumor that the way to a man's heart was through his stomach. "I burn microwave popcorn. I add too much water to packets of instant cocoa. Carryout was invented for a reason, hello. Doug is not going to want to eat anything that comes out of my kitchen."

"It won't be coming out of your kitchen." Lauren climbed onto the bar stool behind the cooking island. "It'll be coming out of Sydney's."

"With too many cooks spoiling the broth, it looks like," Kinsey grumbled, glancing at the latest batch of hovering fairy godmothers. Calm. Collected. *Ohhmmm.* Why had she let herself be talked into such a ridiculous idea?

Now it was too late to back out.

She'd canceled the regular Sunday morning breakfast she shared with her parents to get in this quick cooking lesson before tonight's date. She'd left Doug a message Friday afternoon after the infamous planning luncheon; he'd left her one last night on his way to a basketball game.

But a phone tag relationship was not what she'd been hoping to explore.

"So, what's on the menu?" Wearing a royal-blue headband to hold back her short chunky dreadlocks bronzed with highlights, Izzy pulled open the refrigerator door and peered inside. "And do not tell me you're thinking to fix up anything low or reduced or light. You will not win a man with a woman's diet. Just ask my Gramma Fred. A man's hunger has to be fed and fed right."

Sitting beside Poe on a third bar stool, Kinsey buried

her face in her hands. "Why do I sense a disaster rather than a home-cooked meal in the making?"

"Have a little faith here, Kinsey." Sydney joined Izzy at the refrigerator's open door. "You know full well Izzy grew up in her grandmother's restaurant. And Ray hasn't exactly wasted away since I've taken over the cooking, though Patrick's been doing a lot of it since he's been home."

Kinsey sighed, then glanced over at Poe, who shrugged and said, "I'm only here for the show."

One less pair of hands in the mix, anyway. And since Kinsey planned to do nothing but take notes… "Okay, then. Where do we start?"

"Hmm." Sydney examined the labels on several packages of butcher-wrapped meat. "I bought pork and lamb and chicken and beef. Whatever you don't use for Doug, I'll freeze for Ray. I guess the first thing is to decide what you're in the mood for, since you'll be eating it, too."

"If I'm supposed to eat my own cooking, then the deciding factor is what's the easiest to fix and the hardest to screw up?" Sad, but true.

"No. The deciding factor is what you want your cooking to say." At the sound of Patrick Coffey's voice, five pairs of female eyes turned toward the doorway where he stood.

His hands hooked into the frame overhead, he leaned forward, his long, lanky body covered by nothing but a pair of low-rise jeans and a ribbed white tank-style T-shirt that showed off an intricately woven tattoo ringing the bulge of his right biceps.

His hair hung in dark twisted strands to his shoulders, hiding much of his face in the shadows. At least until he pushed away from the door frame and entered the room, raking all that hair back into a ponytail he secured haphazardly with a thick red rubber band.

Kinsey released the breath she'd been holding, heard Poe do the same at her side. Having seen him off and on now for over a year, Kinsey still remained clueless how the man managed to inspire equal parts lust and trepidation. But he did.

She supposed it was a normal reaction to his circumstances. After all, how many guys returned home after being held hostage for three years by Caribbean pirates?

Naturally, her heart pitter-pattered in a fan-to-movie-star response—one no more meaningful than the patter inspired by Brad Pitt, or the pitter brought on by George Clooney.

Now the trepidation…that part was real. That pirate thing was too bizarre to let go.

Totally unaffected by Patrick's arrival, Sydney moved away from the refrigerator with a chicken in her hand. She tossed it to Patrick, who caught it without even looking her way.

"Believe it or not, ladies," Sydney began, "here is the member of the Coffey household best suited to showing Kinsey how to turn a meal into magic."

2

KINSEY TOOK THE CHICKEN from the oven and moved the golden-skinned bird from roasting pan to platter. She whisked butter along with half the papaya glaze she'd prepared earlier into the drippings, the way Patrick had instructed her to do.

He'd sent her home after this morning's cooking lesson with the chicken marinating in orange juice, shallots and brown sugar. All she'd had to do was strain the marinade into the food processor she'd borrowed from Sydney, add the Dijon mustard, papaya, garlic and additional seasonings Patrick had measured out, and baste the bird as it cooked.

So far, so good. Nothing burned, nothing broken, nothing blown to bits. Her kitchen had never smelled this mouthwateringly yummy. If the food tasted half as good, well, she'd have to confess to Doug that she was really a terrible cook and tonight's dinner was a fluke.

Or, she supposed, such a confession could wait.

Sydney had even offered Kinsey use of the baking and serving dishes. Expert cook that she was not, she'd had nothing appropriate in which to roast and serve Patrick's Caribbean Chicken with Orange Papaya Glaze.

Her cooking instructor had been equally as generous as his soon-to-be sister-in-law. He'd proposed he come do the cooking for her. Kinsey had declined. Cooking for one man while using another's recipe was bad enough.

But cooking for one man while another worked to seduce her didn't seem exactly copacetic.

Patrick's equal-opportunity flirtation was flattering, but meaningless ten minutes later—a fact to which both Izzy and Poe could attest. Both women had fallen victim to his mercurial moods this morning, one that had him walking out of the kitchen in the middle of a lively conversation.

Still, Kinsey had left the Coffey home feeling much more competent than she had when she'd let her girlfriends talk her into this plan for entrapment. Okay, she admitted, she hadn't actually been talked into anything. She'd pretty much been her own ringleader.

And now the circus was coming to town...no, wait. That was ringmaster. Whatever.

The wine was chilled, the salad freshly tossed, the chicken warm and ready to serve, and the table set with dishes, flatware and linen that actually were her very own. She might not be able to cook, but she knew how to dress a table as well as she knew how to dress herself.

Tonight she wore a brand-new outfit, one she'd just added to the gROWL gIRL partywear line—a pair of low-rise leisure pants with a fold-over waistband and a matching knit camisole covered with a fluttery chiffon top.

Both the pants and the cami were white, a brave decision if she did say so herself, but the red-and-zebra stripes of the sheer topper made it too much fun to resist. And besides, she looked damn good in the black, white and red combination.

Or so said her fashion diva's sixth sense.

Now, as long as she didn't start blabbering incessantly, or throw up due to the unexpected nerves turning her stomach inside out, and as long as Doug arrived before the chicken cooled completely, leaving her with too much leftover food for one person to eat in a lifetime—

The doorbell chimed.

She closed her eyes, took a deep breath, looked up again...and realized she had totally forgotten dessert. Oh, yes. Definitely the start of a great impression. She should've gone with her original instinct not to mess with what was a really good friendship. This trap-setting idea was going to backfire with all sorts of regrets.

The doorbell chimed again, and Kinsey found herself wearing a wry smile. Doug never rang twice; he simply walked in with a loud ''Yo!'' and called out her name. That told her he shared her expectant sense of this evening being different than any they'd spent together in the past.

And since *that* was causing butterfly fountains to bubble in her stomach, she gave up worrying that a lack of dessert meant she'd flubbed the entire evening, and reached for calm, cool and collected. *Ohhmmm.*

But when she opened her front door and saw him standing in the porch's yellowed light, she didn't know how to react, because the idea of never seeing him again hit her like a blow to the center of her chest.

When had he become so integral to her life, and when had she started taking him for granted?

She released the lock on the glass storm door and pushed it open, nearly breathless when she said, ''Hi.''

The smile he'd originally given her deepened, his

eyes going wide and his brows coming down as he took her in from head to toe. "Wow. And hi yourself."

His "wow" made all the effort she'd taken with her appearance worth every minute of the tweaking spent on hair and makeup. "Back atcha." *Back atcha in a very big way.*

He looked better than she remembered, and she had to wonder if she'd really ever noticed him before, or if she was simply caught up in the moment.

He wore charcoal-gray trousers and a heather-green sweater over a pale yellow dress shirt. He walked into her living room, and she turned to close the door, leaning back against it and thinking she'd never seen a guy's backside look better than Doug Storey's did in gray wool.

He stopped, one hand shoved into a pocket, the other holding a bottle of wine, and turned back, smiling. "It smells great in here. You should've told me you cooked. I would've been over more often."

She thought about telling him the truth regarding her culinary skills, but went with a different truth instead. "You would've been welcome. You are welcome. Anytime. I just need advance warning if you expect food."

He laughed at that. "Why's that?"

"Well, actually, I don't cook." She considered the fit of his clothes one last time, then pushed away from the door and led him into the kitchen, her slides clicking from hardwood floor to rich Italian tile. "I don't cook at all."

"Hmm. Not sure if I should be honored here or worried." His chuckle followed close on her heels.

The thrill of the chase was on. "Honored, of course.

No need to worry. This recipe came straight from Sydney's kitchen.''

Doug set the bottle of pinot noir on the kitchen island, leaned a hip on the edge and crossed his arms. ''Now that you mention it, I have noticed Ray getting a little pudgy around the middle. I guess that's a good sign.''

Kinsey decided it was best not to let him know who exactly was cooking these days in the Coffey household. She handed him the corkscrew she'd rummaged in her utensil drawer earlier to find. ''Like I said. No worries. I happen to have this meal totally under control.''

One of Doug's brows lifted sharply as he opened the wine and poured them each a glass. He drank, his eyes never leaving hers even after he'd returned the stemware to the island's tiled surface. ''It's not that I don't trust you, darlin', but I'm wondering if you might need to check whatever it is boiling away in that pot.''

''Oh, shoot.'' Kinsey cut off the gas flame, took up the wooden spoon and stirred furiously. The glaze still smelled incredible, thank goodness. She sighed deeply, glanced back at Doug. ''Thanks. You saved the day.''

He shrugged, winked. ''Saved dinner, at least.''

''I wouldn't go that far.'' But she did want to be sure the glaze hadn't burned before she served it with the chicken. She dipped the tip of a clean spoon into the sweet sauce, blew across the surface to cool it down, then taste-tested.

''Mmm.'' She smacked her lips, then did so again, knowing Doug watched. ''Okay. You're right. You saved dinner.''

''Well, then?'' Doug tapped his lower lip, signaling

that he wanted a taste, too. "How 'bout a little hero respect here?"

Rolling her eyes, Kinsey grabbed another spoon. "I guess this goes to prove that cooking is probably one thing I should learn to do."

"Why's that?" he asked, then added, "Other than the obvious need to avoid burning down the house," as she offered him the tip of the spoon, and he took hold of her wrist.

His hand was so large around her much smaller one, and he never broke eye contact as he opened his mouth. Watching his lips close over the spoon, watching his tongue flick at a smudge of glaze left on his lips, she remembered the intimacy of the kisses they'd shared during last summer's vacation.

She wondered if she'd be able to find her voice to answer his question. "Oh, something about the way to a man's heart being through his stomach," she finally said.

He licked his lips and murmured his approval of the orange and papaya, breaking into a grin that pulled deeply at the dimples in his cheeks. His smile grew wider as he carefully timed his reply. "You're catering to the wrong organ, darlin'. Trust me on that one."

And with that, he kissed her. Still holding her wrist, he moved his other hand to the small of her back and pulled her into his body. He tasted of sweet citrus and the even sweeter promise of sex, and Kinsey melted.

She felt the beat of her pulse in the grasp of Doug's fingers, felt the beat of his heart beneath the palm she'd pressed to the center of his chest. His lips parted and she opened her mouth, smiling as his tongue slipped deftly inside.

So warm, so demanding, so confident. So sure of

what he wanted, and of being able to give her all that her body desired. When he slid his hand up her spine, when he threaded his fingers into her hair, when he cupped the back of her head to hold her still, she chuckled because she couldn't help it.

He felt so good. He made her feel so good, even when way too soon he began to slow what had started as a fast and furious and very sudden need to connect. Damn the man for having the restraint she was struggling to find.

"What are you laughing at?" he asked when he finally put enough space between their mouths to talk.

"Nothing." She shook her head but found it hard to push him away. She had to, for the food and for her plan to have time to come together. "Just a happy laugh. You make me feel nice."

"You make me feel even better, especially since you're not laughing at my technique." He shoved a hand through his hair, which had grown overly long and rakish. "A guy can take only so much rejection in one day."

He let go of her wrist and stepped back, his dejection replacing the thrill of seconds before. But just as quickly, the emotion was gone, and Kinsey wondered if she'd imagined it all along. "Why? What happened?"

He leaned against the countertop and snitched a piece of carrot from her chopping block. "A late flight and a missed meeting earned me a hell of a reaming from Anton, not to mention a butt-chewing by my client."

"A late flight is hardly your fault," she said with a frown, feeling strangely protective instincts kick in. As if Doug needed her to watch his back.

"No, but I cut it too close. I knew what time I needed to be back here and..." He shrugged, grabbed another slice of carrot from the bowl she held. "I got greedy, I guess. Trying to make one more contact in Denver while I was there."

Kinsey paused to consider the best answer to give, not knowing if he was looking for support or censure. "So you've got a go-getter sort of work ethic. You can hardly be faulted for that."

Doug grimaced as he finished the carrot. "Except there are times it seems more of a fault than an asset."

"Like now?" she asked, sensing he wasn't exactly thrilled to have made what he considered an error in judgment.

He nodded. "Reuben Bettis, one of the junior execs... Reuben covered my ass on this end, but it's really bad career karma to forget where you came from. Or the people who helped get you to where you are."

She handed him the salad bowl and the cruet of dressing, wondering if this Reuben Bettis was the one wanting to buy out Doug's part of the architectural firm. "But that isn't what you were doing."

Doug took both to the table, giving her a smile on his return. "When you say that it sounds much more convincing than when I tell myself the same thing."

"So you *were* forgetting?" she asked, offering him a fork and carving knife.

"I don't want to think so." He set about cutting off thin slices from the chicken breast and arranging them on the platter. "Media West is one of my original clients. I guess having Marcus West, not to mention Anton, question my commitment and loyalty doesn't sit well."

Lifting her wineglass, Kinsey swirled the liquid inside. How real was the possibility that Doug was actually more torn about this move and the impending sale of his investment in Neville and Storey than she'd been led to believe?

Lauren had made it seem as if Doug was only waiting to sign, seal and deliver the deal. But now...now Kinsey wasn't so sure the other woman knew what she was talking about.

Kinsey sipped her wine, looking over the upraised glass at Doug, wondering what facets of his personality she might have missed during the time they'd spent together. Commitment and loyalty had never been an issue. She was surprised anyone who knew him would question either, especially Anton, who knew Doug so well.

"What're you looking at?" he asked, refilling both their glasses once she'd set hers beside his on the island.

"Just thinking, wondering."

"Wondering what?"

"What it will be like not to have you around."

A look of guilty relief crossed his face. "How did you find out?"

"From Lauren."

"I was planning to tell you tonight."

"Uh-huh."

"Seriously. I was." She could hear the guilt again, this time with added regret. "It's just tough breaking that sort of news to good friends."

Friends. Well, that *was* all they were, wasn't it? So she shouldn't be feeling the sadness that had her eyes welling. "It's tougher having to hear it. Especially secondhand."

"I *am* sorry, Kinsey."

"For what? Not telling me yourself? Or for going off and leaving me?" When he didn't say anything, she decided to let it go. She didn't want to spend their time together in an inconsolable, emotional state. And something in his pained expression told her she wouldn't like hearing what it was he had to say.

Blinking away the threat of tears, she carried her wine and the platter of chicken to the table. When she returned for the glaze, she found Doug pouring it into the gravy boat she'd borrowed from Sydney, and her heart tripped at how at home in her kitchen he seemed.

"It's going to take a lot of getting used to. You being gone and all that. Especially since you're turning out to be quite handy. I'm sorry I never knew this before."

His grin was amazingly wicked. "I have talents you can only imagine."

"Is that so?" she asked, wishing she still had her wineglass there because she really, really needed something to do with her hands. As it was, she was having a hard time not slipping them underneath his sweater and shirt. She wanted so badly to get close to his body.

"Oh, yeah. Definitely so."

"Well, then. Do you care to share what you know?" she asked, settling on toying with a strip of peeled cucumber skin. "Or are you keeping your skills secret?"

Doug slowly lowered the gravy boat. He stood where he was for a very long moment, his hands flat on the countertop as if he wasn't at all certain what he was doing or why.

But as Kinsey looked on, he came to a decision. She saw it in the tensing of his shoulders, and in the way he finally tossed back his head, blond hair flowing, like a stallion having selected his mare.

The analogy made her laugh, or would have if the look he gave her didn't make her feel as if he was considering the best way to mount. And even though that was what she'd wanted, where she'd wanted this evening to go, she couldn't deny the sting of surprise at the speed with which they'd progressed.

He turned and walked toward her, determination in his step as well as in his bright gaze. Once he stood directly before her, he set both hands at her waist. She moved hers to his biceps, a placement that allowed her to feel the flex of muscle an instant before he lifted her to perch on the edge of the tiled island.

Her hands found their way to his shoulders as he stepped fully between her spread legs. His hands still at her waist, he cocked his head and gave her a smile that had her wondering why they'd never taken the time to get to know each other more deeply.

That smile raised a myriad of questions. And his eyes were as bright as green lights. "My kitchen skills are pretty much limited to dessert. And as great as the chicken smells, I'd rather start with what I know best."

She responded with a bit of a grimace. "I didn't remember to make dessert."

"Trust me, darlin'. What I have in mind is better than anything you could've whipped up."

It was a good thing she wasn't easily taken in by a sweet-talkin' man. "You say that without having tasted any of my cooking."

"Yeah, but I've tasted you." And then he moved forward and pressed his lips over the hollow of her throat.

She leaned her head back to give him better access, wrapped her legs around him and hooked her heels at the base of his spine. Her fingers dug into the tight muscles of his shoulders; he was more tense than she'd imagined, and she began to knead the hard knots.

"Mmm," he murmured, his lips creating a soft buzzing tickle on her skin. "You have no idea how good that feels."

"It can't feel half as good as what you're doing with your mouth." He'd moved down her collarbone, pushing aside the loose neckline of her fluttery top, kissing his way along the bared skin.

He nipped at the edge of her shoulder and growled. "It would feel a hell of a lot better if you'd lose this top."

She couldn't get it off fast enough. It was less a necessary piece of clothing than it was a tease that had accomplished its purpose.

And now Doug could easily get to the rest of her, which he did immediately, pulling the thin strap of her knit camisole down one shoulder and working his way beneath the hem with his other hand.

He surrounded her—his hands, his mouth, his clean and subtle scent. The breadth of his chest, which blocked any movement she might want to make. She didn't want to move anywhere at all, except closer to the beautifully exquisite sensation of his touch.

His skin was on her skin, and all she could think about was the night they'd both been drunk and only half aware of being on the veranda at the house on Coconut Caye. His hands had been all over her then, beneath her clothing, in her hair, inside her body in ways she still imagined vividly when she went to bed alone.

With his hands now on her rib cage beneath the curve of her breasts, she thought again of that previous contact, realizing her memories were nothing compared to the bliss of the real thing.

He was deft in the way he teased her, making sure she enjoyed his touch. He tested her reactions, his mouth whispering his kisses along with his words. Both thrilled her beyond belief.

"Is that good?" he asked, his lips drawing on the skin just beneath her shoulder. "Do you like that?" he added, before she could do more than softly moan. "What do you want me to do?" As if his tongue wetting a line along the upper curve of her breast wasn't enough. "You're so beautiful. Soft. Sweet. Like silk. And you smell so damn good."

She whimpered because she couldn't help it. Her shoulder was bare, the strap of her top long since having fallen to her elbow. He took hold of the edge of the material and began to peel it from her breast. His other hand cupped her other breast fully, his palm circling over the very tip of her budded nipple.

And then her top was around her waist and both breasts bared. Oh, but she felt reckless in such delightful ways, reckless enough not to give thought to anything but the physical joy of the moment, and to the man offering her this pleasure. Doug leaned down, his eyes wide, his gaze locked wickedly on hers, and took her into his mouth.

She remembered everything then, every detail of the way he knew how sharply to tug, how sweetly to kiss, how softly to curl his tongue around her nipple. He'd learned so many things about her in that one dark night of sea breeze and sex, and he remembered. He remembered.

When had any man ever remembered, ever paid the sort of intimate attention needed for such perfect recall?

Kinsey moved her hands to her sides, bracing her weight on the counter. She scooted her lower body closer into his and tossed back her head. Eyes closed, she kicked off her shoes and slid her heels up and down Doug's backside, feeling all that taut resilient flesh beneath his very *GQ* attire.

The sensations of slipping and sliding, of being tongued and tasted, the reality that dinner was going to have to wait… She wasn't sure anything she'd ever felt had been so perfect, any man she'd ever known this amazingly right.

When he moved his mouth to her other breast, she knew that having him now mattered more than waiting to be certain, than wondering if she was making a mistake she'd regret not having the resolve to avoid.

She threaded her fingers into his thick hair. ''Doug?''

''Hmm?'' he breathed against her skin.

She shivered. ''The food is going to have to be reheated anyway.…''

He slowed his very attentive movements, finally looking up, his eyes bright, his hair falling dashingly over his forehead, his mouth red and wet from the kisses. He kept his hands on either side of her rib cage, holding her there as if he expected her to bolt.

As if she wanted to be anywhere else.

''What're you saying here, darlin'?''

She met his gaze candidly. ''Just that dessert sounds really good right about now.''

He closed his eyes, as if to assure himself he wasn't living a dream, then looked back at her with an expression defined by one simple word.

Hot.

"Kinsey Gray, you have made me a very happy man."

The very words a girl wanted to hear. "I expect total reciprocation."

"Trust me, darlin'. You're about to be the happiest woman alive."

3

KINSEY GRAY HAD BEEN responsible for the best time Doug had ever spent naked with a woman, and he doubted that she had a single clue.

His fault completely, because he'd never said a word, and he should have. Damn it, but he should have. His excuse wasn't a good one, but it was real and it was honest and it was the only one he'd been able to come up with.

And that was simply that, when they'd returned from last summer's vacation off the coast of Belize, he hadn't known what to say. He also wasn't sure how much she remembered of what they'd done on the veranda while under the influence of palm fronds in the breeze and the moon on the water and way too much of Nolan Ford's stock of sweet Caribbean rum.

Doug remembered all of it, or so he'd told himself anytime they were together and he wanted to take her to bed. Kinsey, however, had never made a move of any sort that led him to believe she wanted to revisit a connection that had nearly left him blind.

At least she hadn't before now.

But now. Oh, now. Now, with her arms around his neck and her legs around his waist, she was definitely sending out the signals he'd been twitching for months to pick up. And the more he thought about having Kinsey served up for dessert, the worse the twitching got.

He scooped her straight off the cooking island's slick tiles and headed back the way he'd originally come. She had a hell of an oversize sofa that was just the ticket to take them where he wanted to go.

She giggled, raining tiny kisses all over his face, blowing away the hair that kept falling into his eyes. "I love that you've grown your hair."

So much for the haircut he'd been planning. "You're making it hard for me to see where I'm going here, darlin'. If you hold up a minute, I promise we can get back to the kissing here shortly."

"Such a spoilsport," she said, pouting, but she did lean to the side and rest her head on his shoulder, giving him a clear field of vision.

Funny how the kissing was suddenly less important than the way she felt cuddled against him, the way she seemed to be so tiny when he knew she was fiercely independent and didn't need him for anything.

When they reached the sofa, he turned and tumbled her on to his chest, his body bouncing once before he sank into the plush cushions. Kinsey bounced, too, and her bouncing was a hell of a lot more fun against his front than falling onto the stuffing had been that was against his back.

Oh, yeah. He could get used to this. Softness all the way around.

Straddling his thighs, Kinsey levered herself upright with her hands on his abs. Her top ringed her ribs like a white cotton tube, baring both her belly and her breasts. She was stunningly gorgeous, with her straight blond hair hanging down to hide her nipples, her bright blue eyes and her legs, that went on forever, gripping his thighs.

A total Scandinavian turn-on, he thought, right about

the same time he decided her hair was in the way of his northern lights fantasy. He reached up and fanned out the strands behind her shoulders so he could get a good look at dessert.

And then she blushed.

He wasn't sure if she was embarrassed because he was staring, or because his hard-on was making itself known there where her legs were spread apart over his. He reached up and brushed the backs of his fingers over her cheek. "You're so cute when you do that."

"And you're so cute when you do *that*," she responded, sliding her hand over his belt buckle to cover his rapidly expanding fly.

Well, that answered that, didn't it? Thoughts that went way beyond simple lust fired his grin. This woman was a horny man's most erotic dream, and he never wanted to come awake again. "Feel free to take a closer look."

She took him up on the dare, making quick work of his buckle before easing down the zipper of his fly. Her focus remained on her fingers, and as she unfastened his pants, her upper arms pressed her breasts together into two plump mouthfuls.

He was absolutely starving, ravenous, insatiable, but he was looking forward to seeing how far she would go. Besides, what was another minute or two when he'd been waiting for this for a very long time? At least for the sixteen months since he'd last had her.

In fact, why hadn't he gone with his gut and pursued her before now?

Maybe because it had taken this long for him to learn that being pursued could be so damn sweet.

He crossed his arms behind his head, raising his head a tad so he could watch as she worked to get his pants down. As seriously as he enjoyed the physical kick to getting blown, looking at a woman's mouth—Kinsey's mouth—in action was a huge part of the turn-on. Any guy claiming otherwise was lying through his teeth.

Doug had a big thing about telling the truth. And seeing Kinsey scoot on her knees to the foot of the sofa, watching her slender fingers take hold of the waistband of his pants and his boxers, following every movement she made as she stripped him down to his bare essentials, was better than any skin flick he'd ever seen.

His pants were binding his ankles when she slid back up his body, her bare breasts pressing on either side of his thickly rigid cock. She leaned down, her hair like strands of white silk on his skin, and pressed biting, sucking kisses all over his belly.

"Kinsey, I'm dyin' here, darlin'."

Without even lifting her head she answered, "I do believe that's the point," and then went right back to torturing him in ways he'd never considered possible. Where the hell had this woman been all of his life?

His cock strained upward, pushing into her chest. She slipped one hand between their bodies to hold him, squeezing rhythmically as her kisses came closer but never in contact with his erection. More than anything he wanted to feel her sweet lips around him, and he told her so with a sharp upward thrust.

She tsk-tsked against his skin, her hair now hanging between his legs and tickling mercilessly. Then again, it could've been her lips and her tongue and his wicked expectation causing the tingles.

Whatever it was, he wasn't going to be able to take much more of this before he grabbed her and flipped her onto her back. He wanted to be inside her in the very worst way. He didn't think he'd ever ached like this after nothing but a few kisses and a hand job that would've admittedly been a whole lot better if she'd actually stroked.

When he heard the phone ring, he groaned, but Kinsey didn't stop what she was doing, except to slip both hands underneath his thighs. She pushed his legs up and toward his body until he lay there with his ankles caught up tight where his pants wrapped around them and his knees in the air and all of the family jewels exposed.

The phone stopped, and Kinsey sat up and grinned, not looking at his face, but at his package, which sent another surge of blood that direction. He pulsed, bobbed, and her grin widened. Oh, yeah. He knew it.

He was going to die.

A slow agonizing death by sex, he thought, might just be worth it, especially when she squirreled around down there between his spread thighs where all of America could have been getting a close-up view of every hair on his—

"Mmm," Kinsey murmured, licking her lips and preparing to kill him. He watched as she opened her mouth into the most perfect O known to mankind. Then she wrapped those beautiful lips around the head of his cock.

Yes, yes. Oh, yes. This was what it was all about. This was what he'd been wanting, been waiting for, been…oh, good ever-lovin' sweet… He groaned, and the sound came straight from his gut.

"You like?" She pulled away to ask the question.

Him? Like? He'd like it a whole lot better without having to talk about it. "You have no clue."

"Oh, I don't know." She ran the tip of her tongue,

the sweet little pointed tip only, around the head of his erection. "It's quite nice from this angle."

Was she talking about his taste? His size? What? Why was she talking at all? "That angle totally works for me."

"Hmm." She blew a long stream of warm air over the wetness her mouth had left behind, and he pretty much had to start thinking about elephant dung to keep from coming right then and there.

"I'm going to try something a little different here. Tell me if you like it."

"Go for it, darlin'." *Elephant dung, elephant dung, big stinkin' elephant dung.*

His cock twitched, his balls drawing up into his body like two blue hockey pucks. Kinsey adjusted her position so that she was coming at him from directly above, and damn if she didn't swallow him whole.

Un-friggin'-believable. She had all of him in her mouth. The grip of her hand was as firm as that of her lips as she slid up and down, sucking the life out of him. But he was going to be the only one here getting anything out of this if she didn't stop. *Oh, Mama, stop…* "Kinsey?"

"Mmm?" she murmured, vibrating him from belly to balls.

"You are amazing." *Suck in a breath.* "You are incredible." *Suck it in, bub. Suck it in.* "But you are really going to have to cool it down there or dessert's gonna be over, and you're still going to be hungry."

She chuckled. She had him in her mouth and she actually managed a laugh. But then slowly, as if she were counting each lick of a Tootsie Pop, she pulled her mouth from the base to the head of his cock and, *pop*, he was free.

He reached down between his legs and pressed hard against the pounding rush of blood. He squeezed his eyes shut, his panting breaths his only chance at salvation. He heard Kinsey rustling around, and when he finally found the control he needed to open his eyes without his geyser spouting...

Oh, hell and a half. *Here we go again.* All that rustling had been Kinsey stripping off her clothes.

Damn, but he'd wanted to do that.

Damn, but he didn't care anymore.

Not when she stood there at the edge of the sofa, her bare skin glowing with the last of a summer tan. All of her skin, it seemed, but for a tiny strip where two strings would've tied a triangle of a bikini bottom over her mound.

Her nipples were a luscious peachy-pecan in the center of breasts too perfect to be real. Lucky man that he was, he knew that particular truth, however. His mouth began to water; his John Henry began to bob.

Enough with the ankle bondage and Kinsey not being underneath him. He sat up and swung around and was out of his sweater before his shoes hit the floor. He kicked them off; his pants followed. His shirt lost more than a button or two; his patience went flying off in the same direction.

She was just standing there, enjoying his struggle and looking as if being naked was as natural as not. Once he'd dug a condom from his billfold, he wasted no time in letting her know how much he liked her lack of inhibition, pulling her to stand between his legs and using his mouth the way he'd been waiting to forever.

As she took the condom from his hand and opened the packet, he held her hips and settled his mouth over her sex. He licked his way in and out of her folds until she whimpered and squirmed and did everything she could to push him down on to his back.

"Not yet, darlin'," he mumbled into her sweetly swollen pussy. She tasted wonderful, clean and salty, as if she spent her days sunbathing after a Mediterranean swim. He swirled his tongue over and around her clit, then used his fingers to spread her open and push his tongue inside her.

She gasped even as she widened her stance and shoved her fingers into his hair to hold him where she wanted. He didn't mind, but it wasn't as if he was going anywhere just yet. He was having too much of a good time tasting and teasing and slurping her up to let go.

Except Kinsey decided she had other ideas, and moved a step away. He looked up into her mischievous eyes, a blond nymph toying with his condom packet as if he were a donkey and she held his carrot in her hand. In a manner of speaking, he supposed she did.

He sat back, his legs spread in a wide V, his hands laced on his belly behind his erection, which was more than ready for some action.

She tapped the condom wrapper to her chin as she considered all he had to offer. When she seemed to make up her mind, she dropped to her knees before him and rolled the sheath to the base of his shaft.

Thing was, while she was down there she made sure to let him know she wasn't the least bit intimidated or put off by the male anatomy. For at least five minutes worth of what seemed like forever, he sat like a statue through kisses and forays she made with her fingers and tongue. He felt every end of every nerve fire off round after round of sensation that was not the least bit wholesome, but was sweet in ways that had him biting down on a mouthful of instructional expletives.

Just when he was ready again to grab her and toss her on to her back, she moved away, pushed his knees together, turned and straddled his lap in reverse. *Sweet, gorgeous, baby, doll.* The movement gave him such a memorable view of her ass that he swore he'd take the picture to his grave.

Then, reaching between her legs, she took hold of his cock and guided him to where he needed to be, lowering herself until he was completely buried in the hottest sweetest piece he'd ever had the pleasure to know.

Pleasure. No, that was weak. The word failed to cover half of what he felt when she took him inside. But he had to keep this physical. Feeling he could deal with; feeling rocked his world. Feeling meant he didn't have to think.

He wasn't sure what to do with his hands, finally setting them at her hips, where he could guide her angle, control her speed. He hated having to hold her at all; sitting back and just enjoying the view suited him just fine.

Seeing the sloping arch of her back, the wide-open space between her legs that revealed exactly what she was giving him and where his cock was buried...

He groaned, watching Kinsey slide down until his entire shaft disappeared, her hands braced on his knees for leverage and balance. Her tiny breathy moans had him clenching his gut and slipping one hand between her legs the next time she rose enough to give him the room.

He slid a finger through her wet folds to her clit, fingering the tight knot, testing her response, whether she liked soft and slow or hard and persistent or teasing butterfly flicks.

She liked all of it, judging by the way she pushed against him, ground against him, covered his hand with one of hers and pressed hard.

She cried out, softly at first, then with more volume as her contractions hit. She tightened around him, shuddering as she came, and then he couldn't wait another single second. He unloaded hard and fast, thrusting upward and spilling himself until he was totally empty and spent.

He sank back into the sofa; Kinsey settled on to his lap, turning to face him without ever springing him free. How she managed, he had no idea. But he was glad that she still held him inside.

For a few more seconds, he needed this connection. He needed it more than he'd thought he could need anything from a woman. No. Anything from *Kinsey.*

And it was his Kinsey-specific need that made it hard to let her go.

Made it hard to admit that he wasn't ready to go.

Made it hard to know if he ever would be.

KINSEY PULLED her bathrobe back up on to her shoulder and jabbed her fork into her salad. She was famished; earlier, she'd been too edgy to eat. Dessert first was a policy she'd have to adopt. At least when dining on Doug.

Dining on Doug.

She liked the sound of that, and she had certainly enjoyed the reality. "Mmm," she moaned around a bite of chicken. "I don't know why I was so worried. This is actually pretty good."

One of Doug's brows winged up as he looked at her

over his glass of wine. "I thought you said you *weren't* worried."

"Did I?" she asked in all innocence.

"Yes. You did."

"Hmm," she hedged, ignoring his laugh at her lie. "Well, maybe I was a bit. But now I'm thinking I'd like to do this more often." She reached for another slice of chicken breast. "You can be my guinea pig. At least for as long as you're here."

She hated adding that last part, but she had to face that one round of sexual Olympics was not going to convince him to continue calling Houston home. One round hadn't even convinced her that she wanted him to stay.

Or so she deluded herself into thinking.

"I'm definitely game." Doug reached over to drizzle papaya glaze onto her chicken. "On one condition."

"What's that?"

He paused, waited until she looked up from cutting her chicken before dropping his bomb. "That you'll serve dessert first every time."

He was so incredibly cute when he teased her. She loved that they were so comfortable together already that neither one of them hesitated to speak their mind.

After they'd showered and dressed and reheated the food, he'd made sure that his chair and hers were as close to the same corner of the square table as possible.

The result had been a lot of bumped knees and a very crowded table, but Kinsey adored him for wanting to keep her near. "Sex does rather stir up the appetite, doesn't it?" She suppressed a grin while cutting her food. "I kinda like the idea of dessert first."

"Kinsey." Doug's eyes flashed as he pulled his

chair even closer. "Don't tease me like that unless you mean it, darlin'."

"Why, Doug Storey." She swirled a bite of chicken through the puddle of glaze. "When have you ever known me to say something I didn't mean?"

"Sixteen months ago on the veranda of Coconut Caye."

Whoa! A blast from the past out of nowhere. If she'd had anything in her mouth, she would likely have choked. "During the group's vacation? What did I say?"

He sat back in his chair, his knees spread wide, his unbuttoned shirt hanging open. She wanted to crawl into his lap and bury her nose in his skin, but decided this was not the right time.

No matter that he looked terribly dejected.

Strange. Why would he be dejected over something said so long ago in the heat of the moment and under the influence of rum?

"Then you don't remember."

She finished with the bite of her chicken, then moved to toy with what was left of her salad. "I remember…several things."

"Like what?" He laced his hands over his flat abs and stretched out his legs even farther, hooking a foot around her chair leg and dragging her practically into his lap.

Two could play his game, she mused, abandoning her plate and propping her legs, ankles crossed, over his thighs. "Like the fact that we don't fit well together standing up. Your legs are too long."

He shook his head. "Your legs are too short."

"My legs are not short." She angled them this way

and that until Doug did as she wanted and touched her, running his palm from her ankle to her knee.

"Not too short if you're standing over my lap, but for normal vertical sex?" His mouth curled into a deliciously wicked grin. "Definitely too short."

Kinsey tossed her open robe back over her legs, which he'd bared. "Then I suppose we were lucky the veranda had such a sturdy railing."

"Then you do remember."

"I told you I did. Would you like any more chicken?" she asked, not quite ready to give everything away.

But Doug wasn't ready to let it go. "Do you know that I still have that pair of your bikini bottoms? String ties are truly a man's best friend."

She was not going to let him get to her. She was not, was not, was not. She had to let him know he'd met his match if a match was what she was looking to explore. Calm, cool and collected.

Ohhmmm. "Personally, I'm a big fan of those little tiny mesh pockets in swim trunks. The perfect size for stashing a condom."

"Be Prepared, that's my motto."

"Stealing from the Boy Scouts these days?"

"Why not? Thousands of kids can't be wrong."

"Maybe not." She went back to innocently moving lettuce and carrots around on her plate. "I just would've thought you might have more originality about you."

She waited for one beat, two beats, three beats, four, and then she looked up. But the teasing Doug of seconds ago was gone. In his place brooded the Doug from earlier in the evening, the one who'd been fairly hard on himself for missing the meeting with Media West.

Her phone rang again. She ignored it. She wanted to know what was going on behind those intensely focused green eyes. Sure, they could banter and bed their way through a relationship, but she was certain, she *knew,* he had so much more to offer than a sexual good time.

And if she discovered that all this time she'd been wrong, well, then—

"Aren't you going to get that?" he asked before the phone rang one last time.

She shook her head. "That's what voice mail is for. I'm more curious to hear the voices in your head."

"The ones telling me to haul you back to the sofa?"

That one she wouldn't mind listening to herself. "No, the one that shut you down the second I questioned your originality."

Doug snorted, glancing toward the living room, ignored her question the way guys usually did when they haven't yet worked out the best possible reply in their minds. She supposed that was one thing she liked about him so much.

He was one-hundred-percent-predictable male, even while surprising her constantly.

He finally returned his hand to the leg he'd bared again, stroking her ankle in a circular motion, as if the movement allowed the gears in his head to engage. "The meeting I stayed in Denver to make?"

She nodded. "The one that caused you to miss the one here."

"Yeah. That one." He twisted his hand around her foot, stopped, started again. "It was over a restaurant design. A café, really. Two women who'd arranged their financing and were looking at models and plans."

"And they didn't like what you gave them."

His mouth quirked. "Who's telling this story, sister? You or me?"

She made the motion of zipping her lips.

"That's better."

"Hey," she said, before remembering her virtual zipper. She mouthed the word, Sorry, and waited for Doug to go on.

"Warren Sill Group, the firm where I'll be working in Denver, tossed the café my way. A welcome boon. Or so I thought." He smirked. "The joke was on me. I learned the hard way that the café's owners had turned up their noses at at least six top-notch concepts already."

"And they made you number seven." Kinsey broke her silence solely because she could sense what was coming and how painful the admission was going to be.

"Always been my lucky number, seven." He shifted in his chair, moved her feet closer to the V of his legs and began to massage her soles. "Thing was, I'd seen what they'd vetoed and I'd read every word in the original proposal. I knew I'd nailed it. I knew it."

But he hadn't. She could tell he hadn't, and that the setback had been a hard one to take. "I'm sorry. That must really suck. Especially with the added blow of disappointing your client here."

"'Blow' just about covers everything," he said with more than a touch of sarcasm. "I'll get over it. Hell, I'm over it now."

He obviously wasn't, but she played along, wrapping her robe tighter around her shoulders and settling her legs more comfortably in his lap. "So, tell me about it."

He frowned, stopped massaging in midrub. "About what? The meeting?"

"No, duh. The café's design." She smiled. "Astonish me with your brilliance."

"I thought that's what I just did in the living room," he said, and the look in his eyes left her breathless.

Incorrigible flirt, making her heart beat like a jungle tom-tom. "Which part? The astonishment or the brilliance? Because I seem to recall doing most of the work."

He squeezed her foot hard. "Do you want to hear about the design, or do you want to take this outside?"

"Bring it on, tough guy."

He stared at her for several seconds, an expression on his face that she couldn't define. His hands on her feet stilled while he seemed to consider where to take the conversation.

And then he shook his head; his lips quirked in a wry smile. "You don't make it easy on a man, do you?"

Poor baby. He was not having one of his better days. She pulled her feet from his lap, tucked her robe around her body and leaned forward to kiss him. A simple kiss. Just a quick brush of her lips to his.

But Doug had other plans.

The moment their mouths made contact, his hands were in her hair, holding her head for a kiss that escalated beyond a comforting gesture into a desperate and needy embrace. He devoured her, and Kinsey's mouth trembled.

She'd intended to soothe him, yet he seemed resistant to being easily calmed…as if…as if…nothing. She couldn't express what she sensed in him except for a strange sort of despair.

And despair did not fit at all with what she knew of Doug Storey.

His kiss, on the other hand, was the one she remembered from Coconut Caye. Wild and hungry, reckless and hot. His tongue possessed her mouth, stroking over and around and along the length of hers, stirring both her body and her blood. Her heart raced, her breasts tightened, her sex quivered.

And then he was done, setting her away as quickly as he'd struck.

She sat back, stunned speechless by his shift in mood and emotion, thinking that she really had no idea what it was that made Doug tick. For months she'd enjoyed his company, but until hit with the news of his upcoming move, she hadn't thought about Doug's deeper appeal.

She'd really been stupid not to take him more seriously, not to learn what she could while she'd had the chance. A chance she now might never have.

"So," she began, reaching for her napkin and dabbing it at her mouth. "What were we talking about?"

Doug sat up, stabbed at a bite of chicken, swirled it through a smear of papaya glaze on his plate. "About what you said to me during last summer's vacation."

"No. I'm sure that wasn't it." *Think, think, think, Kinsey. Think.* Why could she remember in great detail her rum-soaked ramblings from over a year ago, but nothing they'd said before that kiss? "The café. We were talking about the café and your design."

Doug sighed, then shook his head, a momentary surrender, but she knew he'd be back. "My idea would actually have given the place more the look of a diner. But I went there with a reason after seeing what they'd been offered previously."

"Which was?"

"They wanted retro." He snorted. "And, no offense to anyone at Warren Sill, but I didn't see a lot of thought in any of the concepts."

Interesting. He wasn't even settled into the job yet and the penis wars had already started. "Maybe it was a case of the group's frustration in dealing with that particular client. I mean, why go all-out when faced with what sounds like guaranteed failure?"

"I don't buy it." He shook his head. "That's a bogus way to work."

She should've known he wouldn't understand anything less than a commitment of two-hundred-plus percent. "Maybe, but it's human."

"Well, it would certainly account for the cliché after big stinkin' cliché I saw. Booths and counters. Red vinyl. Black-and-white-checkerboard floor tiles. As if the designs were all dialed in."

"Booths and counters say retro to me."

He shrugged. "Sure. They say retro to everyone. But there's a difference between retro and authentic. I read a *New York Times* quote once that basically said when it comes to retro fashion, historical accuracy is often beside the point."

"And your diner design was authentic."

He shook his head. "It was actually more reminiscent of a railroad dining car. True historic diners were prefab, usually stainless steel with porcelain enamel skins. I didn't go quite that far."

She felt her mouth tipping up in a smile. "Actually, I know that about diners."

Doug blinked and then he grinned. "So? Astonish me with *your* brilliance already."

"It's a long strange series of coincidences that make the entire thing sound like fiction."

"I'm not going anywhere," he said, and settled back into his chair.

There he went again, making her feel like she was the center of his world. It was the sort of attention she was used to receiving before sex, not after, and it raised Doug's rating a number of notches on her mating scale.

"I'm not sure if you've ever heard Sydney talk about her friend Izzy? Isabel Leighton?"

Doug shook his head. "Don't think so."

"I've heard her talk about her off and on, but only met her last year. The funny part is that I already knew her. Or I had known her, way back when we were kids and last names didn't matter," she explained, adding a cheery laugh.

"This is the truth being stranger than fiction part, right?" he asked, and she nodded.

"Izzy's uncle works for my parents. He does lawns, theirs and several of their long-time neighbors. He put in my mother's backyard pool garden." She fluttered one hand expansively.

"Anyway, Izzy and her mother lived with her uncle Leonard for a while after her parents divorced, and he used to bring her along when he worked weekends. He'd take me with them to lunch at his mother's diner, where her mother worked."

"And it was original."

"Yep. The whole long counter, the stainless-steel panels and spinning stools that Izzy and I had way too much fun playing on." She shrugged, grinned. "They lost most of the original structure years ago during Hurricane Alicia. Anyway…" Ugh. Why was she rambling on?

Her cooking might not kill him, but she was definitely on the right track for babbling him to death. "That's the extent of my diner-specific brilliance. And I really am sorry your concept didn't work out. Nothing like starting off on the wrong foot, huh?"

Doug made a face as if blowing off her concern. "I suppose being the brunt of an inside joke didn't sit well, but I'll live. And I'll hold on to the design."

"And you should. You'll get a chance to use it later. The railroad car idea sounds like a lot of fun. I can see the serving staff dressed like porters or engineers."

"My thoughts exactly." He pushed his plate away, rubbed his hands together with way too much glee and returned them to her legs. He tossed her robe open so that she was exposed from her toenails to her panties, before pulling the garment completely off her shoulders.

And then he reached for the papaya glaze.

Kinsey held her breath as Doug lifted the spoon toward her, and she curled her tongue to catch the sweet drizzle he poured. Except that he continued to pour even after she'd closed her mouth, dripping the sticky fruit glaze over one bare nipple before moving to the other.

Shudders rippled through her as she waited for Doug's next move. Finally, he made it, leaning forward and lapping his way around one breast, from the underside to the upper curve before settling his lips over her tightly drawn nipple and licking her clean.

Any minute now she was going to die, because then he moved to the other breast and repeated the process of savoring the tastes of citrus and her skin. She had no doubt that he savored because his grip on her arms tightened.

The throaty purr in his throat sharpened into a near feral growl before he pulled back, leaving her panting, and sticky with sugar and sweat.

"Now," he said, eyeing her pruriently. "I think it's time for a second helping of dessert."

4

KINSEY HAD BARELY WALKED through the door of her office before Lauren verbally pounced from behind. "What is wrong with you that you never answer your phone anymore?"

Rounding her desk, Kinsey booted up her PC, noticing the early distribution of weekend mail filling her in-box, and the message light blinking on her phone. She blew out a heavy sigh. Back to work without even a chance to sit and daydream after last night's fantasy feast.

Reality definitely bites, she mused, looking up and greeting her hovering partner-slash-fairy-godmother with a smile. "Good morning to you, too."

Even though Lauren rolled her eyes, this time she had the courtesy to wait until Kinsey stored her purse. And this time the pouncing was not quite so fierce. "When Syd couldn't reach you last night, she called me, and then I called both your home and your cell."

"And neither one of you managed to leave a message on either." Even so, concern rapidly replaced Kinsey's annoyance as, slowly, she sat. "What happened? Is everyone all right?"

Lauren seemed to nod and shake her head at the same time. Wispy strawberry-blond curls settled around her shoulders. "No one's hurt, but Izzy's uncle

Leonard? There was a fire at the house his church is building for Habitat for Humanity.''

"You're kidding!" Kinsey's heart lurched; her hands grabbed the edge of her desk tightly. "But her Gramma Fred's okay, right? And Leonard, and her mother? God, Izzy would die if anything happened to Rose.''

Once again, Lauren nodded. "Everyone's fine. No one was on-site when it happened. A group from Leonard's congregation had headed out there after Sunday evening service and found the structure a total loss. It was like a fire-breathing dragon, it hit so hard and fast.''

"Oh, God." *Oh, God.* Placing her elbows on her desk, Kinsey pressed her mouth to the back of her fingers. She shook her head, even as she imagined hammers swinging in rhythm to "I'll Fly Away." "Do they know what happened?''

"First indication is that it was electrical.''

"What about homeowner's insurance?''

"It's arranged through Habitat, but it'll take time, as all settlements do." Lauren shrugged fatalistically at the prospect of dealing with bureaucracies and neverending red tape.

Kinsey slumped back in her chair. "This is unbelievable.''

"Yeah, and apparently this particular family is in serious need right now. The dad and the boys are staying with Leonard in the parsonage, while the mother and the girls are in one of the women's shelters Izzy works with. It really sucks.''

"Izzy must be going crazy. What are we going to do?" Kinsey asked, because she knew the company would do something. Sydney would see to that.

Lauren settled into the plush armchair in front of Kinsey's desk. "I talked to Sydney earlier and just sent out an e-mail. We have a meeting this afternoon at four. Apparently she's had a Sydney brainstorm."

"Okay. Good." Kinsey was too overwhelmed to even know what to say. "Where's Sydney now?"

"With Izzy and the others, sifting through what they can before the bulldozers move in. From the way it sounds and what Anton says, I doubt they'll be able to salvage any of the donated materials or supplies."

The very idea made Kinsey sick, especially knowing how important it was for Izzy to be able to give back the good fortune with which she'd been blessed. Izzy's family had always emphasized the importance of caring for those less fortunate, a tenet that served as the driving force behind her charity and volunteer work. "I can't imagine. What a waste. And I hate doing nothing. I feel like we should at least take them breakfast."

"Izzy's Gramma Fred has that covered. All we can do is wait to hear what Sydney has on her mind." Lauren leaned back and crossed her legs, swinging one foot and narrowing her gaze to focus on Kinsey's face. "But speaking of food..." She let the sentence trail off until certain she had Kinsey's full attention. "How was the chicken?"

Doug! Kinsey's heart turned over in her chest. She wondered if he'd heard about—

Wait. What was she thinking? He'd told her last night that he and Izzy had never met. Funny how she assumed everyone who belonged to the circle of friends she thought of as family shared the closeness she felt to each.

She definitely needed to introduce Izzy to him.

"Amazing, really. I had no idea that cooking was actually something I could manage."

"With a little help from your friends, you mean."

Kinsey smiled, giving Lauren her due. "My friends and one swarthy pirate."

After a moment's pause, Lauren's foot stopped swinging. She lifted one perfectly tweezed brow. "Patrick wasn't exactly a pirate, you know."

Kinsey cringed, drawing up her feet to sit cross-legged in her oversize chair. "Yeah. That was really insensitive of me, wasn't it? I desperately need to stop spouting the first thing that comes to mind."

"Ooh, let me guess." Lauren's mouth pulled into an I-told-you-so smirk. "Your big mouth is getting you into trouble again."

"Not exactly trouble," Kinsey hedged. "More like...*trouble light*."

"With Doug?"

Persistent wench. "Over Doug, anyway."

Lauren glanced at her watch. "I've got twenty minutes before Macy starts yelling that she needs me to upload her gIRL gUIDE updates. So give it up."

"I'm not sure twenty minutes is enough time to explain it and have it make sense." Kinsey frowned, drilling Lauren with a pointed gaze. "Besides, you sleep with Doug's business partner. I tell you, and the details end up spilled all over your pillow."

"Puh-leez. I have much better things to talk about with Anton in bed. Now, speak. And no leaving out the juicy stuff."

"Like I said, it's not that big of a deal," Kinsey said, hoping to minimize what she feared was big-time damage. "Except in that really maddening way things you've said while under the influence come back to bite you in the butt.''

"When were you and Doug ever that drunk to-gether…?'' Lauren's blue eyes widened dramatically. "Coconut Caye. I knew it. All that sun and surf and skin. The perfect setting for sin.''

Kinsey scoffed. "As well you should know, since you were doing more than a little bit of sinning your-self.''

"Me? Hardly. Well, other than thinking murderous thoughts about Poe…thoughts that are long since noth-ing more than a memory,'' Lauren hurried to add. "I was simply trying to save what I had with Anton, thank you very much. You were the one on the deck humping a pole.''

Again with the reminders of her intoxicated behavior Kinsey didn't need. "If you want to talk about that particular party, let's not leave out what you were do-ing with the clothes you were taking off.''

Lauren huffed. "Fine. Forget about the sin. Just tell me what you said to Doug.''

"It's not that simple.''

"Of course it's that simple.'' Lauren's brow went up. "I don't have to know all the details of what you were or were not wearing at the time.''

Kinsey really was going to have to talk to Doug about returning her bikini bottoms. They happened to belong to her favorite-and-now-useless suit.

Okay. That thought had nothing to do with what Lauren had just said, but the other woman's comment had brought back last night's entire discussion with Doug. Not to mention reminding her of the circum-stances under which she'd lost the lower half of her bikini.

Glancing from her fingernails to Lauren's face, Kinsey hesitated, wondering how much to say. Surely her girlfriend would understand. It really wasn't the end of the world to have completely exposed her heart. Or so she tried to convince herself, since she was afraid that was exactly what she'd done.

"Uh, Kinsey? I'm waiting here. What did you say to Doug last year at Coconut Caye?"

Kinsey took one last huge breath and plunged forward. "I told him he was the man I wanted to marry."

"As soon as Lauren gets back with copies of my memo, we'll get started," Sydney said, glancing around the gIRL-gEAR conference table at Izzy and the six seated partners.

Kinsey's gaze moved from Izzy to Sydney and back. The two women looked like hell and, quite frankly, smelled as if that's where they'd been. They'd worked the site of the fire all day before arriving at the office, and appeared to have skipped over exhaustion and slid into the realm of the walking dead.

Kinsey wasn't sure she'd ever seen the totally put-together and elegant Sydney Ford look so frazzled and fried. And Izzy, usually dressed in vibrant colors and artistic prints that fit her larger-than-life personality, didn't look any better in baggy blue jeans and a Houston Rockets jersey.

If Kinsey had had her way, she'd be suffering and smelling much the same. Once Lauren had left her office this morning, Kinsey had called Sydney and volunteered to help. Business-minded Syd, however, preferred having the rest of the staff at the office to cover appointments. It was help, but not exactly the sort that Kinsey had had in mind.

Working behind the scenes was all well and good, but it was an assistance she found too passive when there was so much physical labor needing to be done. And now, seeing both Izzy and Sydney sweat-and-soot streaked and totally disheveled, Kinsey wished she'd ignored the request.

She should've gone to the cleanup site to do what she could, even if it was nothing more than delivering drinking water. Appointments could've easily been rescheduled. Seeing to the needs of friends who were as close as family should have taken precedence—a mantra the Gray family had lived by all of Kinsey's life.

She reached out and squeezed Izzy's hand. "Are you doing okay?"

Izzy offered a tired smile in return, her usually bright eyes bloodshot and grim. "I'm fine, and I know what you're thinking. Trust me, you were more help here. I promise you that. Between Gramma Fred's friends and Leonard's congregation?" The way Izzy rolled her eyes said it all.

Kinsey grinned. "A madhouse, huh?"

She nodded. "Most everyone ended up being in the way, but—" she gave a weak shrug "—it was all good. They hooked us up with fried chicken and chocolate cake to die for. Way more than a body could ever be expected to eat."

"I would've been another extra, I know," Kinsey said. "But I felt so useless all day. Like I needed to be out in the trenches with you guys. I talked to Mom earlier, and she's *still* worried about Leonard and Rose, not to mention Fred."

Exhaustion sent Izzy's nearly black eyes drifting shut; she opened them again. The corners crinkled slightly with her smile, which was as wide and sunny as always against her light cocoa skin. "Your daddy came by to check on Uncle Leonard right as Sydney and I were leaving. That meant a lot to him. To Mamma and Gramma, too. They really do love your folks."

At Lauren's approach with a sheaf of memos, Kinsey glanced up and took a copy before turning back to Izzy. "Daddy's such a softie. He thinks of Leonard as a brother, you know."

"I have never seen two men with nothing in common but the love of a good lawn and the good book grow as close as Leonard and your father." The weariness waned from Izzy's expression. "You Grays are good people. Gramma Fred says so. And it takes a lot to impress that wonderfully bossy old woman."

Kinsey wrapped an arm around Izzy's shoulders and hugged hard. "She'd smack you around for saying that, you know."

"Tell me about it," Izzy said, and blew out a big puff of air.

Standing at the head of the table, Sydney cleared her throat and waited for the chatter to quiet. Kinsey squeezed Izzy's shoulder once more, then fixed her full attention on Sydney.

"By now, all of you have heard about last night's fire at the Habitat for Humanity home Izzy's congregation is building for one of its own. And I know you're aware of what a big part Izzy's family has played in my life. In Kinsey's, too.

"Homeowner's insurance will, of course, eventually take care of replacement costs, but many of the original donors to the project don't have the means to replace the supplies. That leaves an immediate deficit I'd like to help fill."

Sydney shifted from one foot to the other, then leaned a hip on the table's edge. "I've put together a very brief outline of a fund-raising idea that I'd like to run by all of you before I pass out."

At the obvious weariness in Syd's voice, Kinsey glanced from the memo's introduction to her boss lady's ashen complexion. This was not good, not good at all. "It's okay if you sit, Syd. I swear we'll pay attention."

Sydney smiled, shook her head. "If I sit, I'll need a hunky fireman to hoist me back out of my chair."

"I'm pretty sure that can be arranged," Lauren offered. "Ray called while you were in the rest room. He'll be here any minute."

A look of relief brought color back to Sydney's face and she sighed, sinking down into her chair at the table's head. "Thank goodness. A hunky fireman to clean me up, and his amazing brother to feed me. What more could a girl want?"

"This girl would like it if you shared," Poe said, arms crossed defensively over her electric-blue blazer.

Sitting at Poe's side, Lauren scoffed. "Sounds to me like work and school are getting to you."

Poe gave Lauren a piercing look. "If anything is getting to me, it is simply my lack of time for recreational dating."

"As opposed to serious relationship-type dating?" Lauren asked, brows arched knowingly.

This time Poe simply returned her attention to the head of the table. "I do not have time for a relationship. And Sydney does not have time for this conversation."

"Unfortunately, that's true," Sydney said, getting back to business. "Now, as I was saying, insurance will cover the loss and the rebuilding, but insurance takes time. And with Kinsey and I both considering Izzy's family as part of our own, I need the company to do something. You have a rough sketch of my initial idea on the memo Lauren handed out.''

"Anything, Syd. Count me in,'' Kinsey said.

Sydney gave a weak laugh accompanied by a rather sinister grin. "I appreciate your enthusiasm, because you and Izzy and Poe are all a big part of the plan.''

Uh-oh. Gung ho until seconds ago, Kinsey glanced from that grin to the memo, trying to turn down the blaring alarm bells in her head as she scanned the text. "A bachelorette auction?''

She wondered what Doug would think. She wondered how much Doug would pay. She wondered...*wait a minute.* "Wait a minute. How fair is this? You plan to auction off only me and Izzy and Poe? What happened to *all girls for one and one girl for all?*

"Besides,'' she continued, ranting as her objections grew, "how much money are you anticipating the three of us will bring in?'' She skewed her mouth to one side. "Not that I'm admitting to being cheap or worthless or anything, but I would think more bachelorettes would equal more cash.''

"Well...'' Sydney seemed to hedge. "You and Poe *are* the only two partners still single. And since Izzy is directly concerned, she wanted to be included.''

"Then it's a done deal?'' Kinsey really needed more time; she'd stopped thinking of herself as single last night. "I have no say in this?''

"Of course you do. You can say yes,'' Lauren offered with a friendly little snort.

But Sydney was shaking her head and smothering a

weary yawn. "You have a say, definitely. It's just with the timing being what it is, I wanted to make the pitch so I could get home and shower before I pass out."

Officially single or not, Kinsey knew she wouldn't say no, not when this was as important as it was to Sydney. gIRL-gEAR was a partnership that went far deeper than any official corporate arrangement.

Her musketeer comment hadn't been spoken off the top of her head. That had been the group's catch phrase since their senior year at University of Texas and the fateful night at Starbucks when gIRL-gEAR as a dream had been born.

At least Kinsey wouldn't be alone on the auction block. But she wouldn't be there without making damn certain the agreement was clearly for no more than one date. As a semisingle white female, she could give up one night of dinner and dancing for the cause.

In fact, the entire experience might prove to be quite interesting. She doubted she'd bring in more than five dollars, but that wasn't the point. The point was to gauge Doug's reaction to the idea of another man wanting her enough to pay through the nose.

Okay. Five dollars wasn't exactly nose-paying funds. And then there was the fact that she had no guarantee she'd be bought. But still, if her date wasn't a man she was going to marry, but only a very legitimate part of her wicked Doug-winning games...well, why not?

All was fair in love and making Doug jealous, right? She studied the printed pitch one more time, not finding much at all in the way of details. "How exactly is this going to work?"

"That's what we're all going to think about this week," Sydney said. "We'll meet back here next Monday afternoon and see what we've come up with as far as ideas go. For now, I'm going home. I have a fire-fighter there wearing my name.''

"No. You have a firefighter here wearing your name.''

At the sound of Ray Coffey's deep voice, Kinsey—along with everyone else at the table—glanced toward the conference room doorway.

Ray stood in the entrance wearing crisp blue jeans, black roper boots and a navy polo-style pullover emblazoned with the insignia of Texas Task Force One—the urban search-and-rescue team with which he worked.

"Oh, sweetie. Am I glad to see you.'' Sydney breathed an audible and visible sigh of release.

At the same time a chorus of, "Hey, Ray,'' went up around the room. Kinsey joined in, but Izzy's voice was barely a whisper—a contrast to the intensity of her bone-crushing grip on Kinsey's hand. Kinsey knew exactly what—or rather, who—it was that had captured Izzy's attention. The bedroom-eyed man standing beside Ray Coffey was at least six foot two, with shoulders broader and harder than Ray's, bulging biceps and quads, and skin the color of sweet pecan pie.

"Hey, all. This is Joseph Baron, a buddy from the station.'' Ray crossed the room and draped an arm over Sydney's shoulders, helping her to her feet. "Baron, these are Sydney's girls, uh, women. I'll let them all introduce themselves.''

With that, the meeting was unofficially adjourned, and Kinsey was off the hook, with one week to come up with alternative fund-raising ideas she could live with. Though Sydney with an idea was like a dog with a bone....

Right now, however, there was a much more interesting mating game underway at Kinsey's side.

While introductions were made, she watched Izzy watch Baron make a circle around the room, surreptitiously doing what she could to wipe away any dirt remaining on her face. She smoothed back her short chunky dreads, as well as the loose hairs curling over the wide cloth headband—today in bright red—that held her hair out of her eyes.

Love amid the ruins. Kinsey chuckled to herself. "Uh, Isabel?"

Izzy waved off Kinsey's teasing. "Hush with that. I'm busy here naming my children. Eloise Rose Baron has a nice ring to it, don't you think?"

Kinsey could only laugh, chuckling again when Izzy let out a long, lustful moan and whispered, "Damn, but that man is hard, and so very fine."

Izzy pushed up out of her chair as the chatter fizzled and Ray herded Sydney toward the door. Kinsey walked with Izzy into the hallway and toward the lobby, sensing the twitching of the other woman's man radar as she waited for Baron to follow. "I wonder what Sydney knows about him?" Kinsey asked.

Izzy blew out a breath and shivered. "The only thing that matters right now is the lack of a wedding band on his left hand and what exactly that means."

"That shouldn't be too hard to find out." The two women reached the lobby where, eyes closed, Sydney stood with her forehead resting on Ray's chest. "Except it doesn't look like Sydney's in the mood right now to be pried loose from Ray for girl talk."

"No need," Izzy said with a shake of her head. "I'm spending the night in her guest room. Mamma needed my room for visiting family."

The corner of Kinsey's mouth quirked upward. "How convenient for you."

"Girl, you had better believe it."

Sydney stepped away from Ray then, pushed her hair from her face, telling him with her eyes that she wanted to go. Nodding, he glanced beyond the receptionist's station and lifted his chin in a questioning gesture. "Hey, dude. You ready?"

Both Kinsey and Izzy turned their gazes toward Joseph Baron as he entered the lobby. He grabbed Ray's hand in one of those intensely complicated male handshakes that Kinsey had never understood.

Izzy simply sighed one more time, whispering for Kinsey's ears only, "Fine, I tell you. Fine."

"Right behind you, dawg." Baron spoke to Ray, but his gaze had found Izzy's and had yet to leave. Kinsey would've wanted to run to the rest room and wash her face had a man been looking at her with such dark intensity.

But not Izzy. Chin held high, she wore the remaining grit and grime of the day's labor with pride, and Kinsey had a feeling that her attitude as much as her clear cocoa skin, was responsible for Baron's attention.

Sydney sliced the tension by clearing her throat. "Kinsey, why don't you—"

The front door opened, bringing a burst of heat, the glare of the setting sun and, surprise, Doug Storey. Kinsey swore her grin spread all the way to her ears.

"Kinsey, hey," he said, coming toward her, flashing a smile as wide as hers. Then his expression became concerned again. "Anton told me about the fire. Oh, hey, Ray, Syd."

Sydney looked up at Ray imploringly. "Ray? Please?"

"Yeah. We're outta here." Forgoing more introductions, Ray tucked her against his side and took charge. "Doug, you and Kinsey come on out to the house. Patrick's cooking, and I've got to get Sydney home. Baron, you good with driving Izzy out in Sydney's car?"

"You got it," Baron said, tearing his gaze from Izzy to glance back at Ray.

Nodding his thanks, Ray spoke to Sydney. "Baby, where are your keys? Good girl," he added when she dug into her pocket and handed them over.

He tossed the key ring to Baron, who crossed the lobby and pushed open the door, then waited for Izzy to head out after Sydney and Ray. Izzy waggled her brows at Kinsey and followed. That left Kinsey alone in the lobby with Doug.

"Whoa. Talk about a whirlwind. Ray certainly knows how to get things taken care of, doesn't he?" Kinsey turned and walked back toward her office, assuming Doug would follow. He did, and his warmth at her back was nicely comforting. "I thought you were catching a flight out this morning."

"I was." Doug stood just inside her doorway as she straightened her desktop and logged out of the computer network, shutting down her PC for the night. "But I called Marcus West first thing, and he wanted a lunch meeting. I wasn't about to say no. And then Anton told me about the fire when I stopped by the office afterward. Is everyone okay?"

"The structure's a total loss, but no one is hurt. We're working on fund-raiser ideas." Or idea, singular. One she did *not* want to tell him about yet. "So, how'd the meeting go?" She loved how they had already settled into discussing one another's days. "Things better between you two now?"

Doug nodded, leaning one shoulder against the doorjamb. Today he wore black-pinstriped suit pants and a dress shirt just this side of rust. He looked very continental in the buttoned-up, sans-tie combination, and Kinsey had to force herself not to drool. "Marcus bought new property at the edge of downtown's Westmoreland district."

"And he wants you to design his space," she said, grabbing her purse from a drawer in the credenza behind her desk.

Doug grinned. "You know, Kinsey, you really are getting into a bad habit of finishing my sentences for me."

She grinned from the inside out. "Is that what you think I'm doing?"

"What would you call it?"

Shrugging, she checked her purse for her keys, not quite ready to agree that she'd unconsciously done exactly what he'd claimed. "I'm merely making conversation."

"Good."

"Why so worried?" She frowned.

"No worries. Not really. Just making sure we're on the same wavelength here."

"And what wavelength is that?"

He pushed away from the door and strolled toward her, taking his own sweet time as he rounded the side of her desk.

She stayed where she was, keeping the lacquered-mahogany workstation between them. The desk was wide and broad, giving her tons of space on which to work, but the open design offered absolutely nothing behind which to hide.

Not that she was hiding. She just liked the idea of Doug having to chase her before she gave in. And he did, sort of, rounding the end of her desk and stalking her as she backed up into the credenza.

She'd gone as far as she could go, yet he kept on coming, stopping only when his body was pressed to hers so completely that she could feel muscles and buttons and his belt buckle and his thick sexual package beneath.

He trapped her by bracing his hands on the credenza on either side of her hips, trapped her further when he bent to nuzzle the side of her neck there at the spot she loved—the one he never missed and nuzzled oh, so well.

He even managed to nuzzle as he mumbled against her skin. "The wavelength that says no one in this office is going to be getting married and doing that sentence-finishing thing on a regular basis."

"Please." She lifted her chin to give him better access, proud of herself for keeping her voice steady when she felt the strange urge to slap him silly. "The only reason I'm here with you is to get back my stolen bikini bottoms."

"I've been thinking about that."

"Oh, yeah?"

"Yeah." One hand moved from the credenza to her waist, slipping beneath the crop top of orange-and-avocado silk she wore over matching ankle-length pants. "I've been thinking a deal is in order."

"What sort of deal?" she asked, though the minute his skin touched hers, she was afraid she'd agree to anything.

"A bet." His hand cupped her rib cage, sliding upward until the heel of his palm brushed the full curve of her breast. He groaned, and she did the same.

"What sort of bet?" She sounded like a CD on repeat, but thinking of a witty response was out of the question. In fact, thinking at all had become damn hard to do, now that he'd moved his hand to rub the flat of his thumb over her nipple covered with the filmy, gauzy lace of her bra.

"Football," he said with gritted teeth, as if anything more was too much to push past his binding erection. "Why the hell are you wearing a bra?"

She'd asked herself the same question seconds ago, even as she'd wondered if getting up to lock the door would spoil the moment. "In case you haven't noticed, I need one. What about football?"

"This weekend's game." He wedged her legs apart with one knee and didn't even pretend to ask permission as his other hand settled possessively between. "The Texans win, I keep your bottoms. The Texans lose, you model them for me."

"How fair is any of that?" she asked, then gasped as he pressed the long edge of his index finger up against her sex.

"I like winning." His hand beneath her top made quick work with the hooks of her bra. "And getting my way."

"I can tell," she said as her breasts fell free, and he moved both hands to cup her fully. She couldn't help herself; she placed her hands over his and pressed herself into his palms.

He growled and shoved his erection against the seam of her pants, grinding against her until she whimpered and edged toward orgasm.

"Why the hell are you wearing pants?" he demanded.

"I like pants."

"Learn to like dresses."

"Bossy."

"Damn right," he said, and stepped back completely, leaving her panting and hanging on the edge.

She stared at him, looking for signs that he'd truly lost his mind. "What was that all about?"

His grin was bigger than that of a cat with a canary, sexier than a devil given his due. He smacked his lips as if he couldn't wait to eat her up.

"That was about having dessert before dinner. Now, let's go before the traffic kills us."

5

AFTER THREE AND A HALF hours spent indulging in fine wine, conversation and even finer friends, Kinsey waved a final goodbye to Ray Coffey.

He shut his front door, and she and Doug headed down the suburban home's long pebbled walkway toward their cars. Dinner had been great; even Sydney perked up after a shower and a plate of Patrick's cooking. Who wouldn't when faced with a meal like the one he'd just served?

Seafood and fruit in an amazing combination of sweet citrus and hot spice, and a pudding or custard sort of dessert, the likes of which Kinsey had never eaten but could easily find herself addicted to.

Patrick hadn't even stayed to eat, Ray explaining away his brother's vanishing act as the norm. The ravenous group of six had simply gone on to praise Patrick in absentia as they ate.

They'd avoided talking about the fire or the fund-raising auction, and had instead chatted about Izzy's recent humanitarian efforts working with Doctors Without Borders in Mexico.

Having listened to her stories, Izzy's dinner partners all admitted to their feelings of inadequacy in the charity department. Izzy had rolled her doelike eyes at such ridiculousness, as she called it, and turned the conversation to Baron's and Ray's lifesaving efforts.

At the end of the evening, Kinsey had felt like a toad for complaining about being scheduled for the auction block. It was the very least she could do to help. And who knew? She might meet someone to whom she wouldn't mind being sold.

Someone who wasn't Doug Storey. As if.

Using the light from the moon and the streetlamp, she dug through the contents of her purse for her car keys, trying—but failing—to stifle a groan. She was stuffed. Miserably, uncomfortably stuffed. "I don't think I've ever eaten that much at one sitting in my entire life."

"I gotta agree." Doug followed close on her heels— close enough that his shadow was in her way; she shifted her purse to her other shoulder. "You'd think Patrick wouldn't have any problem getting a position as a chef."

"True, except I'd guess his training is pretty much limited to Caribbean fare." Her keys, finally. She really needed to downsize her bag. Not to mention upsize her usual number of sit-ups tonight. "And it's probably not even real training at that. More like survival skills."

"What was that he did to the fish?"

"I'm not sure I want to know," Kinsey admitted, keys jangling. "There are a few things better left to the imagination."

"Afraid he laced it with an island aphrodisiac?"

"You wish." She tossed a laugh over her shoulder. "Actually, Patrick was probably the one doing the wishing."

Where the hell had *that* come from? she mused, walking down the driver's side of her new Saturn Vue, which was parked behind his Nissan 350Z and beneath the spreading oaks that lined one side of the drive.

She unlocked the door, tucked her purse down next to the center console, then turned back to ask the question she'd calmed enough to voice. "Why would you say something like that?"

Hands tucked in his front pockets, Doug gave a careless shrug. "It's obvious he's all about getting into your pants."

"If he was, then don't you think he would've stuck around instead of taking off the minute the food was on the table?" She blew out a huff of frustration. "Patrick's come-ons don't mean a thing. I know that. Izzy knows that. He's simply…intense."

Doug snorted in disbelief. "How can someone be *simply* intense? Isn't that an oxymoron?"

"I don't know, Doug. Is it?" She wished it wasn't so dark; she wanted to see his eyes. To see if she could tell what was going on in his all-too-male mind. "That's just the best way I know to describe Patrick."

"Okay. Sure. Whatever."

She bit down on her first choice of smart comebacks and stated, "Envy does not become you."

"Don't you mean jealousy?"

She shook her head. "Envy means you want what he has. Jealousy would imply he's a threat to something belonging to you."

He waited a moment, then said, "Maybe he is."

"Oh, really." Now *this* was getting interesting. Crossing her arms over her chest, she leaned back against her SUV. "And what would that be?"

He looked off toward the dark street, then back in the direction of the Coffeys' garage, where a floodlight burned brightly. Finally, he pulled his hands from his pockets and, soles scuffing on the concrete drive, moved closer.

Leaning his shoulder against the car next to her, he hesitated, his mouth drawn into a grim line. "I don't have a right or a reason to be jealous. That's what makes this so hard to deal with."

She stopped her automatic response, which was to demand an explanation, and treaded carefully instead—a very hard feat to accomplish when he stood so near, when his body heat stirred her, when he smelled wonderfully of nothing more than warm skin and a long day.

"What's so hard to deal with?" she asked.

He glanced down at his feet, away to the lights of an oncoming car, waiting for it to pass before turning again to face her. At this range, at this angle, she could so much better see the emotion he fought.

A visible emotion that tugged on the loose threads of the defensive covering she'd woven over her heart. It was sad, really, how weak she was. One strong pull and he had her coming apart. Oh, but it was going to be hard, harder than she'd expected, letting this one go.

Finally, Doug found his voice. "It's tough, Kinsey, feeling this way, feeling…jealous, when I know full well that you and I don't have a committed relationship." He waited, as if unsure about saying anything more.

She liked the idea of making him sweat—especially considering her own rise in temperature and the racing pace of her pulse. "I see."

"C'mon, darlin'. You know it's true." Frustration tinged his voice, a frustration she sensed was the result of losing an argument he was having with himself to justify what he was feeling.

She wasn't about to give him any ammunition to shoot down those feelings. "What's true?"

"We're having a good time. That's it. That's all it can be. You're here. I'm on my way to Denver." He shrugged. "Like I said, it doesn't make a lot of sense."

"But you're still jealous over me." She wanted to get this part straight, because this part was the only part that mattered. "Over Patrick flirting with me."

"It doesn't even have to be Patrick. It's just that…"

"Just that what?"

He hung his head, shook it, moved his hands to his hips and surrendered. "It's just that ever since you told me I was the man you wanted to marry, I've thought of you as becoming my wife."

THE STARBUCKS on South Shepherd made for a much better conversational arena, even if the drive back into town from The Woodlands had given Kinsey too much time to think.

From the look on Doug's face as he stared at his caffè mocha sitting on the table between them, he had a lot on his mind, as well.

It made sense, considering the word *marriage* had cropped up between them.

And since Doug had used the word *wife*.

Kinsey blew across the top of her latte and sighed as she sipped. She hated introducing tension into what so far had been an advertisement for a fun-filled evening.

But as uncomfortable as this subject for some reason made her, talking about their intimacy on Coconut Caye was a big part of taking their relationship to the deeper level she was beginning to realize she wanted.

And Doug did deserve her honesty. She just hoped she didn't freeze from the exposure.

She laced her fingers around the wide mug and

stared down into the milky espresso as she gathered her thoughts. She looked up again before admitting, "You know I was drunk when I said that."

His mouth quirked as he lifted his eyes to meet hers. "I was drunk when I heard it."

"So, then, it shouldn't be that big of a deal. Right?" She shrugged with forced indifference, easing into feeling him out. Sipping again at her latte, she sat back in the plush armchair like the consummate actress she was.

"It shouldn't, no." He reached for his mug, cradled it between his large hands. "I mean, it can't happen, this thing between us. I know that. You know that. Maybe if I wasn't leaving…"

"Sure," she said, getting even deeper into the role of understanding female-but-not-girlfriend. Lee Strasberg would be proud. "I mean, a long-distance relationship would be pretty tough to manage."

He shook his head, grimacing. "Yeah. The reality sucks, but trying to make a go of a relationship like that is a recipe for disaster."

She forced out a laugh, wishing he hadn't been so quick to agree, then wondered why she'd even wish such a thing. It wasn't as if she was a big fan of an emotional involvement played out over thousands of miles.

Still, if the choice was having Doug on those terms or not having him at all… "I've never put myself in a position to know. I still live within ten miles of my parents. And I'm only five miles from work and family number two. I can't imagine not having my family close."

"I don't even know the last time I saw my folks." He was quiet for a moment before adding, "They moved from Abilene to Tulsa a couple of years ago, and I haven't even seen their new place. My brother and his wife are still in Abilene, and it's been years since I've been back.''

Wait a minute. He didn't visit his family? Not that everyone shared her apron-strings issues, but still. ''You're kidding! Why not? I mean, it's your business, of course,'' she added, backing off hurriedly. ''I don't mean to pry.''

''Then why are you?'' he asked, his tone teasing, his eyes not quite so light.

She gave a small laugh that probably didn't sound quite as casual as she meant it to. ''I don't know. It's just that I have Sunday morning breakfasts and Thursday night dinners with my parents every week. I tend to forget that not everyone has the close relationship—'' *dare she say codependent relationship?* ''—with their family that I do.''

''It's not about closeness.'' At a long hissing blast of steam, he glanced toward the barista and simply shrugged. ''They have their life. I have mine.''

And that was that. His tone left no holes for Kinsey to poke at and widen, no cracks for her to pry apart. But she didn't need to be beaten on the head with a hammer to realize the truth he'd just handed her.

Doug Storey was not a family man.

Then again, he had used the word *wife*. He'd been thinking about the possibilities. And he hadn't yet tucked tail and run. So…where did that leave her plan for winning him away from his bachelor life?

Family man or not, she wasn't quite ready to let him go without knowing more about where he came from. Hey, a girl could always dream that she had it in her to change a guy, right?

"Well." She ran an index finger around the mouth of her mug and decided to table any further personal probing about his dealings with his family for the moment. "I don't mind if you're jealous over me, but seriously. You don't have anything to worry about. I'm not the sort to stray."

He drank, then considered her over the rim of his mug. "I'm more curious to know if you're the sort to spill your guts while wasted. Was that you or the booze talking last summer when you made the marriage comment?"

The way he was staring—his brows up, his chin down, his smile impatient and tight, his gaze focused on her eyes—she knew he wasn't seeing just the telltale pulse in the hollow of her throat. He was seeing more, seeing every one of the warring emotions his question had sent into battle.

"Do you want me to be honest?" she asked, and he nodded. "Okay, then. At the time? Would I have said it had I been sober? Definitely not."

Leaving her reply at that would've been the smart thing to do, the easy thing to do. But since she'd never been known to do either, and since the look in Doug's eyes had grown cold, she took a huge leap of faith.

"Would I say it now? Tonight? If I were drunk, most definitely. Under the influence of no more than espresso and your dimples?" She allowed herself a small smile when he gave her the same. "Yeah, there's a good chance it would slip out."

He crossed one ankle over the opposite knee and sat back, seeming to fill up the entire chair more than he had moments before she'd so thoroughly stroked his ego. Kinsey wasn't sure her stomach would hold all the butterflies swarming while she waited for his response.

When he finally gave it, she wished she'd kept her big mouth closed, her daydream fantasies private. "Then we have a problem. I don't want to hurt you."

"No, you just want to screw my brains out." She shot the words back before even thinking to stop her reckless tongue. Fuming at herself for being so stupidly honest, she mentally cursed him for being the same. "Or at least that's what you're trying to tell yourself, isn't it?"

"What're you talking about?"

"C'mon, Doug." Ugh. This was exactly why she'd been avoiding this discussion. Men simply shut down when the truth cut too close and they hadn't had their secret cave time to work things out. "You may have had a glass of wine with dinner, but that wife comment was not drunken rambling."

He waited, stalled, kept silent while she shifted and stewed, until she was sure she'd blown any chance they might've had to work through their issues. Even when he finally looked her straight in the eye and said, "I think we've both probably said more than is wise," she wasn't sure.

She held her breath until the reverberations from the shot to her heart settled. Doug was the only man she'd ever dated who she'd thought of as husband material. And in typical male fashion, he wasn't in the mood to give up any of what he was thinking or feeling. Instead, he put down his big size-twelve foot and brought the conversation to an end.

Fine. Let him be that way. Let him miss out on the best thing that might have ever happened to him. She'd back off for now, give him time to miss her while he was gone this next week, let him think about what he was leaving behind. Plant a seed that would germinate while he slept, and strangle him anytime he got too far from her Houston, Texas, roots.

The picture caused her to grin, and she finally looked up from her latte to change the subject. "Are you going to be in town next Sunday?"

He frowned. "Yeah, why?"

"You know that football game you wanted to make that wager on?" she asked, casting a glance from beneath lowered lashes as she drained the rest of the coffee from her mug.

He nodded, his expression intrigued.

"Well, Izzy gave me two tickets." Kinsey didn't add that the other woman had slipped them into her hand earlier tonight along with a whispered reminder of the male animal's innate love of sport. Step two in her man-trapping plan.

His eyes lightened, the tiny laugh lines at the corners deepening as he grinned. "Oh, yeah?"

"Yeah. With the fire and all, her mother doesn't have time to use the tickets, and Izzy thought we might like them."

Nodding with enthusiasm, Doug sat forward, moving to the edge of his chair. "I'd love to go. I haven't made a Texans game yet this year, so this'll be great. It's a date. Thanks."

"You're welcome." Their mugs empty and the hour late, Kinsey got to her feet, definitely feeling more hopeful than she had five minutes ago. A false hope? Maybe, but at least she'd been proactive in her campaign.

And that, to her, was the most important distinction, because she was still not ready to give up her pursuit of this man. Which brought her to the next subject on the agenda. "Well, maybe you wouldn't mind doing me a small favor in return?"

Doug pushed up out of his chair. "Shoot."

"If it works with your schedule for Halloween weekend, maybe you could put in a bid for me at the gIRL-gEAR bachelorette auction?" That had to be one of the strangest requests she'd ever made of a man, and the question's shock value seemed to have had the desired effect.

Slack-jawed, Doug stood there, holding both mugs. "Bachelorette auction?"

Nodding, Kinsey went on. "It's a fund-raiser for the family who lost their home in the fire. I have absolutely no details. We're getting together during next week's Monday meeting to work them out." She followed Doug toward the service bar. "But I'll feel like such a big loser if no one wants to buy me for the night."

"Trust me, darlin'. That won't happen." Doug left the mugs on the counter before ushering her toward the door with a hand at the small of her back. "Wow. A bachelorette auction. I guess it's a good thing I've already gotten past feeling jealous, huh?"

"Yes. And so quickly, too," Kinsey said, her sarcasm evident. He didn't have to take her completely at her word that he had no need to worry. He didn't, but it would appease her ego in a big way if he did.

"Yep." His hand moved to her shoulder, and he didn't let her get more than a step from his side. "I've decided to work on more of a Zen-like attitude. Job stress is wicked enough. I'll be doing my blood pressure a favor this way."

"Sure. Don't want you stroking out or anything," she said, and mentally rolled her eyes.

They'd reached their vehicles, parked side by side in a lot that was small and deserted and edged by a high privacy fence. Kinsey appreciated that fact when Doug, under the guise of seeing her safely to her car, backed her into the side of her SUV.

He pressed his body along the length of hers, imprisoning her hands at her sides. She opened her mouth to tease him about Zen and the cosmos and serendipitous karma, but he gave her time to do nothing but gasp before his mouth covered hers and settled in to devour and feast.

Even when she struggled to touch him, he held her wrists still, almost as if he wanted to be the one who decided the extent of their contact. Fine, whatever. He could have his way as long as he didn't stop what he was doing, because the contact he was making stole her ability to breathe.

He touched her from knee to nose, his leg wedged between hers and pressing upward to stir coals of last night's flame. She widened her stance as far as her skinny-legged pants allowed, giving him better access and waiting on a sharp cutting edge for him to take it all.

He did, his tongue slipping inside her mouth, his thigh rubbing back and forth, pushing her panties up into the folds of her rapidly steaming sex. She moaned; Doug swallowed the sound, moving their joined hands down between their bodies.

She couldn't speak to ask him what he wanted from her, what he wanted her to do, what he wanted to do in return. His deft mouth kept hers too busy to do anything but kiss him back the way he demanded she do. She did, playing along with his teasing Pied Piper of a tongue.

Yet his hands were even more insistent. He moved one of them around to her pants' back zipper, taking it down and baring her backside to the night air. She was with him all the way, even when he slid both of his hands and both of hers down her belly and into her panties, which were nearly soaked through.

He forced her to touch herself, dragging her fingers through her slick folds to spread the wetness from her clit to the opening of her sex. His mouth moved from hers in a kissing, nipping, sharply sucking line down her neck, and she thought she was going to die.

Sensation consumed her from skin to core, plucking at her nerves as if she were a sexual instrument and Doug her maestro. *Oh, oh, oh.* Why the hell was she making poetic when all she wanted to do was drop her pants to the ground and strip him out of his?

He leaned further into her body, and then dipped down enough to slip an index finger inside of her, urging her own finger into her tight sheath, as well, until she wasn't sure how much of the thrill she felt was from his touch or her own.

She wasn't a stranger to the sensation of self-pleasure, but this…this…she'd never known…

"Oh, Doug." She breathed out his name at the same time he increased the tempo of their slick, thrusting fingers. The next sound she made was less of a moan and more of a whimpering cry. "Oh, Doug."

His mouth continued to arouse her, his lips drawing on the spot he remembered, that one there, *oh, yes,* right there on the side of her neck…. She whimpered louder, breathed in, breathed out, so close, so close….

And then he pulled away from her neck and from her body and dropped down to crouch there between her legs. Tugging her pants down her thighs, he exposed her bottom to the cool metal of her SUV's door and her sex to the heat of his mouth.

He used both of his thumbs to open her fully; his tongue swirled around her clit, down her labia and back before he entered her, licking his way in and out and around the whole of her sex. When he returned to suck on her clit, she threaded her hands into his beautiful long hair and held on, pushing her mound against his mouth.

One of his hands slid around to squeeze her bottom and pull her open, and then he pushed two fingers as far into her as he could, withdrawing immediately, shoving his way inside again and then pulling away. He repeated the process with his fingers, continued the magic he was working with his mouth. Her knees shook; her belly clenched.

She slammed her palms against the cold metal door. Orgasm consumed her. She panted and gasped and moaned through seconds that went on forever, seconds of Doug's rhythmic stroking with both fingers and tongue, seconds of pressing back on the vehicle for balance while a wave of pleasure that was as fiercely emotional as it was physical crashed over her.

He completely took her apart; the shattering continued far beyond any she'd ever experienced. And the return to solid ground lasted almost as long. Never had she imagined anything so intense, anything that sent her to the edge of consciousness.

She barely recognized the fact that Doug had returned her clothing to rights until he practically crawled back up her body, kissing her thoroughly once he reached her mouth, and tasting of what she swore was the salty flavor of the sea.

The way he pushed his hips into hers and ground

roughly against her belly left no doubt about his state of arousal, and she pressed hands to the fly of his pants.

He shook his head, pulled his mouth from hers. "It's okay. I'll be okay."

"I know you will," she whispered back. "I want to do this. For you."

"If you want to do something for me, I'd rather you do it naked in bed than on your knees in a parking lot."

Her smile was as twisted as the thoughts running through her mind. "Rather chauvinistic, aren't you? In this world of equal-opportunity oral sex?"

Laughing out loud, he opened her door. The interior light shone brightly enough to illuminate the wild intent in his eyes. "I'm a pig of the worst order. Greedy and selfish enough to want more of you than I can get to here. Besides, I like to look. And this parking lot is too damn dark."

He helped boost her up into the driver's seat. She buckled up, squirming a bit as her panties bunched again between her legs.

"You okay?" he asked, standing in the V of the open door.

"Girl stuff." She shrugged. "Trying to fix what you didn't adjust quite right."

He took a step closer and didn't even ask before sliding his hand between her legs. She just looked up at him as if he'd lost his mind while he fiddled with her there where the seam of her pants ran the length of her sex.

The fact that she was fully clothed didn't matter. In fact, it raised the level of sensation, increased her pulse, which raced with the tempting fear of discovery. Her door was open; the light was on. They were no longer hidden behind the vehicle in the parking lot's shadows.

She stared into Doug's eyes; his look dared her to stop him, dared her to close her legs and push him away. Instead she turned the tables, pressing her head into the headrest and her mound up to rub against his wrist.

He worked her through her clothes, turning her into another wet mess. Her eyes rolling closed, her abs clenching, her hands gripping the edges of the seat cushion as she held on for the ride.

Easing her eyes open, she looked up to find his body bathed in the light from the open door, while his face remained eerily in the shadows. Perspiration and gooseflesh prickled over her skin, tightening her nipples and the hold she had on the seat. "If you don't move and let me close the door, I'm going to come again all over the place."

He did move; he came closer, ducking his head so that he could rest his forehead on hers. When he forced her legs even farther apart, she complied with a sharp gasp, squeezing her eyes closed when he slid his hand beneath her bottom. He cupped her fully, pressing the heel of his palm into her sex, which was waiting and ready. His breathing came raw and ragged and hot on her face.

She whimpered then, and he wedged one long, thick finger along the entire length of her, his thumb circling her clit, his fingertips probing and rubbing and...*oh, oh, oh*. Three seconds and she was done.

She cried out the way she'd wanted to minutes ago, verbally letting go and spilling everything she felt. He continued to work her, rubbing and pressing and squeezing in and out and ruthlessly around until she shuddered from a pleasure that reached close to being pain.

She collapsed, slumping down into her seat and wondering if she'd even be able to drive. Aw, who the hell cared. Eyes closed, she managed a halfhearted grin. "Please stop doing that."

"You know you love it."

God, but she did. "Yes, but a girl can take only so much intensity before she goes blind."

"Hmm. I thought that was a situational hazard proprietary to men."

"Situational hazard?"

"Going too long without a real woman."

"A real woman? As opposed to one you've blown up?"

"As opposed to one who talks it up in an Internet chat room."

"Eww. You do Internet porn?"

He looked at her for a long moment before he tossed back his head and laughed out loud. "You are way too easy, darlin'. You know that?"

She slapped the center of his chest. "You're just plain mean."

Before she could even think to pull away, he grabbed hold of her hand. "Come spend the night with me."

A thrill rushed through her. "What? Having trouble seeing?"

That strange flash of despair winked in his eyes, then was gone. The same one she'd seen last night over dinner when he'd spoken of the decision he still had to make about selling his share of his company.

There was something deep going on with Doug Storey, and Kinsey was absolutely dying to figure out his secret. But for now, she kept her mouth closed and waited.

His expression shifted again and he leaned in to kiss her. A briefly fleeting tease of his lips to hers, and then he pulled back. "Come home with me. I've got a flight out first thing and won't be back until Saturday. That's just too long to wait."

"For sex?"

He shook his head. "No, darlin'. To see you again."

6

DOUG LAY ON HIS BACK, his head pillowed on his crossed forearms.

He stared up at his bedroom's plain white ceiling, counting the narrow stripes where the courtyard's security lights shone through the slats of his miniblinds.

Eighteen, nineteen or twenty-one.

He had yet to come up with the same total twice.

And he'd just started in on his fourth try when Kinsey stirred beside him.

He willed his body to perfect stillness so as not to wake her if she were doing no more than turning over and cuddling up to his heat. If she came fully awake, she'd want to talk.

And he wasn't up for spilling any more of his guts than he had while they'd made love.

No, he hadn't gone and blabbed out anything about falling in love. He wasn't that stupid, though he was a very short centimeter from disproving that fact.

What the hell was he thinking, getting involved with a woman when he was weeks—if not days—away from walking out on any sort of life they might share?

They sure couldn't share much of anything from a couple thousand miles apart. He'd been shooting as straight as he knew how when he'd told her that a long-distance relationship was a no-go.

He'd been talking from experience with that one.

He'd long since quit entertaining such a possibility, having learned his lesson, having accepted the truth about letting what he loved out of his sight.

If he were staying in Houston, he'd be making sure she saw into his future, saw what he wanted to do with his life, saw how he was coming to want her to be a part—

"You're not asleep."

"Hmmph." He wondered how well she read minds.

"If you were asleep, your breathing wouldn't be so obvious."

"If I'm breathing hard, it's your fault," he said with more of a growl than he'd intended.

She sighed, turned and curled into his body. "I love your sleepy voice."

His heart jolted. God, she was amazing. "Didn't you just accuse me of not sleeping?"

"That doesn't mean your vocal cords are as wide-awake as the rest of you." Her hand slid to the center of his chest, where she plucked lightly at his hair.

"I'm not wide-awake. Just not quite asleep."

"What time is it?"

"Four-thirty."

She yawned. "Have you slept at all?"

"For a while," he lied. He'd been afraid to drift off, not wanting to miss the reality of holding her close even for the few hours of rest he needed.

She stirred enough to prop herself up on an elbow. Her hand stirred as well, slipping around to his far side, then up his ribs to his armpit. "You have to be up soon for your flight, don't you?"

"Yeah," he grumbled.

She gave a quiet tsk-tsk. "That doesn't sound like the gung ho Doug Storey I know."

He heard the disappointment in her tone as clearly as her words. "That's because it's the lazy-ass Doug Storey you don't know."

She paused in her exploration of his underarm and his triceps. "So, introduce me to him."

"I don't think so."

She pinched him softly right above his elbow, then rubbed her finger in a soothing circle over the spot. "I do think so. I'm terribly nosy. And I'm dying to know everything about you that you're dying not to share."

Why? he wanted to ask. *So we can compare dysfunctions?* Though he doubted she had any, unless being too nice and wholesome counted. Then again, he'd experienced a fairly huge range of her unwholesome abilities....

"Yeowch," he yelped when she pinched him again and this time didn't bother to soothe. "That hurt."

"Answer my question."

"What question?"

"Why aren't you in contact with your family?"

"I don't remember you asking me that just now."

"I asked the other day."

"I'm pretty damn sure I answered the other day."

"A lame answer. 'They have their life, I have mine.' I want something better."

"Then take your hand south about twenty-four inches."

She growled, tugged at the hair in his armpit. "You are such a guy."

"I should hope so."

"Well, stop it for a minute. See if you can't get in touch with your feminine side and talk to me for a while here before you have to leave."

"Miss me already, do you?"

"Actually, yes. More than you can imagine."

His heart thudded; his stomach rolled end over end like a dropped football. "Then I can think of a much better way to spend our time than talking."

Her hand had drifted down his side, over his rib cage to his hip. But then she stopped her exploration, far short of where he would've halted her had he been in charge. And so he rolled away from her and pressed his penis into the cup of her hand.

She chuckled as she cuddled close to his back and took him into her hand. She rubbed her palm in circles over his sensitive, swelling head. He hardened and let out a long sigh of tortured relief.

"Time to come clean, buddy."

"You need to work on your threats, darlin'. Not a lot of meat to that one."

"Speaking of meat…" She let him go, moving her hand up his belly and threading her fingers into the hair that grew between his navel and his cock.

He thought about stroking himself; it wasn't as if he was a stranger to taking care of his own business. But he really liked the way she touched him, and so he reached for her hand instead.

With their joined fingers wrapped around his shaft, he prepared to sing like a sissy.

"What do you want to know?"

When she wedged her knee between his thighs from behind him, he lifted his top leg enough for her to settle her leg between his.

It was as if she was trying to climb completely into his skin, and the closeness he felt with her then scared him more than telling her the story of his life.

"Everything. What do you want me to know?"

That was easy. "No more than you do."

"Uh-uh. Nope. Not part of the deal."

If he could talk her into turning over and spreading her legs, they wouldn't have time to talk. He liked the concept, liked it a lot. But not quite as much as he liked what she was doing with her hand.

"Okay then," he said. "I was twenty inches long and nine pounds, ten ounces at birth."

She reached down and lightly cupped his balls. "You don't have to go back that far."

"All right." He'd pay her hard cash to never stop what she was doing. "Though you should feel free to go back as far as you want."

For only a moment she hesitated, then wedged her knee closer to his groin, lifting his upper leg in the process and exposing his back door.

"Is that what you had in mind?" she asked as she slipped her hand between his legs from behind, fondling his tight balls from this new and intimate angle.

"That'll do," he said, though his voice came out strained and his cock surged toward his belly as her wrist snugged up between the cheeks of his ass.

What a place to have one woman's hand while he talked about another. "I was supposed to marry the girl next door. Literally."

"Literally marry her? Or she was literally the girl next door?"

So far Kinsey hadn't pulled away, and he took that as a positive sign. "Both. We grew up together. Kindergarten through high school graduation."

"What was her name?"

Why was that what women always wanted to know? "Doesn't matter. It's long over and done."

"It's a girl thing. I just want to know."

The way Kinsey was playing with him, moving her

hand to squeeze the base of his shaft, he'd be lucky to remember his own name, much less Gwen's.

He snorted, and grimaced at his recollection. "Gwen. Her name was Gwen." Might as well tell the entire truth. "Her name *is* Gwen. Gwen Storey."

And with that, Kinsey stopped feeling him up.

She paused, and he counted the seconds until her decision—one, two, three—a decision that had her pulling her hand from between his legs and rolling away.

He didn't want her to go, not this way, so he rolled in her direction, trapping her legs by throwing one of his across the top of her thighs.

She stared at him, her eyes wide and blinking as she digested his news. "What do you mean, Gwen Storey?"

"Just what I said. Gwen Storey."

"You're divorced?"

Funny. Even he hadn't thought that would be Kinsey's reaction. "Would it matter?"

"No. Not really. But why keep it a secret?"

"It's not a secret. I'm not divorced and, no," he hurried to add, "I'm not married, either. Gwen is my sister-in-law."

After another never-ending, heart-stopping moment he spent waiting to breathe, Kinsey waved both hands, then scooted up in bed, bracing herself on her elbows, her face inches from his. "Wait. Just wait. Could you maybe start this at the beginning? Skipping over the details of your birth."

He looked away from her face to the blanket she'd pulled up to cover her breasts. "In that case the beginning would've been when I was five. That was the year her family moved in next door. Gwen and I were inseparable from then until we graduated.''

Kinsey seemed to let that settle before she went on to ask, ''College? Is that when you split up?''

''I can't say when we split up.'' He toyed with the blanket's edge, avoiding her probing gaze. ''Gwen stayed in Abilene and got her associates degree locally. I came home from Houston the Christmas of my third year at U of H to find her engaged to my brother, Adam.''

''How could she be engaged to both of you?''

Doug shook his head. ''She and I were never officially engaged. I didn't think we needed to be.''

''And you were wrong.''

She didn't stop him when he pulled the blanket down enough to bare one of her gumdrop nipples. ''Apparently so.''

He leaned down and sucked her into his mouth. He didn't want to talk. He wanted to bury himself in her body and forget everything but the sex.

He especially wanted to forget one of the most stupid mistakes he'd ever made. It was over and done with, as he'd said to Kinsey, and this trip down memory lane was interfering with his need to get laid.

''That's it?'' she asked, though she didn't push him away. ''That's all?''

He opened his mouth but spoke against her skin as he answered, ''You want more?''

''Yes, I want more.''

''Insatiable wench,'' he said, and climbed on top.

She pressed her hand to his chest. ''Not that more. More of the story.''

''Why doesn't that come as a surprise?'' he asked, and collapsed to the side.

"Well, there has to be more than that. How did she end up with your brother?"

He shrugged. "He was there. I wasn't."

"But after all those years?"

"What can I say. Absence does not make the heart grow fonder."

"And no one said a word to you?"

"There's a reason I say that my family have their lives and I have mine."

She shook her head, rolling it back and forth on the pillow. "This isn't right."

"Kinsey, this is just the way it is. And it's history."

"It's not history if it still keeps you and your family apart."

He levered himself up onto one elbow so he could look down into her face. He didn't want to chase her away, but he'd be damned if he let her dig into and reopen wounds that had long been healed. "It's going to keep you and me apart if you don't drop it."

"Fine," she said, before she clamped her mouth shut and rolled over and away to go back to sleep.

Ah, well. Hers wasn't the first cold shoulder he'd slept with, he mused ruefully, plopping onto his back. No doubt there'd be more. And, besides. He needed to get up and shower in a minute, anyway....

"Doug?"

God, but her voice sounded so tiny and so faraway. "Yeah?"

"I'm sorry for prying. Your business is none of mine."

He sucked in a huge breath, let it out slowly to prevent himself from saying things he didn't need to say. Things about his feelings for her, the clawing need for stability he'd never thought a woman would help him to find.

When he had a better grip and the moment had passed, he allowed himself a private smile.

And then he smacked her on the ass. "Apology accepted."

"Apology retracted. If hitting me is going to be your response."

"Hitting you? That was a love pat, darlin'."

"Then it's a good thing our relationship is all about sex if that's your idea of love."

The thought of loving Kinsey made his heart hitch. "If our relationship is all about sex, then it's not much of a relationship at all."

She turned over then and faced him, mirroring his pose with her head pillowed on one arm. "What makes you say that?"

He raised a brow. "The fact that there's no sex going on that I can see."

"That's right. You told me you like to watch."

His heart hitched again, followed by his belly and his balls. "You have something you want to show me?"

"I might."

"I'm all-eyes over here."

She leaned across his body, pressing her bare breasts to his chest as she turned on the lamp at his bedside.

When she cuddled back down and faced him, he knew he was going to have a hell of a time walking away and leaving this woman alone in his bed.

As sleepy and sexy as her expression was, he saw how much she wanted him, how ready she was to give up anything he asked, how she couldn't keep her feelings for him from her eyes even if she tried.

His cock had already made its preference known, but Doug wanted to take his time. He pushed his knee between her thighs, separating her for the exploration he had in mind, the trip he wanted to take her on while watching her expression.

He slipped his hand down to brush over the closely clipped hair where her legs came together, seeking out her clit and playing ever so lightly there where he'd played so much harder last night.

She gave a small shudder; her eyes drifted closed as she smiled in pleasure, and he stopped.

Pouting and frowning, she looked back at him again. "You stopped."

"You closed your eyes. I told you I like to watch."

"My eyes?"

"Your eyes, your mouth. You've got a nice face."

"Oh, well, thanks," she said with a laugh. "I just thought being a visual type of guy and all…"

"What?" He slid his index finger down her slit, which was so juicy and warm. "That I only want to look at your pussy?"

It was almost as if she blushed without the color staining her face. "Well, that, yes."

He shifted, moving his other arm to capture a nipple between two knuckles and tug. "And that, too?"

She nodded. "The covers are in the way. You can't see any of what you're wanting to see."

"Ah, but that's where you're wrong." That's all he could afford to say without explaining how the look in her eyes grabbed him so tightly he thought he would choke.

Then she totally blew him away by throwing sheet, blanket and bedspread to their feet. "Well, I can't see anything of what I want to see. So there."

Saucy wench. He rolled over on to his back, crossed his feet at the ankles, his arms behind his head. "Is that better?"

"Do you remember that childish taunt? 'Take a picture. It'll last longer'?" She pushed up to her hands and knees and scooted down in the bed to straddle his lower thighs. "I wish I had a camera right now."

His cock, already straining, bobbed with pride. "I've got a digital on my desk."

"Is that so?" She grinned, her brows waggling in time to his cock's up and down show.

She was so beautiful, sitting there all sleepy and disheveled, not the least bit inhibited by her own nudity or her apparent enjoyment of his.

It scared the crap out of him how quickly they'd reached this place of comfortable intimacy. And it pissed him off that he wasn't going to be around long enough to enjoy her as fully as he might like.

Still…there wasn't a damn thing but his own stupid descent into touchy-feely, talkedy-talk-talk hell stopping him from enjoying her now.

He bucked with his legs and tumbled her onto his chest. She grabbed at his shoulders, but he didn't give her a chance to find her balance before he had her pinned flat on her back.

"I changed my mind."

"About?"

He sat up on his knees, straddling her. "Looking at you."

She slipped her hands beneath her breasts and plumped them up. "Is this what you wanted to see?"

By some wild force of will, he stifled a nearly painful groan. "It's a start."

She pinched her nipples into tight buds, her bottom

lip caught between her teeth as she played. His fingers gouged into his thighs; his gaze moved from her breasts to her eyes, which never left his.

He didn't know which one of them he was trying to kid here, faking his strength of will, when he'd never be able to walk again if he didn't pry his fingers away from his thighs.

He shifted position and settled between her legs, spreading her wide open; he could smell her sex and see how wet she was. If he'd been wearing a condom he'd already be buried inside.

Instead, he leaned down and lapped from her vagina to her clit. She came up off the bed and pressed her mound to his mouth; he used his hands on her thighs to push her back to the bed, and pulled her sweet pussy lips apart with his thumbs.

"Are you getting the eyeful you wanted down there?"

Her voice was no more than a raw whisper, and he answered her by shoving his tongue into her hole and eating her up.

She cried out, thrust upward. He let her go with a quick sucking kiss to her clit. "It's a great view. I wish you could see it."

She reached toward his bedside table again, found a condom and passed it along. "I know that view well. I've lived with it all my life. I'm much more about watching the action."

She wanted to watch him screw her. She wanted to see him slide his cock as far as he could go. Nothing else she could've said, could've asked for, would have blown him further away.

The women he'd known rarely wanted the lights on,

much less a full visual. But this one… "I knew there was a reason I was crazy about you."

"Why's that?" she asked, watching him roll the condom from the tip of his cock to the base.

"A guy would have to be mad not to appreciate a woman with your appetite for sex." One hand holding his shaft, he positioned himself between her folds, spreading her juices from her clit to the button of her ass.

She boosted herself up onto her elbows, spread her legs wider, pulled up her knees and braced her feet flat on the mattress. She watched him circle the head of his cock around her, waited until he pushed inside before she looked up and said, "No, Doug. Not sex. My appetite for you."

He stopped.

Buried as far inside of her as he could manage in this position, he stopped because he knew he was faced with a choice here. A choice to simply feed both their sexual appetites or to make love to her the way his gut urged him to do.

"Well?" she asked, an unholy gleam in her eye that sealed his fate.

"Well what?"

"What are you waiting for?"

And with that, he made his choice, taking hold of her hips, pulling her close and draping her thighs over his. "Is that better?"

She glanced down to where their bodies were one, glanced back up to meet his gaze. "You're getting there."

"Oh, so I'm gonna be doing all the work here, is that it?" He pulled out, pushed forward.

She shivered; her nipples drew up into morsels meant to be enjoyed, and his mouth watered.

"Let's see." She wiggled, gasped, caught a breath. "It seems to me I'm the one here who was roused from a perfectly good sleep. It's only fair that you make sure I'm a happy woman when you leave this bed."

"Or else?"

"Or else?" she echoed.

He ran his palms down her thighs, his thumbs rubbing slow circles all the way until he reached the joint where her legs met her hips. "That sounded like a threat. That I'd better make you a happy woman, or else."

When he slid his thumbs farther and captured the knot of her clitoris between, she tossed back her head and reared her lower body up toward his.

He surged forward because he could hardly do anything less, what with the way she was working his cock. Not to mention that he wasn't exactly a saint or anything when it came to having Kinsey in his bed.

She blew out a staccato series of breaths as if pulling herself together and away from orgasm's edge. And then she lay back on the pillows, looking as if she was queen of the harem. "I'm assuming you might want the pleasure of my company next time you're in town. So making me happy now would be a very good thing."

He really didn't like the way she sounded as flippant as she did, the way she made what they were doing sound like nothing but a cheap fling—though he'd given her every reason to do just that, hadn't he?

He hadn't exactly shared the battle going on among his mind, his emotions and the head he kept in his pants. "Hey, I still live here, ya know."

She scooted farther down in the bed, sliding herself up the length of his shaft, her eyes soft and sleepy and sexy as hell as she watched her sex swallow his. "Yeah, but for how long?"

He pushed forward then, leaning over her, his hands braced on either side of her head. This had to be his favorite position, looking down into her face, watching the shifts in her expression as he moved.

Oh, good, sweet, gorgeous doll... He groaned, loving the way she pressed her lips together to hold back the sounds that made him nuts, loving the way her breasts, all round and plump and incredibly edible, teased him.

He grunted as he slid into her fully, growled as he lowered his weight and paused. Her legs went around his waist and he lost all grasp of his mental faculties. He couldn't even think to answer. All that mattered was how long he could hang on right here, right now.

But she was giggling and making it hard for him to concentrate. If he didn't concentrate, the volcano would blow and the only one in this bed to be happy would be John Henry.

"What's so funny?"

"I absolutely love the sounds you make."

"Is that so?" he asked, mentally running through the opposing team's stats for this weekend's Texans match-up.

She nodded eagerly. "And it's not even like the noises come out of your mouth. I mean, obviously they do." She stopped, hissed as he rotated his hips, shuddered before going on. "But it's more like they come straight out of your..."

"My cock?" he finished for her.

She shook her head. "Your gut. Right here," she

said, her fingers pushing into the muscles supporting his pelvis.

This time his moan was feral and deep, and her grin was as wide and bright as the moon. "Right there. I can feel it vibrate against my fingers."

All he could feel were the vibrations thundering from his balls to the head of his cock. "I don't think I've ever experienced sex with a partner who cackles."

She pouted and frowned. "I do not cackle."

"Yeah, you do." He thrust in.

"Do not."

"Yeah, you do. And you huff." He pulled out.

She huffed.

"And you puff."

She puffed.

"Doug?"

"Kinsey?" he answered, his voice as strained as he expected.

"Why don't you blow my house down?"

"Is that a bad architect joke?"

"No. It's an order," she said as she reached up and pulled him down to meet her thrusts.

That was all it took; he was done. He covered her completely, buried his face in her fine-smelling hair, breathed in the scents of grasses and herbs and gave himself over to her body's sweet demands.

His hips set a rhythm that hers eagerly met, a slow in-and-out motion that he felt no need to speed up. Not yet. Not when his enjoyment of the moment was heightened by hers, and when hers was so hard to deny.

She wasn't still for a moment, her arms moving so that her hands ran from his shoulders to his ass. Her legs winding around his, the soles of her feet rubbing his calves. He wanted her to come, wanted to feel her contractions grip and squeeze and—

She cried out and grabbed his backside with greedy fingers, one leg thrown over his hips to guide him to where she needed him to be. He waited, waited, until he couldn't wait anymore. *Oh, sweet, yes, baby, oh, baby.*

Grunting and groaning, he shoved his cock home, pumping with fierce abandon as his gut ripped open to spill more than his seed.

He spilled all that he felt, and he did so in utter silence as his body shuddered with spasms that felt as if they were killing him. And then he was done, exhausted, depleted, spent beyond his ability to understand.

Kinsey Gray was like no woman he'd ever known. She'd taken him apart, and he was going to have to work his butt off to find all the pieces. But first he was going to have to say goodbye, to get up out of this bed and literally fly away.

He didn't think that he'd ever regretted leaving a woman behind before he'd even pulled out of her body. But this time, this time… How the hell was he supposed to walk away knowing what he was leaving behind?

7

LATER THAT MORNING, Kinsey settled into a chair at the gIRL-gEAR conference table, fearing imminent death by starvation. Lauren followed, fresh from a stop at Einstein Bros. for bagels and shmears. Poe arrived moments later with a pot of green tea.

Kinsey's favorite cream cheese spread was the maple, raisin and walnut. The bagels were a secondary consideration. She'd come to their informal meeting armed with two lattes from Starbucks, hoping the wake-me-up caffeine charge would see her through the day.

After Sydney's announcement yesterday afternoon, the three partners had decided during a brief after-work, drive-time phone call to do breakfast together this morning, Kinsey and Poe being directly involved in the auction and Lauren being a voyeuristic busy-body.

Each was to have come to the table with thoughts on implementing the fund-raiser, or even with alternative ideas that might have popped up overnight. It was rather short notice, yes, but over the years each of the partners had discovered they shared an aptitude for brainstorming on the fly.

Other than her coffee, Kinsey hadn't managed to show up with much of anything but a sex hangover—that and a decided reluctance to being bought by any man but Doug. Doug, who was off to the Rocky Mountains for the next four days.

Funny how the weeks she'd gone without seeing him in the past seemed like nothing compared to the Dougless days that loomed ahead. God, but she had it bad. Having it so good and so often did that to a girl.

"What is wrong with you?" Lauren asked, plopping into the chair at Kinsey's side, the bags rustling as she set the bagels on the table. "That shade of purple under your eyes would make a great color of eye shadow."

"Just your usual Tuesday morning sex hangover." Kinsey shook her tired head. "I am definitely not as young as I used to be."

"Whoo-hoo! I knew it." Lauren slapped the table. "You and Doug are going to be perfect for each other."

Perfect for each other or not, this distance thing sucked in a really big way.

"Though," Lauren added, waggling both brows, "I doubt your exhaustion has anything to do with your age, girlfriend. You're just not as used to sex marathons as you need to be—or as you're going to have to be to keep up with that man."

"And what would you know about keeping up with Doug Storey?" Poe pointedly asked.

Lauren shrugged. "All a girl's gotta do is watch the man in action to know that he pours the same energy into everything he does. That's why poor Kinsey here is so tired."

They had no idea. Even she couldn't believe how exhausted she was, nor how much she missed Doug already. "Too true. Plus, I'm a total sleep addict. I'm dysfunctional without eight or nine hours."

"So?" Poe inquired succinctly, pouring her tea as Lauren set out the bagel bounty.

"So, what?" Kinsey answered Poe's probing question with her own. "Be more specific. My powers of intuition aren't yet working this morning."

One of Poe's dark brows arched curiously. "I'm assuming Sunday night's dinner was the start of something good?"

Kinsey slumped back in her chair, her head lolling to one side. Bed. She needed to go back to bed. "It was definitely good, though I'm not sure if it was the start of anything."

"Two nights in a row with Doug?" Lauren gave a low hissing whistle. "I'd say that gives you bragging rights."

Kinsey frowned. "Why would I brag about my time with Doug?"

Lauren rolled her eyes. "I don't mean you *have* to brag. Not really, and not to me. I just know from Anton that Doug doesn't date. He hasn't dated in months."

"Hmm." Kinsey's heart gave a small blip. "I wonder why."

Poe sliced open a cranberry bagel. "Are you seeing him again?"

Kinsey nodded. "Izzy gave us tickets to next weekend's Texans game."

Lauren chose the sun-dried-tomato bagel and garden-veggie cream cheese. "Like I said. Bragging rights."

No. Kinsey wasn't going to get her hopes up. The flight to Denver was almost three hours. And her life, her family was here. "Three dates doesn't mean a hill of beans."

"If we were talking about any other guy, I'd agree,"

Lauren said, thinning out the cream cheese she'd just spread. "But this is Doug."

Kinsey still wasn't ready to buy into Lauren's scenario. "I don't get it. What makes Doug different?"

"Hello? What did I just say?"

"Doug doesn't date."

"Exactly." Lauren gestured with her knife. "Doug works. He goes to ball games with his buddies, stops off for a beer. And then he works some more."

"Has he always been like that?" Kinsey couldn't help but wonder about the girl back home who'd betrayed him, and if that entire incident had impacted Doug beyond anything he was willing to admit....

What was she saying? He was a guy. Guys were never willing to admit to anything involving emotion.

Yes, they might admit to wanting to hang around, to get to know a woman better, definitely to take her to bed, but what was that in the scheme of things when Denver was not exactly a reasonable commute?

Lauren nodded. "As long as Anton has known him. I think there was a girl for a while in college, but that obviously wasn't anything long-term."

Not after she married his brother, anyway. "Well, sister, don't start in with the smug face, because Doug still doesn't date."

"Perhaps he'll buy you at the auction," Poe suggested, pinching off a bite of bagel.

"I'd rather he didn't." Which, of course, was a total contradiction to last night's teasing plea for his bid. Kinsey wrapped both hands around her first latte. "I'd rather no one who might recognize me even knows about the auction."

"C'mon." Lauren licked a smear of cream cheese from the edge of her thumb. "It won't be that bad."

"That's easy for you to say." Kinsey suddenly wondered what had happened to her appetite. "In fact, that's easy to say for all of you who don't have to suffer the possible humiliation of bringing in the lowest bid."

"It's not about the money," Lauren said.

Kinsey countered with, "It's all about the money or else we wouldn't be doing it."

"Okay, true." Lauren nodded, considering the truth as she considered her bagel. "But what I meant was that it isn't a competition to see which one of you brings in the biggest bucks."

Poe chose that moment to interrupt. "Actually, it's completely about which of us is the most expensive. Why would you think anything else?"

Kinsey smiled semisweetly. "Dear, dear Poe. There are times when you really don't have to speak your mind."

"I have yet to experience any situation that required me to—"

"To bite your tongue?" Lauren interrupted. "Trust me. This is one of those times."

"Perhaps a private wager then." Poe lifted her delicate china teacup with equally delicate fingers. "As to which one of us will bring the bigger prize. The money to be donated to the cause, of course."

"You're on," Lauren said, causing Kinsey to slap at her friend's shoulder.

"Are you out of your mind?"

Lauren frowned and rubbed at the spot. "It'll be fun, and it'll give us a reason to campaign."

"Campaign?" Kinsey groaned. This was getting out of hand. "Campaign how? For what?"

''We'll enlist marketing's help. We'll paint you as a prize no man can live without.''

Lauren's excitement was not the least bit contagious, and Kinsey grumbled, ''This is only about one date, Lauren. Not happily ever after.''

''You never know.''

What Kinsey did know was that her enthusiasm was definitely waning more than waxing. But did she really want or need to tell the other women that her lack of interest in the auction was due to her recent decision to go after Doug?

That thought brought a frown. Lauren and Poe had both been there for that conversation. Had they already forgotten her plans? Either that or neither of them put much stock in her commitment to the ideas they'd laid out.

Now here they were, off on another competitive, game-playing tangent. And all Kinsey wanted to do was tell them the deal was off—the auction, the wager, all of it. She didn't want to be sold to another man when she was in love with Doug Storey.

''Kinsey? You still with us?'' Lauren asked, jostling Kinsey's elbow. ''You look like you got hit by a bus.''

Calm, cool, collected. *Ohhmmm.* ''I'm fine.''

As fine as anyone could be having fallen in love with a man who only wanted to play when he wasn't working, who was but weeks away from walking out of her life.

A man who wouldn't even return a girl's bikini bottoms, and would most certainly never continue what they'd started from a distance of two thousand miles.

''You don't look fine,'' Lauren insisted.

''She's contemplating her imminent loss,'' Poe stated.

Truer words had never been spoken. Not that Kinsey was going to correct their misconception about what it was she was losing.

After all, she could hardly lose what she'd never really had to begin with, could she?

IZZY WALKED AROUND the perimeter of the ashy-black and still-smoldering rubble that two days ago would have been a family's home. It was bad, this sort of loss, but definitely not the worst she'd ever seen.

The house was gone, but the love that would rebuild it, the love that would fill it, still existed and bloomed. It was the sort of love that put the needs of another before the needs of one's self. The rarest kind of love that many never had the privilege to know.

Izzy had known enough love in her lifetime to share with an entire village. At times she felt as if she'd been loved *too* much, that what was intended to be concern became confining, smothering, an attempt by her family to take charge of her life because…why?

Because they thought there was too much work to be done at home. That she needed to concentrate her charitable efforts on friends and family and not worry so much about the needs of those relying on the relief and humanitarian organizations with which she worked.

What her family seemed to forget, or perhaps saw only through eyes clouded by insular perception, was that the kind of love they shared and practiced was rare. The Golden Rule did not top any etiquette list for living on the street.

At least none that Izzy knew of. And she knew a lot, having worked with the homeless, with gang-bangers,

with girls without mothers who were mothers themselves.

But her goal had always been the larger global picture, third world countries with unsanitary living con-
ditions, rampant disease and malnutrition. And she was
beginning to believe her degree in nutritional anthropology would turn out to be nothing but a waste.

Time after time, nothing changed. She'd get away
for a bit, be hip-deep in dedicating her energy and re-
sources where needed, then another calamity at home
would call out her name, and she'd be back to help out
her Gramma Fred and uncle Leonard and her mamma
Rose.

She kicked at a chunk of burned two-by-four, ag-
gravated by the reality. Truth be told, the calamities
were usually nothing more than her mamma missing
her, and Gramma Fred looking out for Mamma, and
then Leonard deciding it would be in Rose's best interest for Izzy to come home.

As hard as it had been, she'd finally found the
strength to say no. Saying no was the only way she'd
managed to hold on and finish her education, though
she was paying for it now by having her career choices
openly ridiculed. And all of that done by those who
claimed to know her and love her the most.

For some reason, their idea of love seemed to require
a loyalty to her family's wishes above her own, no
matter where the calling of her heart took her. They
saw no reason for her trips abroad or for the energy
she devoted to caring for those around the world when
she could find plenty of charity work to do at home,
within a distance they deemed suitable. She felt torn
by what seemed to be a conditional acceptance, a qual-

ified approval, of her career choice. A conflict that translated into wondering about their acceptance of her.

She kicked again at the two-by-four, this time with a different anger than before.

"Some kind of mess, isn't it?"

At the sound of Joseph Baron's voice behind her, Izzy caught her breath, but wasn't able to stop the shiver speeding down the train tracks of her spine. Since she'd first laid eyes on him yesterday, and spent last evening in his company, not an hour had passed that he hadn't been on her mind—even during her dreams.

In the middle of the night, she'd heard his deep voice and his laughter. She'd relived the initial rush of awe inspired by his intelligence, the thrill at discovering a kindred spirit with a calling to help others. And then, of course, as dreams were wont to do, they took him out of his clothes and brought him into her body.

That memory, though only one of her imagination, was too real not to elicit a physical response. She felt her breasts swell, showing her exactly how it could be between her and this man. Tight and intense and as bitingly sharp as a bee sting.

She pictured his hands discovering what he caused her to feel, and turning to face him brought a stabbing pain to her belly. Wanting to bed a man the way she wanted to bed this one would cause her a world of hurt—some good, some bad and some a fierce combination.

Hugging herself tightly, she nodded. "The worst sort of mess imaginable. But I suppose you see this a lot."

He came closer, his hands stuffed into the pockets of the baggy gray athletic shorts, which reached his knees but did nothing to hide how fine his legs were beneath. "I do."

His voice rumbled through her like storm clouds on the horizon of the life she'd determined to live serving others. She didn't want a relationship to get in the way of that dream, to conflict with her life's goal, but it was going to be hard not to wonder about this man and what might have been.

Baron went on. "But it's always tough when it hits close to home. The personal ones are what get to you."

After last night's dinner with Sydney and Ray, Izzy had wondered if she'd ever see Baron again. Ray had driven him home late in the night; Izzy knew because she'd watched from the guest room window as they left, and she'd wondered if he was returning to a woman he hadn't mentioned.

The thought shouldn't have tortured her so.

Last night, more than any night she could remember, she'd felt vulnerable, lost and alone. And it didn't matter a bit that she wasn't a woman used to depending on a man. Strong arms still felt damn good when the world was swirling destructively down a drain.

She allowed herself a private smile. Oh, the drama she managed to conjure up. Her mamma would be so proud…right before she smacked Izzy across the back of the head and told her to reel it on in. "This one hit especially hard. The family that was to live here? They were so close to being back together. So very close."

Baron moved into her sunlight; his shadow covered her with a warmth of a deeper color and heat. "It'll work out. You'll get it built again. No one got hurt. That's the main thing here to think on."

She nodded, knowing he was right. "Physically hurt,

no. I do worry about the emotional pain. How much does it take before a body gives up?''

"It's all about faith.''

She turned to him then, shaded her eyes with one hand to look up into his, which were clear and confident and intent on taking her in. He wasn't looking at the destruction that surrounded them but at the personal devastation eating at her heart. "Are you a dreamer, Joseph Baron?''

This time he did glance away, turning to face the rubble and crossing his arms over his chest. His biceps bulged, and his lean stomach lay tight and flat beneath his sleeveless white T-shirt.

She couldn't help but allow her gaze to drift lower, and boldly took in the fullness beneath the elastic band holding his shorts at his waist. He was doing nothing, just standing still, yet he reminded her of how beautifully a man moved into a woman's body.

He started out by shaking his head. "It's like I said last night. I've seen a lot, Isabel. Ray pulls the victims free. Then I have to see if they're worth putting back together.'' He paused, and she heard him clear his throat lightly. "Making that call can be the hardest thing a man has to do.''

His words compelled her to move to him, to slip her fingers beneath his arm pressed tight to his side, and into the warmth of his bare skin. "You're right. No one here was hurt. The building will be replaced, and the loss of this dream will heal.''

He was quiet for several long, pulse-beating moments before he spoke. "You like talking about dreams, don't you?''

She clasped her other hand to his arm and laid her forehead on the hard muscle beneath his shoulder. "My

Play the
"LAS VEGAS"
GAME

Play the "LAS VEGAS" Game and get 3 FREE GIFTS!

1. Pull back all 3 tabs on the card at right. Then check the claim chart to see what we have for you — 2 FREE BOOKS and a gift — ALL YOURS! ALL FREE!

2. Send back this card and you'll receive brand-new Harlequin® Blaze™ novels. These books have a cover price of $4.50 each in the U.S. and $5.25 each in Canada, but they are yours to keep absolutely free.

3. There's no catch. You're under no obligation to buy anything. We charge nothing — ZERO — for your first shipment. And you don't have to make any minimum number of purchases — not even one!

4. The fact is, thousands of readers enjoy receiving their books by mail from the Harlequin Reader Service®. They enjoy the convenience of home delivery...they like getting the best new novels at discount prices, BEFORE they're available in stores...and they love their *Heart to Heart* newsletter featuring author news, horoscopes, recipes, book reviews and much more!

5. We hope that after receiving your free books you'll want to remain a subscriber. But the choice is yours — to continue or cancel, any time at all! So why not take us up on our invitation, with no risk of any kind. You'll be glad you did!

Play the
"LAS VEGAS" Game

PEEL BACK HERE ▶
PEEL BACK HERE ▶
PEEL BACK HERE ▶

YES! I have pulled back the 3 tabs. Please send me all the free Harlequin® Blaze™ books and the gift for which I qualify. I understand that I am under no obligation to purchase any books, as explained on the back and opposite page.

350 HDL DNYQ   150 HDL DQD6

FIRST NAME	LAST NAME

ADDRESS

APT.#	CITY

STATE/PROV.   ZIP/POSTAL CODE   (H-B-09/02)

7 7 7   **GET 2 FREE BOOKS & A FREE MYSTERY GIFT!**

🍀 🍀 🍀   **GET 2 FREE BOOKS!**

🍒 🍒 🍒   **GET 1 FREE BOOK!**

🔔 🔔 🔔   **TRY AGAIN!**

▼ DETACH AND MAIL TODAY ▼

The Harlequin Reader Service® — Here's how it works:

mamma has called me a fool more times than I can count. She's all about practical doings, not about what her daughter wishes would come true.''

Baron uncrossed his arms, disturbing Izzy's anchor, but only for the seconds it took him to pull her into his side. "Dreams are what keep me going. Every time I head out to answer a call, I dream that we'll walk away without losing a single life. Without sacrificing a single limb. If I didn't dream, the reality would shoot me down.''

"It takes a special man to do that work."

He shook his head. "Just one with a need to give back.''

Erasing the words *soul mates* from her mind, she reached up to hold his hand, which cradled her shoulder. "I hear you about the giving. That's what I was wanting to do here. What we were all doing here until two days ago.''

"And it's what you'll do again."

She hesitated, sighed, wondering how much of herself she was ready to reveal. "Sometimes I feel like…well, like it's too little, building one home when there are villages in the world without a single roof to cover even the tiniest of babies.''

Baron squeezed her shoulder and tucked her even closer to his side. "And what drives you to take on the whole world, Isabel?''

She waited for a moment, not sure she knew him the way she would want to before spilling all of her secrets. "Did you know only Mamma Rose and my Gramma Fred call me Isabel?''

He laughed at that, this time a deep, rolling, thunderous outburst that rattled every last one of her bones. "Izzy just doesn't work for me. I cannot bring myself to call such a beautiful woman by such a...scratchy-sounding name.''

''Scratchy?'' She pulled her head away and to the side, looking up as he looked down. ''Scratchy?''

Again he laughed, with a joy more infectious than the sadness surrounding her in this place. ''I should have known you'd latch on to that, rather than the fact that I just called you beautiful.''

''Sweet-talkin' ain't gonna get you nowhere, Joseph Baron,'' she said, but she went back to cuddling against him all the same.

''It sure has worked in the past. Guess I'm gonna hafta work on my game, huh?''

Oh, yeah. And she planned to be there for every move he made.

IF KINSEY HAD EVER HAD doubts as to whether step two in her Doug-trapping plan would be worth sitting through three hours of football on a Sunday afternoon when she could've been taking care of at least a dozen errands, well, she had her answer—even if the Texans didn't win.

The animation that gave Doug the look of a boy at his first big-league ball game had been nothing if not contagious. She couldn't say she'd paid as much attention to the game as he had, but that was okay. She'd had an amazingly great time watching him, instead.

Having known Doug now for three or four years, she'd never questioned that he was a kid at heart. And since she couldn't have taken herself seriously if she'd tried, they got along like Forrest Gump's peas and carrots.

Still, it would have to be an awfully big bowl of vegetables to hold both Houston and Denver. There was all that real estate, not to mention the other carrots and peas to deal with in between.

She hadn't yet decided on the third crucial step in her plan to convince Doug that he couldn't live without her, but wondered if there was really any need to continue the game. Nothing she'd learned thus far led her to believe he had any intention of changing his mind about leaving.

He'd be gone soon, she'd be auctioned off to the highest bidder and that would be the end of their succotash.

Her plain white Keds scuffing along on the concrete, Kinsey walked beside Izzy out of Reliant Stadium, having watched the Texans lose by a last-minute field goal. With Doug and Baron not far behind, the two women headed for the shuttle bus staging area to catch a ride back to the Metro lot where she and Doug had hooked up with the other couple earlier today.

"So?" Kinsey asked, needing a distraction from her depressing thoughts. "How're things going between you and Baron?"

"Is this more of that gIRL-gEAR all-for-one thing?" Izzy asked, gesturing with an expressive wave. "I give you the lowdown on Baron and you tell me about Doug?"

Kinsey shrugged. "There's not a lot to tell. I'm wild for him, and he's moving to Colorado."

"Crazy woman." Izzy smacked Kinsey's arm. "Talk him out of it."

"Right." Kinsey dodged a pair of playful boys waving their Texans banners as they ran. "He told me on the drive over that one of the Warren Sill secretaries gave him the grand house-hunting tour."

"Did he buy anything?"

"No."

"Then, as long as that's all she gave him, what's the big deal?"

"He's committed to going."

Izzy didn't say anything. She didn't have to. Her big bad wolf huff blew a hole in the defense Kinsey was building on the fly.

"At this point, there's not a lot I can do except lick my wounds and hope I bring in a bundle at the auction. Otherwise, I'll be a big fat three-time loser."

"And how do you figure that?"

"I told you about the bet Poe conned me into, right?" she asked, and Izzy nodded. "Okay, so I'll be losing out on being the pricey piece I bragged to Poe that I was. Then, on top of being worthless rather than priceless, there's the fact that I'll be out that money. Plus..." This part was the hardest to put into words.

"Plus?" Izzy prompted, when Kinsey continued to delay.

"Hey, I'm getting there."

"Just making sure."

"Fine. Okay? Fine." Might as well rip out her own heart. "I'll be losing Doug. When I first heard he was leaving, I wasn't sure how I felt. Now I do, and I hate the idea. I'm absolutely beyond miserable. So there. Happy now?"

"Happy about what?" Doug asked from behind before wedging between the two women and draping an arm around both. "Or did I catch you bad-mouthing me again?"

Kinsey felt the flush of heat rising from her collarbone to her hairline. She was sure he'd overheard everything and was seconds away from running screaming into the night. "What makes you think we were talking about you at all?"

He leaned toward her, nuzzled the hair above her ear. "The fact that I heard my name."

"Yeah, dawg. I heard it, too." Baron moved to Izzy's far side and pulled her closer when Doug let her go. "You women are outnumbered here."

Izzy shook her head. "Outnumbered? Wanna bet?"

"No." Kinsey waved both hands. "No more bets. I'm already on the verge of losing my shirt."

"You mean losing your bikini." Doug, aka Dracula, tossed back his head and laughed diabolically.

"What's this about a bikini?" Baron asked, earning himself a punch to the biceps from Izzy as the foursome reached the queue of people waiting for a bus.

"Nothing about a bikini." *Think fast, Kinsey. Think fast.* "I was talking about a bet I made with Poe having to do with the auction."

As the bus pulled up to the gate, Doug lifted his sunglasses to glance down at Kinsey. "You girls really think you can raise money that way?"

"As opposed to a bakesale or a car wash?" *Grr,* but she hated even the suggestion of condescension. "First of all, we are women. We are not girls. And second, there are men willing to pay a lot for what we have to offer."

"Yeah, but aren't those men called johns?"

Kinsey ducked from beneath Doug's arm and pushed him away, slugging him soundly in the shoulder when he came close. "You are not the least bit funny."

"Hey," he yelped, hands up, eyes twinkling. "It was a joke, darlin'. I'm kidding. You know I'm kidding. I bet you'll make a bundle. What man wouldn't want to try his luck with you?"

Kinsey didn't even attempt to answer. All she could think of was the reality that Doug obviously wouldn't be there making sure he was the one to win a night in her company.

He'd tried his luck. He'd gotten everything he'd wanted. Given the opportunity, he'd probably personally pass the torch.

Except she had a feeling the idea of the auction was bothering him a lot more than he cared to admit. The way he was acting, the jerk he was being, the teasing that wasn't the least bit funny but rather caustic and sharp, offered more in the way of honesty than his words.

She shoved herself in front of him. They got onto the bus, taking the seats directly across the aisle from Izzy and Baron. Kinsey settled into the one by the window, and Doug slumped back, pressing against her side.

"You do have a seat of your own," she grumbled. She still did not like his comments about girls and johns, even though her true pique was self-directed for allowing him to get to her when she'd known what she was letting herself in for from day one of this ridiculous scheme.

"I like yours better," he stated, tucking her shoulder under his.

"I see," she said, realizing how good he felt beside her, how right, yet how wrong it was to feel anything at all when guarding her emotions would be so much smarter. "And why's that?"

"Because you're in it."

That was it. She was weak and worn down, and she could not stand how cute he was; she wanted to gobble him up like the hot muffin he was. A hot studly muffin. One she was getting too used to having share.

She sighed, then sighed again, looking down at his faded blue jeans, which were baggy where they needed to be and snug in all the right places. He'd sprawled out as completely as the seats allowed, one leg in the aisle, one beneath the seat in front, acting like the total guy he was.

She wanted to close her eyes and sleep off this bad dream, but she sensed his stare and turned. "What are you looking at?"

"You. What are you thinking?"

She didn't even hesitate, but forged ahead with complete honesty. "About you. And me. And our incredible knack for bad timing."

When he didn't say anything else, only closed his eyes and laced his hands over his belly, she felt a strange stirring of alarm. Alarm she shouldn't be feeling, because they weren't officially an item.

Their imminent breakup from their unofficial entanglement was just that—imminent. Nothing she could say or do at this point would change a thing.

"What about you?" she finally asked after several minutes of silence. "What are you thinking about?"

Doug turned his head, opened his eyes. Gave her a look that made her want to retract the inquiry because of the regret-filled expression he let slip before his lashes drifted down. Regret that he wanted what she wanted but had no idea how to manage having it all. Then he offered a careless sort of shrug, as if that would rub out what he had revealed.

He took another chunk out of her heart when he finally said, "My breakfast meeting with Marcus West."

All-business, all the time. Why wasn't she surprised that yet again he'd taken refuge in the one thing he did have a handle on? "That rift seems to have healed nicely."

"Yeah, but finishing up with Marcus is making it really tough to schedule a start date with Warren Sill." Doug shifted where he sat, scooting even closer and moving a hand to Kinsey's thigh. "I'd been set to leave here the first of November, but now I'm not sure what I'm going to do."

He felt incredibly good there, holding her, his palm so warm and so large, his fingers so strong, his ease at touching her so compelling. "Will the Denver group have a problem with you splitting your time for a few months?"

He shook his head, shrugged. "I don't know. I haven't talked to them yet about this newest holdup. I'm not thrilled with the idea of dividing my energies. As far as work goes, I'd like to cut my ties here and go. A clean break, a fresh start and all that."

"And as far as your other ties? The ones that don't have anything to do with work?"

"You mean you?"

She nodded, because there was really no need to deny what was such an obvious truth.

He looked up and caught her staring. His face softened; his expression grew strangely sad. And then he leaned toward her and nuzzled his mouth to her cheek. "Trust me, darlin'. The thought of leaving you is making all of this damn hard."

This time it was Kinsey who couldn't think of anything to say. Not that she'd have been able to speak, anyway, what with sorrow lodged like a big red ball in her chest. How could the loss of a relationship-that-wasn't hurt like this?

After several more minutes of silence, it was Doug who asked, "Now what're *you* thinking?"

Way more than she wanted to share with a man who was about to walk out of her life. She cleared the tears from her throat. "Wondering how hard this move really is going to be for you, especially having to sell your part of Neville and Storey."

The bus reached the parking lot then, turned and rumbled through the entrance, shuddered to a stop. Doug didn't say a word. He seemed, in fact, relieved by the timely interruption of their arrival.

"Well?" she asked, because she wasn't ready to let the subject go.

"Well, what?" He stood and gestured for her to move out into the aisle.

Rolling her eyes, she stepped in front of him. "You have a terrible habit of avoiding what you don't want to talk about."

"Oh, this from the woman who refuses to say a word about what happened on Coconut Caye."

She was coming to realize how often he brought that up, and, not for the first time, wondered why. Whether his tactic was one of simply changing the subject. Or if all the things that had passed between them that night—the words and the deeds—were weighing that heavily on his mind.

"I said a word. Just the other night."

"Yeah. You said you were drunk. That doesn't mean you don't remember."

"And if I do remember? What difference is that going to make?" She stepped out of the bus onto the raised walkway, turning to Doug as he joined her.

"You tell me."

Tell you what? How aggravating you are? "We've all done things and said things we regret later. Add alcohol to the equation and the possibility of those regrets rises considerably, don't you think?"

"I dunno, Kinsey. I'm not the one here who proposed marriage." Doug raised a hand to wave farewell to Izzy and Baron as the couple headed across the lot in the opposite direction.

Groaning, Kinsey waved, as well. This marriage-proposal-that-wasn't seemed destined to haunt her forever. "I did not propose. I just…"

"You just need to get a move on, sister." And then Doug actually smacked her on the bottom. "We'll talk about this after we settle up our bet. The Texans lost, which means you've got some bikini bottoms modeling to do."

8

HANDS AND ARMS TUCKED beneath and between her breasts, Kinsey leaned her forehead on the warm tiled wall of Doug's shower enclosure. Hot water and steam slicked her skin, stripped her muscles of tension, the worries from her mind.

On the drive back from the Texans game earlier, she and Doug had stopped for a quick dinner with Izzy and Baron, arranged via a cell phone call.

Starving as always, Kinsey had hoped that a break for food and from the subject of her drunken marriage proposal would wash that particular conversation from Doug's mind.

So far, so good.

Too good, unfortunately.

Once back at his place for the ridiculous bikini bottoms modeling session he'd teased her about, she'd followed him into his bedroom. Instead of pulling her swimsuit from wherever he'd stashed it, he'd pulled out his suitcase and started packing for his upcoming week away.

She'd simply sat cross-legged against the head of the bed, watched and listened as Doug talked of Denver.

He hadn't talked of anything else, as if his travel preparations required one hundred percent of his concentration precluding his focus from drifting, his attention from returning to the conversation they'd started hours before.

Minutes ago he'd taken a call from Marcus West, and the two men had continued to talk until she was certain Doug had forgotten her existence. So she'd decided a shower was just the thing to warm and wake her, not to mention numb her mind, which was racing to depressing assumptions she'd never intended to entertain. Assumptions such as the one that said she really *was* nothing to him but a temporary good time, when she'd been hoping to convince him otherwise.

Until tonight, until ten minutes ago, she hadn't realized how right Lauren's assessment had been of Doug as a workaholic. Sure, Kinsey knew that he stayed busy, that he commuted two thousand miles on a regular basis, that he worked his butt off to balance commitments in both cities. But all his teasing bikini-bottom talk...what had that been about if he'd only brought her here to hang out while he packed? Did he really consider her simply a decorative accessory for his bedroom? Had she been imagining that his interest seemed to be taking root in deeper emotions?

Well, his moodiness was about to earn him a fat karate chop where it counted. She was not going to be ignored or treated like a flesh-and-blood *Maxim* model he kept around for times of horny frustration.

If all he really wanted was for them to remain friends, fine. They'd remain friends. They just wouldn't be playing friendly between the sheets.

And that sucked. That really, really sucked, because she enjoyed their closeness—even as she recognized that she'd reached a place where she needed more than that explosive physical intimacy.

She pulled in a deep breath, releasing it slowly as

the water beat down on her left side and left shoulder, and sluiced over her back. Spray fizzed and spewed into her face; she couldn't even be bothered to move.

She was drifting in that gauzy place between consciousness and sleep, trying—and failing—to convince herself that her feelings for Doug were simply her imagination's romanticism run amok, when she heard the shower's frosted glass door slide open.

Roused from her lethargy, she listened for the latch to catch, remaining still and continuing to breath in the same relaxed rhythm though her skin began to prickle and burn.

She didn't want to make any sort of first move, or to lay into Doug when she wasn't sure her aggravation for his inattention was justified. It was quite possible she'd been borrowing trouble all of this time. That Doug was simply clearing his schedule, getting business out of the way in order to spend the rest of the night with her.

As long as she knew where they stood, she could handle the straightforward sex. But they were skirting the edge of too much strange emotion here. The ups and downs were nauseating and were wreaking havoc with her perpetual good mood.

When Doug moved to stand behind her, her mood instinctively lifted. Anticipation popped in the shower's sizzling steam—an anticipation all the more potent for her current unrest. When he pressed his body fully to hers, she came awake completely, shuddering as he replaced the soothing warmth of the spray with the heat of his body.

He placed his hands on the wet tile on either side of her head, surrounding her with so much of himself, she wasn't sure she still had it in her to breathe. This was so unfair, the way he took her apart when she had been working to keep herself together.

Nuzzling her neck, he ground his hips into hers, his erection already strong and seeking a place to settle. He followed his kisses with sharp nips, then with healing laps of his tongue, feasting on the skin of her neck until she thought she'd surely dissolve into a boneless mass of sensation.

"I'm sorry," he mumbled between bites. "I shouldn't have taken that call."

"Business is business," she answered, trying to remember that not five minutes before she'd been on the outs with this man.

"Business could have and should have waited." He dipped his knees, dragging the full package of his sex along the crevice of her bottom as he came slowly upright. "I'm sorry. That's all I know how to say."

She wondered if he was sincere, saying what needed to be said, or if an apology was only what he thought she wanted to hear. She went on to wonder if he'd take the next call that came even if it happened while they were in bed.

The thing was, sex shouldn't hurt. Not physically, not emotionally. Not with the sort of pain she was feeling in places she had no idea how to heal. And that meant what they were doing here together was no longer about sex.

It was about love.

Her heart lurched; her breath became hard to draw in. When she turned to him here in a moment, when she faced him again, looked at him again, when she let him into her body, she'd be doing it all because, without question, he was the man she loved. Truly loved.

The admission rocked her until tears welled in her

eyes. She tried to breathe, and gasped instead, unable to bypass the hard knot of emotion bulging at the base of her throat. She didn't want to be in love, not when it made her feel wondrous one moment and miserable the next.

"Kinsey? Darlin'?" He pushed her hair away from her neck and nuzzled her nape. "You're not saying anything and you're starting to scare me here."

"If this is just sex, why are you scared?" she whispered, not sure if he would hear her over the rush of running water.

He did, and stopped the nibbling kisses though he didn't move away. Instead, he moved even closer and whispered into her ear, his voice a throaty echo of his normally upbeat tone. "How honest do you want me to be?"

"As honest as it gets," she said, before she finally turned to face him. Oh, but he was beautiful, a sight for her weary heart to hold close, though in this moment she felt a curious distance descend.

With her back pressed flat to the tiled wall, she settled her palms in the center of his chest, loving the feel of his smooth skin, the way the water heated him, the way his muscles were so strongly defined yet shuddered beneath her touch.

Steam rose around them from the water and from Doug's body like heat waves off a sunbaked road. She didn't even try to measure the level of heat in his eyes. It was a compelling and devouring sort of hunger, the need to take her, to possess her and own her, consequences be damned.

A hunger that had her blood running hot and her body opening to take him in.

For several long, silent moments he held her gaze

without blinking, without moving a muscle but for the hard tic that pulsed in his jaw. She watched helplessly, hopefully, as his emotional battle fired and flashed, continued to watch as it fizzled.

It was when he pushed wet strands of hair from his face, looked down and away, that she knew it was finally over.

He was going to break her heart.

She closed her eyes, did her best to reach for an inward place of calm, yet knew she'd failed miserably when she had to struggle to speak. "Forget it. It's not that important."

"Since when has honesty not been important?"

Since I decided being ripped apart was too much to take. "Not honesty. My question. My question isn't important."

He shook his head. "Wrong. It is important. I've told you straight out that this isn't about a commitment, yet I still can't stop treating you like you belong to me. And, yeah. That scares me. It scares me a lot."

She was as contemporary as a woman came, but the idea of belonging to the man she loved? Anachronistic or not, she thrilled to the idea. "Yeah. I've noticed that belonging thing."

He slammed his palms to the wall on either side of her head and glared down, his chest heaving with raw, ragged breaths. "So why do you let me?"

"Because I love you."

That wasn't what she'd meant to say. That wasn't what she'd meant to say at all.

If she hadn't blown it before... She pressed her head back against the tiles with a thud, closing her eyes.

It was time to soap and shampoo and get out of here. Before she could make a move, however, Doug moved his body into hers, chest to chest, belly to belly, his erection searching out and finding the space between her legs designed for his fit.

He slid up and down her body, the friction supplied by the shower stall's wet heat, sending shiver after shiver along her spine.

And then his mouth was on her neck, beneath her chin, lovingly nipping a line to the hollow of her throat. She moaned, rubbing her nipples through the swirls of wet hair on his chest.

He stood tall, towering over her and remaining still until she opened her eyes. Her heart plummeted before rebounding into her throat. Never before had she wished to capture an expression the way she wanted to now.

She was so afraid no man would ever look at her this way again. As if everything in her life had led up to this moment. As if what passed between them now would determine future events. As if he wanted her in ways he'd never be able to tell her, yet showing her would fall far short of the truth.

"You don't want to love me," he murmured.

"I know."

"I can't love you back."

"I know."

"I won't be around. I won't ask you to go with me."

"I know."

"You're way too understanding."

"I know."

"I know what you're doing," he said, his mouth quirking up on one side. "You're trying to get me to talk. To explain myself. To give in."

She shook her head. "No, I'm not, really. I know

you have to do what you have to do. That means you'll be leaving. And I'll be staying.''

''It'll be lonely in Denver without you.''

''You can come see me anytime you're in town.''

''What about all the other guys you'll have in your life?''

''You told me you wouldn't be jealous.''

''I lied,'' he said as he cupped his hands beneath her bottom and lifted her to meet his thrusts.

He impaled her, and she gasped. Nothing had ever felt so right as being filled the way Doug filled her. She wrapped a leg around his hips, standing on the toes of her other foot.

Both of her hands found their way to his face. She held him still for her kiss—a kiss he wanted to deepen, to intensify. A kiss she kept simple.

And into that simplicity she poured her love. The love his voice rejected.

The love his eyes hungered to know.

The fact that he was leaving soon, that he wouldn't be here to share her life, meant nothing in this moment. At this very instant, she loved him with her mind and her spirit as well as with her body.

With her body she was able to show him her feelings as she kissed him tenderly, gently, even as he tried to increase both the pressure and the pace. She continued caressing him softly, moving her hands from his face to his shoulders, down his arms to his waist and then to his hips.

Once there, she urged him to a stop. He fought her firm hold and growled when she insisted he obey.

It was then that she began to move over his body, rubbing her swollen and aching sex along his shaft, her pelvic mound against his lower belly. He bent his knees and she returned her feet to the shower floor, aligning their bodies completely.

Skin to skin from feet to face. The sensation overwhelmed her; she had never felt the urge to laugh and cry at the same time the way she did now. She couldn't think of their parting when they were joined as they were. A joining that completed her fully.

And so she showed him the capacity of her love, showed him with fingertips and tongue. Showed him with the lifting and lowering of her hips, the slide and squeeze along his shaft.

She kept the rhythm to the slowest pace she could for as long as she could, but it didn't take long until speed became as necessary as taking her next breath.

Doug panted against her neck, his hands braced against the tiles, his knees bent as his hips thrust, thrust, thrust.

Her grip on his backside tightened, and she urged him to hurry, to push, to press, to rub, to slip and slide and…she cried out as she came.

He took her apart as his own knees buckled and he collapsed into her arms. She held him as he shuddered, held him as he calmed. Held him until he recovered and eased away the weight of his body.

She held him because it was what a woman did when she loved a man the way Kinsey loved Doug. And then she cried, softly at first, silently, waiting for him to shift his weight from her body. Wanting him to move, but only so he wouldn't feel the hitch in her chest when she breathed.

He moved, but not until after she'd caught only half of her audible sob. "God, Kinsey. I hurt you, didn't I? What hurts? What can I do?"

Rescind your acceptance of the Denver offer. Stay

*here so we can shower together every night before we
share a bed. Don't leave me. Ever.*   ·

"You can answer one question for me."

"Anything, darlin'. Anything."

With a bit of needed distance between them, with
the water now more soothing than stimulating, with
their bodies sated, their mood relaxed, she looked up
into his eyes of springtime green and asked the only
question that mattered.

"Why are you really going to Denver?"

"WE'RE GOING TO CREATE a gIRL-gEAR version of the
'Cell Block Tango' number from the movie *Chicago*."

At Sydney's pronouncement, a flurry of excited chatter went up around the conference room table. The
partners had gone as a group to see the film earlier in
the year, and Kinsey still got shivers remembering that
particular prison dance scene.

She had totally lusted over and envied the female
dancers' bodies. Sit-ups and push-ups and crunches be
damned. She would never have those sculpted abs.

And then it hit her. Cell block. Prisoners. Did that
mean she was going to be auctioned off as a convict?
She hadn't done the crime and didn't want to do the
time.

But she especially didn't want to wear stripes. Talk
about unflattering. "Are we token bachelorettes required to wear jailhouse stripes?"

Sitting in on the meeting as an involved party though
not a partner, Izzy sputtered. "Stripes are better than
jailhouse orange."

"Only if the stripes are vertical," Poe sagely added.

But Lauren simply shook her head. "The dancers in

that number did not wear stripes. Unless you count garters and the boning in their bustiers.''

Kinsey just rolled her eyes. Garters and bustiers. Great. She returned her attention to Sydney. ''Do you want to fill us in on the where and the when, et cetera?''

''Halloween night.'' Having made her initial announcement, Sydney pulled out her chair and sat, crossing one leg and lacing her hands in her lap. ''Unless anyone has objections or plans that absolutely cannot be changed. We have two weeks to pull this together and, yes, I realize this is short notice.''

After they grumbled agreement, the partners hashed out the logistics as questions rose in intensity and volume until they sounded like a gaggle of honking geese.

Sydney waved down the henlike chatter. ''I apologize in advance for putting down my executive foot, and I won't mind lifting it should you all have objections, but I think I've hit on an idea that makes this a totally feasible strategy.''

''You plan to share it?'' Kinsey rather hesitantly asked. Sydney's brainstorms were legendary; this group of highly individual personalities wouldn't be sitting here as partners otherwise.

Sydney nodded with her usual grace. ''Ray and I were having drinks at my father's bar last night. Last year before the name change, Paddington's Ford hosted a book signing for the elusive Ryder Falco.''

Lauren heaved a sigh. ''God, I love his stuff. Anton got me hooked on the Raleigh Slater horror novels. But I'm dying to get my hand on Falco's newest book. It's a romantic drama, and the buzz has been amazing.''

Sydney voiced her agreement. ''Yes, and the publisher actually rushed the book into production. Falco will be signing advance copies at Paddington's this year on Halloween just as he did last year.''

Lauren frowned. "I didn't think advance copies were available for sale.''

"They're not. They're giveaways.''

"And how did your father manage that?'' Poe asked.

"The signing is a fund-raiser for a shelter Falco has established for homeless mothers and children. The copies are available for a substantial donation. As in really big bucks.'' Sydney's grin widened. "That means we'll get to piggyback on the advertising and have an amazing crowd of fat-walleted bidders.''

Kinsey forced back a groan. She was a woman in love; she did not want to be sold to any man with deep pockets. Still, it was too late to back out after giving her word.

And then there was the simple fact that her feelings for Doug didn't mean she had a love life....

All for one girl, one girl for all. "What do you need us to do?''

WEDNESDAY NIGHT FOLLOWING church meant pie and coffee at Fred's Place.

For as long as Izzy could remember, Gramma Fred had closed the restaurant on Wednesday nights at six, opening again immediately after Bible study.

Some weeks, when prayers were short and lessons delivered at breakneck speed, the coffee would be ready to pour by eight o'clock.

Other weeks, slow Southern weeks when everyone's sins needed an extra washing, the pie would be nearly stale by the time it was sliced.

Tonight, Uncle Leonard had more on his mind than usual and had given over a big part of the service to the choir. It seemed a night for song, and a good thing, too.

Singing didn't require a body to do more than embrace the hymns' familiar and comforting words. And tonight Izzy had no mind for listening.

Joseph Baron wasn't up for coming to church, but he'd agreed to meet her for pie.

She pulled her Civic into an empty space facing the front of the diner. From that vantage point, she could see into the brightly lit interior through the windows that ran from end to end.

Baron was already seated at the long counter, swiveling on a stool that seemed too tiny to hold what that hard muscled body surely must weigh.

Izzy wrapped both hands over the top of the steering wheel and leaned her chin on her knuckles. Staring at him fed her sweet tooth in ways Gramma Fred's apple pie never could, in ways she wondered if she'd ever been fed.

But sitting here wasn't going to get her anywhere, so she pulled the keys from the ignition, tucked them into her wallet and grabbed a woven wrap shot with strands of dark paprika, cinnamon and sunflower-gold, draping it over her plain black tank dress.

"Penitent clothes," Mamma Rose called the combination, which was more subdued than the rest of the wardrobe hanging in Izzy's closet. All Izzy knew was that in the humbler clothes, the simpler colors, she found herself able to focus wholly on her spiritual self.

Since she was used to going to Gramma Fred's straight from church, she hadn't even thought to change for her "date" with Baron. That was okay. She had no reason to hide any part of who she was from anyone— even though she did.

She wondered if he had secrets, what they were, how she could pry them out, since subtlety was not one of her strong suits, and since she wasn't yet ready to reveal all of her own. That would come later, after he'd earned her trust.

She pulled open the door of the diner and was greeted by the aroma of fresh brewed Sumatra—one of the perks of being Frederica Higgs's granddaughter. Gramma Fred kept Izzy's favorite roast for Wednesday's pie nights.

Following her nose led Izzy straight to Baron and the cup he cradled between his two beautiful large hands. The thought of those hands...

She eased up onto the stool at his side, but spoke to her grandmother, who was already hovering with pot and cup in hand. "You know, Gramma, I'm going to be really disappointed if you've given away all of my special brew."

Gramma Fred merely filled Izzy's cup, addressing her response to Baron. "Think twice about ever havin' children, Joseph. They produce ungrateful complainers who try to pass themselves off as loving granddaughters."

Izzy lifted her cup and, eyes closed, inhaled before looking back at her grandmother, who stood with one hand on her hip. Gramma Fred's imperially arched brow failed to produce a single wrinkle in her forehead. Izzy prayed on a regular basis that she'd inherited her grandmother's youthful skin.

"And now I suppose Her Ungratefulness will be wanting a slice of pie, not that the sweetness wouldn't be an improvement," Gramma Fred said with a huff.

"Apple, please, if you have any left." Izzy stood up on the bar stool's rungs, leaned across the counter and wrapped her grandmother in a hug. "And vanilla ice cream," she added as she sat back. "Thank you."

Gramma Fred simply shook her head, returned the coffeepot to the warmer and headed to the opposite end of the counter and the pie case. Izzy watched her go, feeling Baron's gaze on her face as she grinned at her grandmother's back.

When she finally glanced up, it was to find him looking at her with a curious expression. "What?"

He shook his head, his mouth caught in a crooked smile that skirted the corners of his eyes. "Interesting bond you have with your grandmother."

"She's amazing. The best. Aren't you, Gramma Fred?" Izzy asked as the older woman slid a plate holding a quarter of a pie and nearly a pint of ice cream toward her.

"Eat up," she ordered, giving Izzy a wink before getting back to her other customers.

Baron watched her go, lifting his cup to drink. "You're lucky to have that."

Izzy didn't think she'd ever seen a man's hand envelop a coffee cup so completely. "It's beautifully smothering and wonderfully challenging."

He lowered his cup to the counter. "Is that a complaint?"

Slowly, Izzy pulled the soup spoon from her mouth, pressing her lips tight to get the last smear of ice cream. The delay allowed her to think of a comeback that wouldn't send this man running into the night.

"Tell me about your family, Joseph."

He picked up the spoon resting on his saucer and tapped the counter with the end. "Well, Isabel, if I had a family, I'd be more than happy to tell you about them."

What a strange admission to make. She didn't think she'd ever known anyone without at least a black sheep or disinherited outlaw sharing the family name. "Would you like to adopt mine? I have more than enough to go around, and not enough business for all of them to stick their noses into."

A smile pulled at his lovely full lips before revealing even, white teeth that she knew someone had been paid to keep that straight. So white against his sweet pecan skin. Staring into his coffee, he shook his head. "Can't say that interference is something I need any more of these days. When I was back running with my boys, well, having a nose stuck into my business would've been a good thing."

Curious, her feelings about this man. "Your boys? Just what kind of running did you use to do?"

He rolled one shoulder, and she wasn't quite sure if he was giving her an answer or simply shrugging off her question.

"Running I'm not exactly proud of, Isabel. I've done some things. Things I shouldn't have done. But that was a long time ago. People change. Circumstances, too."

"So, how have you changed?" she asked quietly, her mood suddenly pensive as she pressed the tines of her fork into her pie crumbs. Yes, she wanted to know, even as she admitted feeling intimidated by his answer.

She'd known former gang-bangers and what it had taken to turn their lives around. But she hadn't known one as intimately as she wanted to know Joseph Baron.

"For one thing, I only strap on blades that are legal." *But no less lethal,* he might as well have said. "And I have a respect for human life that I sure as hell never learned from example."

Something in the way he said it told her.... "You learned it from experience," she finished for him.

He nodded, frowned. "A month spent with a tube up your dick and down your throat'll make a big difference in the way you see your life."

In that instant, Izzy's whole world shifted. All this time she'd been bitching and moaning because everything around her seemed to stay the same. No matter what she did to get away, family obligations kept calling her back.

How petty she had been in her complaints, how small her issues were in comparison. And then it hit her that, if not for his strength of character to overcome his background, his strength of will to switch the track down which he'd run, Joseph might never have lived to come into her life.

He didn't have to give her the details for her to know that a very large thing had happened in his life. "That's why you do what you do, isn't it? You save lives because you almost lost yours."

His gaze dropped almost involuntarily to the number fourteen intricately tattooed on his left forearm, as if covering up an earlier design he wanted to hide. He then dug for his wallet, tossed a ten on the counter and got to his feet. "I want to show you something."

She glanced from the bill on the bar to his face. "Gramma Fred will be insulted if you try to pay."

Baron looked back briefly at the money he'd left before signaling for Izzy's grandmother. She made her way down the counter, refilling cups along the way, stopping when Baron covered his with his hand.

"One cup? That's all?" she asked.

"Shift change is at midnight and I'm on call. I've got to go." He picked up the ten and tucked it into her apron pocket. "Isabel tells me you won't accept payment."

"My girl's got that right," the older woman said, her head cocked in that jaunty way that dared him to argue. And then she looked at Izzy. "He called you Isabel."

"I know, Gramma," Izzy said, her heart swelling with the tingle of anticipation. "I think he's used to getting his way."

"I am. I also tip based on the service, not on the cost of the meal." This time it was Baron's look that told Gramma Fred he wouldn't be putting up with any back talk.

"Thanks, Gramma. Wednesdays without you just wouldn't be the same." Izzy got to her feet and leaned over to press a kiss to her grandmother's cheek. As much as she enjoyed seeing Gramma Fred speechless, Izzy couldn't imagine not hearing that bossy voice on a regular basis.

She was still wondering over her sudden melancholy when she and Baron reached his truck.

The stars were bright in the sky of velvet darkness, and Baron had parked at the far end of the lot, where the floodlights didn't quite shine. Izzy couldn't say that the idea of shadows and solitude bothered her a bit. Nope, not even a little.

In fact, the idea of having Baron and the stillness all to herself brought a warm flush to her skin. She crossed her arms and rubbed her hands over her bare skin and the gooseflesh that had nothing to do with the weather.

"Are you cold?"

Oh, but she loved the rusty and weathered sound of his voice, the way he observed and paid attention, never letting a detail slip past. She shook her head. "Not at all."

He opened the driver's door; light spilled out in a sharp triangle and took away much of the ambience Izzy had been soaking up.

But then he started unbuttoning his shirt, and everything changed.

He kept his gaze focused on hers, his eyes never wavering, not even to blink. As Izzy watched, he bared his chest, one gorgeously muscled inch at a time.

His pecs were amazing, sculpted above an abdomen that was rippled all the way to the waistband of his uniform pants. Izzy held a hand to her throat to keep it from fluttering, feeling strangely light-headed and awe-inspired.

But it was when he shrugged out of the shirt completely that she fully held her breath. Scars pocked his shoulder, deep gouges that stopped at his collarbone, only to pick up again near his waist, a scatter-shot pattern that spilled across his torso toward his ribs and disappeared down into his pants.

Her voice caught at the base of her throat, and her heart thundered. His body was so beautiful, so perfect…and so badly damaged.

When she finally found the ability to speak, she asked the most obvious question. "What happened?"

"I had my ass kicked by a nine-millimeter Beretta." He said it matter-of-factly, as if being shot was no worse than running into a brick wall or getting nailed by flying fists. "A drive-by?"

He nodded.

"How old were you?"

"Sixteen."

And he'd spent weeks in the hospital recovering.

Weeks when he'd been all alone. "Who took care of you?"

"Doctors, nurses." He started to shrug back into his shirt.

"Wait." She moved closer and touched him because not touching him wasn't an option.

She placed her palm squarely over his pectoral muscle where his skin was smooth and warm and resiliently firm. But then she spread her fingers, searching out the closest scar and rubbing a circle around it before dipping into the quarter-size crater.

"Isabel—"

"Shh." She stepped closer and laid her cheek in the center of his chest. His heart thudded; his chest rose and fell. Her fingers continued to explore.

She traced the random configuration toward his shoulder, reversing the path down over his ribs and coming closer to tears with each scar her fingers discovered.

When she reached the last one he'd uncovered, she simply wrapped her arms around his waist and held him, pressing her lips to the ribs that guarded his heart.

Baron sucked in a hiss of breath at the contact, his hands moving to her shoulders as if to set her away. She wanted nothing more than to stay where she was as long as she could.

But at Baron's insistence she stepped back and looked up, catching only a glimpse of the moon before his head descended.

His lips were beautifully full and soft even while firm in pressing down with their kiss. She slipped her palms up his back and held him close, wishing she was wearing anything right now besides her penitent clothes.

She kissed him, moving her body into his, against his, doing the same with her tongue. He pressed harder, deeper, his hands reaching down to cover her backside and pull her fully into his strengthening erection.

He so obviously wanted her that she found herself floundering when, in the next moment, he set her away. "I don't want your pity, Isabel. I've long since learned my lessons and I know how to take care of myself."

Pity was the furthest thing from her mind. He stood there in the truck's open door, his hands at his waist, his chest bared and beautiful as he struggled to breathe.

"Oh, Joseph. That wasn't pity. That was a woman enjoying a man."

His grin started slowly, then broke over his face. "As long as we're clear on the concept."

"Oh, yes. We are."

"Then you're welcome to climb up into the cab of my truck and show me more of what you enjoy."

And, of course, she did.

9

WITH POE HAVING WALKED off toward the dressing room carrying at least six garments over the store's limit of four, Kinsey turned from the rack of clothes through which she'd just uselessly combed.

She tossed up both hands and faced Lauren. "This is totally hopeless. Even with a wig, I will never look like Catherine Zeta-Jones."

Glancing away from the beveled mirror where she'd been smoothing her royal-blue headband, Izzy didn't even give Lauren time to start in before pointing out the obvious objection. "The aim here is to look like Kinsey Gray, no matter how gorgeous Mrs. Douglas might be."

"Izzy's right, you know." Lauren went back to sorting through the clothing items hanging on the rack. "You're selling yourself for who you are and what you look like. So, get to shopping. Find something to play up those two big ol' assets there on your chest."

Kinsey didn't have it in her to argue, and simply gave up trying to reason with her friends. She was stuck, end of story; she'd be selling herself to the highest bidder even if his name wasn't Doug. The thought was more depressing than she'd ever imagined it would be.

The four women had taken off a long Thursday afternoon to stroll through the resale shops and vintage boutiques along lower Westheimer. Taffeta and Timeless, their second stop, once a Victorian style house, was now a maze of rooms filled with period clothing and jewelry.

The store had met all of Poe's shopping expectations; after winding her way through the potpourri-scented rooms, the woman was on her third "narrowing down" of possibilities, any of which would've made the perfect auction costume.

So far, Kinsey hadn't seen a single garment she wanted to try on. At least not the type of thing she felt fit with the theme of the auction. Of course, she was shopping with Doug in mind, and probably breaking every feminist rule around about dressing to please one's self.

Still, wasn't that the entire point of this outing? Coming away with an outfit that would incite a frenzy of bidding? Garters and bustiers, indeed. "I was kidding about the wig. I'd look terrible as a brunette. Though I would love to look that hot."

Izzy narrowed her eyes. "And just who is it that you're wishin' to look hot for?"

Before Kinsey could even think of an appropriate lie, Izzy went on, bringing one foot down sharply on the hardwood floor. "Kinsey Gray. Do not tell me that you are planning to be auctioned off in an outfit that is more about a man's taste than your own."

"It's not that," Kinsey hedged, lifting a sequined flapper-era shift from the rack. Nope. All wrong for her shoulders and, unfortunately, not skimpy enough for the job at hand.

"It is that and you know it." Lauren grabbed the hanger and returned the dress to the rack. "You're trying to decide what Doug would like. I can see it in your face.''

Kinsey schooled her expression into a blank stare. "See what in my face?''

Lauren rolled her eyes at Kinsey's lame attempt to hide her emotional confusion. "You are a woman conflicted. Should you show off what you want Doug to see? Or hide it in case he doesn't put in an appearance?''

He'd damn well better put in an appearance. Not to mention a hefty bid, Kinsey thought. "I just want to look…auctionable.''

"As if you have a worry over that. Blond hair and blue eyes and all that leg?'' Izzy raised a brow, quirked her mouth to one side. "I'd like to borrow about half that length if you don't mind.''

Placing one hand on her hip, Kinsey frowned. "And why would you want to do that? I think Joseph Baron was quite taken with you as you are.''

Izzy's chin went up. "*Is* quite taken with me. *Is*.''

"See, Kinsey?'' Lauren gestured toward the stunning African-American woman who'd been Kinsey's friend when the two had been girls in bare feet and pigtails. "Izzy's working on something with Baron and she's not complaining about being auctioned.''

"Are you kidding?'' Izzy shook her head. "I'm getting a great outfit here, and the chance to show Baron that he'd better get to working on his game if he doesn't want to lose out on the best thing that hasn't yet happened to him.''

"It's not the same thing at all. You're not in love—'' Kinsey bit her tongue midsentence, but not in time for all three of her co-shoppers to hear, as Poe had just walked out of the dressing room.

"Love?" Wearing a pale ivory beaded, thigh-length slip with narrow straps and a square bodice that barely covered the swell of her breasts, Poe stared at Kinsey. "After two weeks of man-trapping, you've decided you're in love?"

Kinsey sighed, fingering a faux mink stole. Calm, cool, collected. *Ohhmmm.* "It happened a long time ago, not only during the past two weeks. It's just that in the past two weeks I've let the truth sink in and I've faced it. The denial just wasn't working anymore."

Lauren finally shut her gaping mouth. "Kinsey. Why didn't you face this a long time ago? You could've saved yourself all this hassle."

Kinsey twirled the circular clothes rack separating her from the dagger-throwing gazes trained her way. "I don't think me facing it sooner would've made any difference in Doug leaving. For some reason, he's determined to go."

"And you've asked him why?" This from Poe as she checked out her reflection in an alcove of mirrors. The ivory silk shimmered beneath the lights; the pleats in the bodice and the sheer lace in the skirt were the perfect decorations for her perfect body and porcelain skin.

Kinsey couldn't help but feel a twinge of envy. "Yes, duh. I've asked him repeatedly."

"What does he say?" Lauren asked.

"He doesn't. He changes the subject. He remembers a phone call he needs to make." *He shuts me up with a sponge and soap bubbles and an amazing massage.* She shrugged. "He kisses me."

"Well, that's good to know. At least there's kissing going on," Izzy said, pulling a strapless yellow camisole off the rack and giving it and the coordinating, very sheer ballet skirt a thoughtful once-over.

Lauren, who had been pacing to the dressing room and back all this time, came to a complete and sudden stop that blocked Kinsey's view of the clothes she was sifting through. "Do you want him to stay?"

The question of the day, the week, her lifetime. "Selfishly speaking? Of course I do. But not if it's not what he wants, not if it'll make him unhappy. Not if there's something in Denver he can't get here."

"Another woman, perhaps?"

Kinsey delivered a withering glare to Poe. "If there's another woman giving him something he's not getting here, then I'd like to know what it is."

"Then it must be all about his work," Izzy offered.

Lauren shook her head, twining a strand of glass beads through her spread fingers. "I find that hard to believe. How could another firm give him anything he can't get from the one he established with Anton?"

Poe left the alcove and joined the others. "So, find out what he's looking for."

"Easy for you to say." Kinsey heaved another sigh, moved to stack her hands on the end of a rectangular rack next to the circular one she'd abandoned. She propped her chin on top. "It's not like I haven't tried."

"So try harder. Time is running out."

"Stop right there." Lauren held up her hand to halt Izzy from returning a rich burgundy-and-black-velvet bustier with matching tap pants to the rack. "Kinsey, this set would be perfect for you. Go try it on."

Poe canted her head and considered the lingerie. "I actually agree with Lauren. And, really, Kinsey, you need to put more effort into winning over this man if he's the one you want. This outfit can't help but grab his attention.''

"Poe, get a grip. I think I know fashion. gO gIRL and gROWL gIRL are both doing phenomenally well.''

"You know gIRL-gEAR fashion. You wear gIRL-gEAR fashion.'' Pursing her bowlike mouth, Poe gave Kinsey a thorough assessment, starting at the floor and working to the top of Kinsey's head.

Today she was wearing a black-and-white polka-dot skirt with a gusseted hemline and a close-fitting black top with a flirty lettuce-edge ruffle at the scoop neck. Poe took it all in, then advised, "What you need is a makeover.''

Kinsey frowned and turned to check out her reflection in the mirror Poe had abandoned. Her frown deepened. "You really think I need a makeover?''

Lauren began to nod. "I see what Poe's saying. Not a permanent makeover. Just enough of one to catch a certain man's eye.''

"Thank you, but I think I have his eye.'' And quite a few of his other parts.

"Don't listen to Lauren,'' Poe argued. "Listen to me. This isn't about catching his eye as much as making sure he knows he's been caught.''

"I sorta think that's obvious,'' Kinsey said, reluctantly taking the ridiculous underwear from Lauren's hand. "We've spent every weekend since the fire together.''

Lauren's eyes went glaringly wide. "Kinsey, wake up. That's only been two weeks.''

Kinsey knew the other woman was right. "It seems like forever.''

"That's because time has no meaning to a woman in love,'' Lauren posited.

Izzy frowned. "That's just plain stupid."

"And incredibly untrue."

At that, all eyes turned to Poe, but it was Lauren who pried. "Speaking from experience?"

"I am thirty-three, not thirteen."

"So? Tell us about this wild experience of yours."

Poe went back to admiring herself in the mirror, tucking up the slip's skirt until it barely covered her backside, and nodding at her reflection. "Which one?"

Lauren harrumphed. "Sounds to me as if someone's mouth is writing checks that she can't cash with her—"

"Enough with the cattiness," Kinsey nearly shouted. Sheesh, but those two got on her nerves at times. "I want to hear about making sure Doug knows that I know that he knows...oh, whatever."

She waved a flustered hand because her tongue and her brain had quit working in sync. "I've caught Doug's eye. Now I'm supposed to do what, exactly?"

KINSEY DUMPED the contents of another paper bag onto the long folding table in front of her and begin the arduous task of sorting the donated clothing by gender, size and wearability.

On the other end of the table, Izzy did the same, while her mother, Rose, and Kinsey's mother, Martine, worked at the opposite end of the Gray family's church fellowship hall.

Thursday evenings Kinsey spent with her parents. The weekly tradition was as long-standing as the family's early breakfast before Sunday services.

With Kinsey's father out of town this week on business, and the recent advent of the fire, Martine had suggested she and Kinsey spend the evening going through donations made to the ministry.

Izzy and Rose had been invited along, which meant Kinsey's time wouldn't be spent with her mother at all. But that was fine. Martine hadn't seen Rose in ages and the two could talk a vegan into eating beef.

"I will never understand why people think anyone else would want to wear junk that should've seen a trash can forty washings ago." Izzy tossed a scuzzy yellow T-shirt into a box beneath the table designated for cleaning rags.

"I'm like that with books," Kinsey said. "It doesn't matter that it's so old and worn that even the used bookstore won't take it. I can't bring myself to throw it away." She held up a pair of denim cutoffs with a missing zipper. "Now trashing these doesn't even cause me to blink." The shorts hit the big rubber garbage bin next to the exit door.

"Score. Two points for number fourteen, Kinsey Gray." Izzy shimmied her hips in a wickedly sexy imitation of a courtside cheerleader.

Kinsey rolled her eyes. "Number fourteen? Which ball player do you have a crush on this week?"

"None." Izzy considered a pair of dingy gray briefs. "Eww, gross." She pinched them between her forefinger and thumb and carried them to the trash. "Fourteen is the number Baron has tattooed on his forearm."

Like prying a bottle from a baby. "And what does the fourteen signify? I ask since I know you're champing at the bit to tell me."

Having returned to the table, Izzy grew still, her expression pensive and disturbingly sad. She hesitated—Kinsey saw the indecision in her face—before she finally glanced up and said, ''That's how many bullets he took in a drive-by.''

''What?'' *What?* The shock literally had her reeling; Kinsey glanced toward where their mothers were caught up in gossip and sorting at the other end of the fellowship hall.

She reached across the table and took hold of Izzy's wrist. ''Let's get out of here.''

Kinsey pushed through the heavy door that led out to the church parking lot, holding it open for her friend to follow. Once outside, the two women walked in silence down the sidewalk toward the sanctuary, where they turned in sync and sat down on the covered steps.

Kinsey stared at Izzy, who had her knees pulled up to her chest, her chin propped on top and her eyes closed, looking so anxious that Kinsey didn't know what to say. ''What did he tell you?''

Izzy's eyes remained closed as she spoke. ''He didn't tell me. Not at first. Not until he showed me. His body is beautiful, Kinsey. So beautiful.''

''But he has scars?''

''His entire right side. His shoulder, his ribs. His hip.''

Kinsey couldn't even imagine. ''When did it happen?''

''When he was sixteen. He spent weeks in the hospital.''

''Wow. Did they find out who did it?'' Obvious question, though one she could've answered herself. Shooters were rarely apprehended.

Izzy shook her head. ''I don't know.''

''His family must have been crazy with worry.''

Izzy shifted, stretching out her legs. ''From what he told me, he didn't have family to speak of. He was put in foster care when he was seven and grew up in the system. When he got shot, the family he lived with basically washed their hands of him. He'd already been gang-banging for a few years, and apparently they didn't want any more close calls."

Kinsey thought back to the protective cocoon she'd grown up in. The life Baron must have lived was one she had only seen in movies and on the six o'clock news. "Incredible. I mean, you'd never guess, looking at him now, all that he's been through."

"It scares me. He scares me. A lot," Izzy whispered.

Kinsey frowned. "What? You don't think he's dangerous, do you? Not now. Not after all this time."

Izzy exhaled a long sigh. "He's dangerous, all right. But not that way. I know the gang-banging isn't a part of his life anymore. He had help getting out. One of the doctors who saved him took him under his wing and got him off the streets."

"And now he saves lives in return."

Izzy nodded. "He's stronger than I've ever thought about being. And I don't know if I can be the woman he wants. After all this time of working to prove to Mamma and Gramma Fred how well I know my own mind, and that I know what I'm doing with my life... I just don't know if any of that is true."

Kinsey watched the other woman shake her head, saw her eyes brim with tears. "How can you say that? How can one man make you question everything about your life?"

How bizarre was it that she felt so clearly justified in questioning Izzy when her own thoughts of late had been to consider Doug's reaction before making a decision? That sudden realization dissolved her original worry that Izzy wasn't thinking straight.

Her friend gave a sharp little laugh. "It's so ridiculously complicated."

"I may look like a blond bimbo, but I'm a pretty damn good listener, you know."

Izzy accepted the offer, leaning back to stare up at the darkening sky beyond the covered walkway. "I've always insisted that I would find my man on my terms."

"And now you have."

"Maybe, yes." She gave a slight shrug. "But what if that means I'm disappointing my family?"

"How could seeing Baron disappoint your family?"

"Expectations. Obligations. All of which I've tried to escape because I felt like my life was my own."

Kinsey listened to Izzy's heavy sigh, realizing that her own family had been protective in their own way, but never in one that either demanded or smothered. They'd always trusted her to rely on the advice they'd imparted over the years.

And though her circumstances were different from Izzy's, she knew the other woman's family only wanted what was best for their daughter. That was the thing about love. "Have they even met Baron yet?"

Izzy nodded. "Last night I took him to Gramma Fred's for pie night."

"And?"

"You know my grandmother. She didn't say much. She just gave me enough pie and ice cream for two people." At the memory, Izzy grinned.

Kinsey followed suit. "Give them time. They just need to get to know him. *You* need to get to know him. It hasn't even been two weeks." When Izzy didn't comment, Kinsey frowned. "You are still seeing him, aren't you?"

"God, yes. And no man-trapping games for me, I can tell you that."

"Oh, fine. Now that it's your turn you've changed your tune."

"I haven't changed anything."

"Then what was that about feeding a man what he needs and playing to his love of sport?"

"Hey, that was you. This is me. And don't pull that all girls for one, one girl for all crap on me. I am not one of the gIRL-gEAR girls, even though Sydney is doing her best to claim otherwise."

"So, is Baron going to buy you at the auction?"

Izzy turned her head slowly in Kinsey's direction. "He doesn't know. And I forgot. How are we going to get out of this?"

"You're kidding, right? We're stuck, girlfriend."

HAVING AGREED TO MEET Marcus West for breakfast in Houston on Saturday morning, Doug had taken the last and latest possible flight out of Denver Friday night.

The way the other man had spent their last few phone calls trying to talk him out of leaving Texas, Doug would've thought Marcus and not Anton made up the other half of Neville and Storey. As hard as Doug tried, he just didn't get the other man's persistence.

Exhaustion was probably a big part of his confusion these days. He was having more than a little trouble thinking straight about a whole lotta things. A big one being what he felt about Kinsey Gray. But right now he didn't have time to think about anything except this meeting and Marcus West's impact on his career.

CuppaCafé was an Internet coffee shop located at

the edge of the downtown theater district. With the influx of new urban dwellers living in the converted lofts and hotels, the café had enough weekend business now to justify remaining open seven days a week.

Doug had never been there, and took a moment to get his bearings, eyeing the high open ceiling exposing duct work and beams, the olive-brown-and-yellow color scheme and the overall streamlined techno design. He liked it. Liked it a lot. Whoever had put the place together knew their stuff.

Marcus was apparently a regular, judging by the banter going on between him and the roller-skating waitress as Doug arrived. He slid into the booth opposite the other man and ordered coffee.

"What kind?" asked the waitress, her spiky black hair giving her the look of comic electric shock.

Doug shook his head. "Just coffee. No flavor. No syrup. No whipped cream."

She rolled her eyes as if to say *Boring...!* "Mild or full-bodied?"

It was definitely a sleep-deprived, full-bodied sort of morning. "As strong as you've got."

She skated away across the glossy concrete floor, her serving tray tucked under one arm. Doug shook off a buttload of skater chick jokes and turned to find Marcus staring—first at the woman, then across the table at him while picking up his mug.

Doug nodded toward the brew, which was definitely more than straight-up java. "What do you drink here?"

"Whatever Alexandra decides I'm in the mood for," Marcus said, the corner of his mouth quirked upward.

Doug lifted a brow. "It's like that, huh?"

Marcus shook his head with a snort. "It's only like that in that she knows her coffee and I don't. She gets a chance to show off and I get a nice strong start to the morning."

The waitress skated up then with Doug's order. "This should do you. Monsooned Malabar. As strong as we're serving today."

Doug blew over the surface and sipped. The bite nearly took off his tongue. "This'll work."

The waitress gave a look that implied there should never have been any doubt, before skating away. Doug went back to waking up.

Marcus laughed. "Man, I don't think I've ever seen you look like such crap."

Doug wasn't about to fess up to the doubts that had to be showing in his face. Especially not to a client. "Let's see you split your time between two media firms. Five hundred bucks says your knuckles will be dragging the ground, too."

"Ah, but that won't be happening. I didn't pour my life into Media West to give it up should some *Forbes* firm come calling." Marcus lifted his coffee and drank, then returned the mug to the table. "I'd much rather be the big fish in the little pond than lost at sea."

"I'm certified to dive to one-hundred-and-fifty feet. I'll be fine." Doug read the skepticism in the other man's expression. "You think I'm feeding you a load of bull."

Marcus looked out the window at the early morning Houston foot traffic, looked back and shook his head. "It's not that, Doug. It's just that I don't want you going half-assed into my build-out, or packing it in halfway through the project."

Doug felt his gut clench tight. "And you think that's going to happen? After all the work I've done for you?"

"I don't think it will happen, no. But things come up. Things go wrong. A screwup in Denver puts you behind on things here."

Yeah. He knew. "Which is why Reuben Bettis is covering me on this end."

"I'm not hiring Neville and Bettis. I'm hiring Neville and Storey." Marcus's gaze narrowed. "I'm hiring you, Doug. And I don't want to get boned because you're stuck at a hundred-and-fifty feet and can't find your way back to the surface."

Doug sipped at his coffee, taking the time he needed to get his temper under control. "Give me some credit here, Marcus. If you can't trust me, at least keep my track record in mind."

"Including the meeting you didn't make it to?"

"If that's going to make a difference, then yeah. Include it." Doug was starting to get pissed off—but, strangely, at himself more than at Marcus.

Marcus sat back in the booth, draped his arms along the smooth gold vinyl. "Just wanting to be on the same page here, man. That's all."

"Then the same page it is," Doug said, wondering for not the first time if any more of the decisions he'd made lately were going to haunt him forever.

WHAT SHE WAS SUPPOSED TO do, exactly, remained a mystery until Saturday and Macy Webb's gAME night. The monthly gIRL-gEAR get-together had been a tradition since the launch of Macy's popular gIRL gAMES column.

Due to Poe's insistence, Kinsey had been forced to put Doug off when he'd told her he'd swing by and pick her up. Poe had hinted at a plan, but hadn't given

Kinsey any details to work with. She'd simply told Doug he was in for a surprise.

Tonight the gAME theme was Junior High, and the gang of usual suspects was getting together at Lauren and Anton's place, as Macy and Leo Redding were having new Italian tile installed in the loft they shared to replace hardwood floors damaged by leaky pipes.

The cast of regulars put Macy's fun-time concepts through their paces, working out the kinks before the ideas went up on the site as sexy party games.

Macy and Leo, in fact, had hooked up during her infamous scavenger hunt a year or so ago. That same game had paired Chloe Zuniga with Eric Haydon, and ended with the winner, Ray Coffey, walking away with the prize of a cruise on Sydney's father's yacht—a vacation trip that had ended up being the catalyst for Sydney's romance with Ray.

Though Kinsey had been a part of the shipwrecked cruise that had landed on Coconut Caye, she had missed that particular gAME night because of her parents' return from an extended European vacation.

As important as she held her extended gIRL-gEAR family, her mother and father would always come first.

And her and Doug's conflicting view on family dynamics brought her back to her biggest worry about their developing relationship. They didn't share the same viewpoint when it came to the importance of keeping family close, and she feared that difference might rear an ugly head between them.

Though why she was worrying so stupidly now when they weren't together and would never be together if Poe didn't get here with her surprise bag o' tricks—

The doorbell chimed. Finally. Kinsey hurried

through the living room to let the other woman into the house.

Wearing slim black ankle pants and a matching black shell, Poe stood in the doorway with a garment bag and a professional-style makeup artist's train case, which Kinsey was sure cost a small fortune.

Poe lifted the hand holding the clothing to remove her sunglasses. Brows arched, she stared unsmiling through Kinsey's storm door. "Are you going to let me in?"

Kinsey pushed the door open. The other woman brushed by, smelling of her trademark light spice. "When you offered to help, I had no idea you were going to knock over the Alley Theater's makeup department."

A knowing smile passed over Poe's face. "They only wish they had my tools and training."

Not that she'd ever had any doubt, but Kinsey decided this was going to be interesting.

The storm door latched; she closed the front door and led Poe down the hallway to the master bedroom. "What kind of training are you talking about?"

Poe set the train case on the bed, hung the garment bag over the top of the closet door. She pulled down the zipper and glanced back over her shoulder. "I've been modeling for about five years."

"You're kidding." The woman never failed to surprise.

"Not runway or any national campaigns. I specialize in local work when a special look is needed." She turned to face Kinsey fully then. "And, no. Not just token Asian chick work either."

The mystery continued to build. "What's the last thing you did?"

"I was the face for an anthropology exercise on bone structure."

"Hmm." Kinsey flipped the latch on the train case, her eyes widening at the amazing array of cosmetics. "How're your classes going?"

"I have finals in December. I'm actually taking two weeks of vacation to relax and celebrate once I'm done."

Kinsey glanced up. "And then what? I mean, forensic anthropology is a far cry from fashion. I'm guessing you'll be leaving gIRL-gEAR?"

"Eventually, yes." Poe frowned. "Do you plan to stay there forever?"

Kinsey had always thought she would, in one capacity or another. But then Doug was moving to Denver, and she had entertained the thought of how she would answer if he asked her to come along. "For now? The immediate future? Yes. All of my family is here and I can't imagine leaving them."

"I didn't ask about you leaving your family. I asked about leaving the company." Poe crossed her arms, pursed her mouth thoughtfully. "But you'd have to in order to be with Doug in Denver, wouldn't you?"

"Well, that's a bridge I'm not crossing because I'll never reach it. Doug's made it clear he's leaving, and he's never even mentioned that he might want me there with him."

"So you're just his good-time girl here, then?"

"I am having fun with him." Kinsey sighed. "And it sucks a lot to think it's going to come to an end."

"Does that mean you've already given up? After one home-cooked meal and one ball game?"

"Fifty home-cooked meals. Fifty ball games. It

wouldn't matter." She shook her head. "He's determined to go. And he won't tell me why."

"Maybe he doesn't know why," Poe suggested, waving Kinsey toward the bedroom's vanity dresser.

Kinsey settled onto the padded bench while Poe pulled up the room's desk chair before returning to the bed for the train case. "I'm beginning to wonder if he does. Whatever it is, he's a master at avoidance and denial."

"Most men are."

"And then there's the way he manages to change the subject so fast and so seamlessly that it's thirty minutes later before I even realize we're talking about something totally inconsequential."

"Don't let it happen tonight. Tonight, you're in charge."

"Well, that sounds good in theory."

"And it works in practice. Once we have you ready to go, you won't forget. That's why we're here, remember. This costuming session is all about making sure Doug doesn't know what hit him."

"So, what did you bring me to wear?"

"I only picked out two outfits. We seem to be about the same size, and I have both of these left from shoots I did months ago." Walking back to the closet, Poe pulled out garments on hangers, holding the first outfit in one hand, the second in the other. She cocked her head to one side, then the other. "Think back to junior high, since that is tonight's theme."

"I'd rather not," Kinsey said, though her interest was definitely piqued.

"Exactly. Now, what I do with your face and your hair will depend on your image, so…"

She offered one outfit first. "Do you want to be

every guy's girl?'' And then she offered the second. ''Or do you want to be an unattainable, off-limits adolescent fantasy?''

Kinsey felt her face break into a grin. ''Oh, Poe. How perfectly, wickedly clever of you. The adolescent fantasy, definitely. Doug won't be able to resist.''

''My point exactly. What are men if not overgrown adolescents?''

10

DOUG STOOD BEHIND the curved bar in Anton and Lauren's spacious living room, the main room of their home seeming even larger due to the ceiling that reached to the second floor.

Anton had bought the warehouse in the Heights near downtown Houston and converted it into a showplace that had Doug envying both the living space and his partner's awesome artistic vision.

Not a lot of the architects he'd known and worked with could've imagined and pulled off such a conversion feat. The fact that he and Anton shared such a talent meant that Neville and Storey's reputation was beginning to reach beyond Texas's borders.

And that was the very reason the Warren Sill Group had come calling.

Doug stared down into his drink, swirled the slivers of ice around in the aged Scotch. He had to admit he enjoyed being wooed and wanted. He equated the experience to a major league scout finding a player on a neighborhood sandlot. The kid's life would never be the same, and he'd been doing the very thing he most loved.

Doug loved what he did at Neville and Storey, loved his client base, took pride in his completed projects, anticipated future ones. He would never have gone looking for a major league scout, but the scout had come looking for him. So here he was.

It was a damn heady feeling, being wanted by the big boys. And it went a long way to feeding an ego that had been busted now for quite a few years.

Oh, sure. He'd had his successes; he'd built his name. He'd gone on with the plans he'd made with Anton even after his plans with Gwen had hit the skids in a very big way.

Did he still have feelings for her? Hell, no. He was long over that resentment. Especially seeing how happy his brother was. And now the couple was expecting their first child. He was going to be Uncle Doug… instead of being Daddy.

And that was what was getting to him, getting to him in ways he never would've expected. Especially now that Kinsey had entered the picture, tempting him in ways that made the associates at Warren Sill look like amateurs.

When the hell had he become so dissatisfied with his life and, more importantly, why? There was absolutely no reason he could come up with for his restlessness of late. And it was driving him crazy, this need to always want more, the looking ahead, his inability to find the sense of accomplishment he'd once known in the here and now.

"Dude, you've been staring at your drink now for five minutes. You got a thing for watching ice melt?"

At Anton's jibe, Doug lifted his glass and drained it of Scotch. "That better?"

"Depending on whether or not you're wanting a refill or if you want to be able to drive home."

"A refill, definitely. Are you kidding? How many of

Macy's gAME nights have you made it through sober?''

"I heard that," Macy said, walking by in bare feet and blue jeans, a lingerie top that sure didn't do anything for her flat chest, and her hair wound into dreadlocks.

"Hey, Macy. Nice tattoo," Doug said, nodding toward the intricate red-brown patterns decorating her feet.

"It's a Mehndi design, not a tattoo."

"Uh-huh," Anton said, echoing Doug's own cluelessness.

Macy rolled her eyes. "It's not permanent." She held out her hands, the backs of which were similarly stained with dots and swirls. "See? It's done with henna." She turned them this way and that. "It's a compromise."

"Compromise?" Doug asked.

"Leo said no more permanent ink," she said then headed toward the front door with her party invitations in hand.

Doug just shook his head. "Leo's a braver man than I am."

"Get real, Doug. Leo knows what counts." Anton returned the crystal stopper to the decanter of Scotch. "You got a woman you want, you compromise."

Doug glanced toward the door, wondering what the hell was taking Kinsey so long. He hadn't seen her since the night in his shower when she'd told him she loved him. That hadn't even been a week ago, yet it seemed like forever.

The thought of Kinsey loving him had his gut clenching like a fist around a golf club grip. The thought of the compromises he'd have to make to keep her... "I thought it was Macy doing the compromising."

"Macy gave up the permanence. Leo gave in to the ink." Anton grabbed another bottled ale from the bar's minifridge. "You're going to need some serious relationship instruction if you decide to pursue this thing with Kinsey."

"What thing with Kinsey?"

"Oh, man. Your problem's bigger than I thought." Anton laughed, shaking his head. "What thing with Kinsey, my ass. Last I heard, the two of you were only having dinner, and now Lauren can't shut up about what a great couple you two are going to make."

Doug huffed, hoping the other man wasn't picking up on the fear that he didn't know shit about being part of a couple. He ran a hand over his forehead to wipe away the sweat. "I don't do long distance. You know that."

Anton turned to face him and stared until Doug acknowledged that his partner wasn't going to go away, even after Doug had flipped him the bird and told him to bug off. God, but he did not want to hear another rendition of Anton's "Gwen" lecture.

But Anton being Anton, Doug's threat didn't do a bit of good. "Man, you have got to get over this idea that you screwed up. You and Gwen were kids. You left home. You grew up. You followed through on your goals, and she didn't stick around to see you through it."

"Yeah, yeah, yeah."

Anton lowered his bottle after swallowing a quarter of the contents. "Doug, don't be an ass. You think if you'd stayed and gone to school in Abilene you would've had half the success you've had so far?"

Doug blew out a snort. "Is that what it's all about? Success?"

"You tell me. You're the one climbing the ladder straight out of our partnership."

That pissed Doug off. "So this conversation isn't about Kinsey or Gwen at all, is it? It's about the business and my bailing."

But Anton's attention had been drawn to the foyer and the front door. "Well, dude. It would be if we had time. But your number just came up."

It didn't take but one jab of Anton's elbow for Doug to turn. Holy sweet poker chips, but he was going to stroke out where he stood if his pulse was any indication. And damn if he hadn't drained his second drink way too soon.

Kinsey stood at the edge of the room looking like the naive ingenue every depraved teen horndog he'd ever known would've given a left nut to debauch.

She wore penny loafers and kneesocks, white ones to match her plain white button-down uniform top. Beneath that she wore a pleated green-and-blue-plaid schoolgirl skirt.

But the skirt was a length no schoolgirl would've ever been allowed to wear. Goddamn, but she had legs. And the blouse... Sweet mother, her tits were about to burst the buttons free from their holes.

He finally managed to make his way from her body to her face, and that was when he was done for, done in, done to a crackly, unsalvageable crunch.

She wore tiny barrettes just above her temples. They held her long blond hair off her face. And, oh, her face.

He knew nothing about makeup except to know it looked as if she wasn't wearing any. But she had to be. He'd seen her at the office; he'd seen her in bed.

And he'd never seen her looking like purity embodied, like her innocence was the only thing with the power to save him from himself. He turned back to the bottle of Scotch before his heart completely tore a hole in his chest. He splashed another ounce over ice with a shaking hand and lifted the glass.

That was when he stopped. Swallowing wasn't going to be happening with his throat closed up this tight.

Having her tell him that she loved him had been bad enough.

But knowing that he loved her?

He would never be the same again.

KINSEY GLANCED DOWN at the sheet of lined notebook paper on which Macy's party invitation had been scrawled, and laughed.

It looked exactly like a note she would've passed to a friend during geometry. And the wording... "My parents are gone for the weekend! Let's party!!!" Oh, yeah. Macy knew her stuff when it came to party planning. She went all out with every one of her thematic concepts.

The gAME night itinerary had Kinsey chuckling more—Spin the Bottle, Chase and Tackle, the Dirty Closet Thirty, Truth or Dare. Oh, yeah. Junior high revisited. And then there was the Bangles, Culture Club, Foreigner and Wham music mix blaring through the Nevilles' sound system.

This was going to be such a blast.

Or as much of a blast as she could manage feeling so out of her element in Poe's schoolgirl uniform. The rest of the party-goers could have easily been groupies in a Jon Bon Jovi or Madonna music video.

Junior high had been Kinsey's first exposure to

cliques and popularity and the always imperative need to stand out while fitting in. She'd grown up and attended school with the same core group of friends—the ones whose parents hadn't been displaced by the bottoming out of Houston's oil industry.

The name Kinsey Gray had been on rosters for the drill team and the cheerleading squad and the student council, as well as on the list of officers for both academic and social clubs.

Playing the part of an innocent was going to be a stretch of her acting ability. Especially since she already felt the intensity of Doug's gaze as he stared from the bar on the far side of the room.

Still, she gave it a shot, rubbing the toe of one shoe over her sock-clad calf, and catching the tip of her tongue between her teeth while she glanced around the room from beneath lowered lashes.

After being handed Macy's invitation, Poe had abandoned Kinsey in the foyer entrance and headed into the heart of the party wearing the second, more traditional junior high era outfit: snazzily buckled and zippered jeans along with a sparkly, spangly skin-hugging top. She'd even managed to work with hot rollers and mousse to give herself big hair.

Kinsey couldn't help but grin as she studied her fashion coordinator. Standing at the French doors to the patio next to a similarly dressed Sydney, Poe looked as out of place as Kinsey felt. Interesting contrast, that.

"Ooh, girl. If you don't look like the epitome of my adolescence," Izzy said with a laugh. She gave Kinsey a head-to-toe once-over before going on, lips pursed, head shaking. "I take that back. You look like what I would've given a million bucks to have looked like back then."

Kinsey laughed in turn. "Wouldn't you just die to live those years again knowing what we know now?"

"Are you kidding? Knowing what I know now I would never go back."

"Well, I think it would be a blast," Lauren said, joining the conversation. She reached out and tugged on Kinsey's buttoned placket. "The boobs are what I wish I'd had. The girls with boobs were invited to all the parties."

"And all the school dances."

"And got to spend football games getting warmed up beneath the bleachers instead of freezing off their booties in the cold wind whipping through the stands."

Kinsey glanced at her two girlfriends and grinned. "Can you imagine what we would've been like in school together?"

Izzy shook her head madly. "Uh-uh. You two with your blue eyes and blond hair? I can see it now. You would've clawed at each other's eyes and pulled hair with all that competition going on."

Laughing, Lauren draped an arm over Kinsey's shoulders. "Maybe it's a good thing we didn't meet until college. I was pretty much over my competitive streak by then."

"Don't believe a word she says," Macy countered, walking by. "Lauren's still a master at one-upmanship."

"You *were* the first to get married, you know," Kinsey accused.

"Well, duh. Anton and I *have* been together forever. And," Lauren continued with a suspiciously secretive expression, "he tells me that Doug is more distracted than usual these days. I'm thinking he senses the trap closing in."

Kinsey sighed. "That means he's probably about to bolt before he's caught."

"Uh-uh. I don't think so. Look at the boy's face. I'd say he's trying to figure out how to trip the catch before you get away."

At Izzy's comment, Kinsey found herself unable to avoid looking at Doug. She turned only her head, slanted her eyes and felt the impact of his gaze in a direct hit to her heart.

He was watching her as if she were the only woman in existence.

She loved him unconditionally, and the rapid-fire beat of her heart came from the realization that he would never know how much. He would be no more than a memory weeks from now, and she'd blubber around, heartbroken, pathetic and sad.

She took a deep breath, brought up both her chin and her gaze and swore to go down fighting. "What has he told Anton about selling his half of Neville and Storey?"

Lauren shook her head. "Nothing yet, so I'd say you have time to change his mind."

"No. Not change it." Kinsey took a deep breath. "I'm going to help him make it up."

WITH ONLY A LITTLE BIT of help from her girlfriends on Spin the Bottle, Kinsey found herself on the floor of the foyer's coat closet with Doug.

Sitting between his spread legs, she leaned back and shifted around to get comfortable. The rules of this game meant they were going to be here for a nice little while; she didn't plan to leave without setting matters straight.

"You know," he began, pulling her snug against

him, "in junior high we called this Heaven in Seven, not the Dirty Thirty."

Kinsey smiled, feeling the rumble of his voice like tickling fingers down her spine. "Just one of the perks of playing as an adult instead of a teen."

"Is that so?" he asked with a laugh.

Oh, but being with him felt so, so right. "Yep. You get a full thirty minutes to show me your stuff. In junior high, guys rarely needed the full seven."

Doug made a sound that was half chuckle and half snort—a sound she would've marked down to jealousy if he'd had reason. "Are you speaking from experience?"

She shook her head, wrapping her arms over his, which were around her middle, and snuggled her head back into his shoulder. She breathed in the scent of his skin as her cheek grazed his jaw.

"I'm a closet virgin," she assured him. "You're definitely going to have to show me what we can do with the time we have."

He nuzzled his face to hers. "Don't tell me you've never had a quickie?"

"Of course I have. Just not in a closet." She grinned to herself and nuzzled back. "And not with you."

"So what are we waiting for?"

"Hello? This is junior high."

"In that case, forget it."

"Why do you say that?"

"You know junior high girls. All talk and no action. They get a guy where they want him, then bam. He pays up or they don't put out."

"Damn prick teases," Kinsey said with a laugh. Against her cheek, she felt Doug grin.

"It wasn't really so bad in junior high. The guy

would only have to promise to take the girl to a school dance and then second base was a given.''

''And as you got older?'' she teased.

''Hey, there. Who said we were talking about me?''

Kinsey lifted a hand, threaded her fingers back into his hair, wondering if he would regret opening this particular window, because she certainly planned to climb in. ''I thought maybe you were relating your own experiences. With Gwen.''

Doug's fingers, which had been twining in and out of hers in her lap, stilled where they rested low on her belly. ''I don't remember ever making out with Gwen in a closet.''

''Just every other room in the house?'' Kinsey asked, finishing his thought.

''A few, yeah. But not all of them.''

''Why not?''

Doug laughed then, but it didn't sound the least bit joyous. ''Because we did most of our making out down behind our houses. Our yards sloped in back toward a creek bed hidden by scrawny pines and underbrush.''

She wondered how long he'd keep talking, how soon he'd realize that he was. ''Hmm. For some reason you don't strike me as the back-to-nature sort.''

''A guy can be any sort a girl wants him to be when second base is within reach.''

Kinsey laughed. God, but they had such a good time together. She laid her hands over his and laced their fingers together, lifting and settling his palms over her breasts. He drew in a sharp breath at the contact; she did the same when he fondled and squeezed.

''Thought you said you didn't have any closet experience,'' he said with a deep, throaty growl.

''I don't. But I have experience with you.'' He

started to open her buttons; she slapped him away. "Uh-uh. Junior high, remember?"

"Then let's blow this joint and head back to my place for some purely adult fun."

She shook her head. "No can do. gAME night is a big part of the gIRL-gEAR experience. But I will move out of your lap if you'd like."

"No. I don't want you going anywhere. I'll just save the groping for later," he said, and returned his hands to her waist.

The simple contact was all she needed. He was here and she was here and the dark, silent closet actually had her in a more reflective than sexual mood.

It didn't matter that they were here because of a game. Playtime was over. She took a deep breath. "Doug?"

"Kinsey?"

"Does your move to Denver have anything to do with your breakup with Gwen?"

"That was quite a few years ago, darlin'. I'm long over that loss."

"Are you?" she asked. Before he could interrupt, she hurried to add, "I don't mean that you still have feelings for her, but maybe you're still looking for what she represented."

A tic started up in his jaw; she felt the pulse in her temple. "You think that's why I'm here with you? That I want you to replace Gwen?"

"No, that's not what I'm saying." She scooted around to lean against the closet's back wall, draping her legs over Doug's once he'd stretched them out. There wasn't enough light to truly see his face, only the hint of his profile. "I'm saying that Denver is replacing Gwen."

Doug turned his head, shifted where he sat, pulling up one knee and draping his arm on it. "Does Macy's game require we stay in here the full thirty minutes?"

She'd hit a nerve. "Tired of me already?"

"No. Not of you." He blew out a long breath. "Just tired of everyone getting in my Denver business."

She reached for his hand. "We're just looking out for you, Doug."

"I'm old enough to look out for myself, you know."

"I know. But this is what friends do. Especially friends who are as close as family."

Doug chuckled. "You and your family issues."

One second ticked by, two, then three before she let go of his hand. "You think *I* have family issues?"

"You're saying you don't?"

"No, I do not." At least none she wanted to talk about now when she had his to get out of the way. She crossed her arms over her chest.

"Then come to Denver with me."

"What?" What? Her stomach plummeted; her heart followed. Damn this dark closet that kept her from seeing his eyes and what he was feeling.

Her life was here, as was the career that had been everything to her since leaving university. She couldn't walk out on something she'd helped build, even if he could.

Then there were her girlfriends, and her family…

Oh, no. *Oh, no.* She saw what he was doing, and she was not going to fall for his tricks.

He thought he was so smart, trying to make their imminent split seem like her fault because she wouldn't leave her parents and gIRL-gEAR to go with him to Denver.

Time to turn these particular tables in a very big way.

She pretended uncertainty, hoping she would be able to pull this off now that her blood had began to boil. "I don't know, Doug. Leaving Houston after living here all of my life…"

"Think about it." He rubbed a palm up her bare thigh, beneath her skirt, all the way to her panties. "No more time wasted in flight. Being together every night. All that kinky fun waiting to be had."

"You do make it sound tempting." She reached for his wandering hand and returned it to his lap with a disciplinary smack. "I'm just not sure I can leave gIRL-gEAR."

She waited for him to insist that she could, to give her a list of reasons. But he didn't try to talk her into it; he didn't have anything more to say.

So she pressed forward. "On second thought, if you can come to terms with leaving Neville and Storey…"

He shifted restlessly.

Exactly the move she'd been waiting for. "Okay. Yes. Yes, I'll come with you."

"You will?"

"Yes." She nodded, though doubted he could see. Just as well, considering it probably wasn't very convincing in its enthusiasm.

Then again, neither was his tone of supposed excitement. "Just like that?"

Excitement, ha! Panic was more like it. He wasn't any more ready for her to pack up and go with him than she was ready to leave. "No, not just like that. I mean, there's my house. Then I'll have to make arrangements for my share of gIRL-gEAR. You know how that goes."

"Uh, yeah."

"This is going to be great." She squirreled around and climbed up to straddle his lap, moving her hands from his chest, where his heart thundered, to his shoulders, where his muscles had seized, to his face, where his breaking sweat gave him away. "We're going to have *so* much time to spend together."

"Well, yeah. But Kinsey, we probably need to talk about this before—"

"Shh." He'd had his chance to talk. Now she planned to make him squirm. He deserved it for being such a rat. For making her fall in love with him when he didn't want to be with her at all.

Fueled by a mixture of anger and hurt, she kissed him and kissed him hard. He met the slant of her mouth with a tilt of his head, covering her hands on his face with his.

She imagined she felt his fingers tremble, or maybe she was feeling nothing more than the shudder working its way the length of her limbs.

She didn't know if she had scared him to death or if he was truly jarred by the thought of her coming with him.

It didn't matter because the moment he parted his lips she was there—ready, wanting, needing, loving him, telling him so with her touch and her tongue and her tiny breathy whimpers.

She moved her hands to his wrists, her fingers stroking the soft skin and the tendons of his forearms.

And then she set him away.

He waited for a long moment before he let what had just happened sink in. And then he hung his head and sighed. "You didn't mean it, did you? You're not going to come with me, or leave gIRL-gEAR. You were just determined to make your point any way you could.''

She gave a shrug, hiding her hurt in the darkness. "Does it matter? I'm staying. You're going. End of story.''

A sharp rap on the closet door came long before she was ready. "Thirty minutes is up, you two,'' Macy called. "Get decent and get your butts out here. It's time to eat.''

Doug moved away with obvious reluctance, and Kinsey pressed her fingertips to her mouth. She started to say something sexy and flip and teasingly risqué, but Doug stopped her by reaching out a hand and tucking her hair back behind one ear.

"Listen, Kinsey,'' he began, his voice raw and hoarse, his tone vulnerable and uncertain. "I don't want either of us to have regrets. And I sure as hell don't want to hurt you.''

She was the one hurting herself, falling in love with him when their situation was impossible to resolve. But she wasn't going to tell him that. She wasn't going to tell him anything else at all. Certainly nothing that mattered, nothing deeper than her thoughts on the barometric pressure, nothing usable as ammunition when she fought to push him out of her life. A fight she intended to take up this very minute.

Or at least by the time the door opened and she could see that there really was light at the end of the Dougless tunnel.

And so she simply got to her feet and said, "I'm fine. I'm hungry. Now let's go eat.''

11

ONCE KINSEY ARRIVED HOME, she changed from her schoolgirl uniform into baby doll pajamas and went straight into her bedtime routine.

Sleep. That was what she needed. Things always seemed clearer the morning after, less hurtful, not so distressing, easier to compartmentalize by trauma factor and exaggerated angst.

Was it over or was there hope?

That was the question.

The party outfit had drawn Doug's attention as planned, but once she found herself sequestered with him in the closet, he'd done a total number on her.

Sure, she'd been a willing participant, had even worked her own reverse scheme in a trap that had snapped shut tighter than any of the others she'd rigged.

That didn't mean she'd come away from their not-so-dirty thirty minutes feeling vindicated. In fact, once the high of the party had flown, she'd come away quite hurt. And she'd left quite angry—at herself for not better protecting her emotions, and at Doug for, well, for being Doug.

He'd told her weeks ago not to love him. He hadn't hinted at sharing or returning her feelings. He'd never actually given her confession more than a cursory acknowledgment, telling her not to love him, that he couldn't love her back.

And then he'd asked her to come with him to Denver without meaning it.

When she'd accepted his invitation, he'd frozen in place before backtracking as fast as allowed by his well-oiled bipedal motor skills. He'd been caught in the act and hadn't even pretended to be sorry for the ridiculous ruse.

He was a rat. A total stinking rat.

Rubbing lotion over her legs, she decided to propose a gIRL gUIDE column about falling for inappropriate tricksters posing as sexy men. And then her doorbell chimed.

Pulse hammering her ears, she glanced at her bedside clock. Midnight. It was either the police with bad news or—

Her cell phone rang. Holding panic at bay, she scurried from her bed to her desk, where the phone sat in its charging cradle.

She glanced at the number displayed, took a huge breath and answered. "What the hell are you doing calling me this late?"

"Come open the damn door," Doug growled.

Kinsey didn't even respond. She slapped the phone closed and marched to the living room, her bare feet smacking the hardwood floor.

She jerked the dead bolt back and the door open. The glass storm door remained locked, a barrier between them, clear and impenetrable unless he decided to kick it in.

She crossed her arms over her chest; Doug's hands went to his hips, his brows up as he took in her very short and very sheer nightie. She pretended she was wearing chain mail and stared him down.

"That was a crappy thing to do, running out on me," he said, his voice muffled but his words unmistakable. His mood was unmistakable, as well; the hard glint in his eyes broadcast his frustrated anger. "We weren't through."

"Through with what?" She wasn't sure she could breathe. She swore the reaction was a delayed response to the midnight ringing of the doorbell and phone. But she knew there was much more at stake here than losing sleep. "The games were finished. Dinner was over. What hadn't we done?"

"We hadn't finished our conversation."

"Oh, I was quite finished," she said, and the responding tic in his jaw had her wanting to take a step back. She held her ground and most of her tongue, as well as her desire to thrust open the door and take him to bed. Damn her traitorous body and heart. "I can't think of a thing we left unsaid."

"I can think of plenty. Now open the damn door."

She waited, her arms still crossed, his jaw still pulsing, his frown deepening until his brow pulled down and the vibrations from his impatience seemed to rattle the glass.

Slowly she took a deep breath and released the hold she had on herself before she released the catch on the door. She inched it open; Doug grabbed the handle and finished the job, stepping through the entrance and into her home before she could do more than back a step away.

Her feet were bare on the hardwood floor; her body was bare but for the flimsy cotton baby doll top and panties. The light, at least, was low, giving her exposed heart the cover of darkness in which to hide. She had no doubt her eyes were at this very moment giving her away.

Doug shut and locked both doors, then turned. Only the low-wattage bulb burning in the base of one table lamp gave the room illumination. Or so she'd thought until she looked into his eyes, which seemed to glow.

She backed up another step; Doug moved forward until he stood within reach, within touching distance, within range of her senses, which blossomed at having him near. She swore her nostrils flared.

His scent compelled her to hold her breath, then to breathe through her mouth so as not to be reminded of how much she loved to tuck her nose close to his skin and inhale. But that didn't help a bit because with her lips parted she remembered both his kiss and his taste.

When the back of her thighs were against the arm of her sofa and her retreat came to a complete stop, she lifted her chin. Her heart pounded. Her pulse raced. Her skin itched and burned, and she wanted nothing more than to claw her way free from the pleasure that was pain.

"I meant what I said."

"I opened the door."

"Not that."

"Then what?"

He took another step, remaining just beyond her reach, but not beyond her body's sexual receptors. He was doing nothing but standing and staring, and she wanted him beyond all common sense.

"I want you to come to Denver with me."

"Bull. You didn't mean that at all."

"Maybe not then. But I do now."

"Why?"

"Because I asked you to."

"That's no reason."

"Because I want you to."

"That's not enough of a reason."

Again he moved closer. She gave up completely on trying to keep her voice steady, her hands still. She buried her fingers in the tufted arm of the sofa behind her and held on.

It was too late for sweet talk or for promises she doubted he'd really want to keep once he made them. She'd vowed days ago not to sit back and watch him gnaw off his leg to escape the traps she'd set.

"What do you want from me, Kinsey?"

"I don't want anything."

"Liar."

"Same to you."

"What do you think I'm lying about?"

Where should she start? She doubted any man would appreciate having a woman enumerate the lies he was telling about himself.

She took a deep, shuddering breath. "It doesn't matter what I think, Doug. Nothing matters but what you believe about yourself."

"You know that's not true. No one exists in a vacuum."

"Isn't that exactly what you're trying to do? Isolating yourself from your family. Now leaving your friends."

He spat out a foul curse and shoved a hand through his hair. "I'm not leaving my friends. I'm following a dream."

"I thought Neville and Storey was your dream."

"It was. It is." He paused, looked to his feet before returning his gaze to hers. "It was."

Her heart broke, fluttering in her chest like a bird with a broken wing. In the barest of whispers, she asked, "What happened?"

"Nothing happened. Just…" He shook his head. "Just nothing."

She curled her fingers deeper into the plush sofa stuffing because she wanted to reach out to him, to open her arms and hold him close. But she had herself to protect, and her emotional safety mattered more than her longing to soothe his sadness.

The next step he took brought him close enough that his knees bumped hers. The denim of his blue jeans rubbed roughly against her skin, but she remained still—at least until the weary hunger in her eyes, the way he rubbed tiredly at the back of his neck, tugged her off the sofa and into his arms.

She pressed her cheek to his chest; her arms went around his waist and she drew him close, tucking herself up into his body and loving him in that moment more than she'd ever imagined possible.

How would she ever be able to let him go?

His hands roamed her back, from her shoulder blades to the base of her spine. The clingy cotton nightie tickled and teased, transferring the heat of Doug's hands but disallowing the skin-to-skin contact she wanted desperately.

She wiggled her butt, hoping he'd get the message even while she worked to get closer, spreading her palms across his lower back before bunching her fingers into his shirt and pulling it free from his pants.

And there was his skin, so healthy and resilient over muscles so firm. She tiptoed her fingers up his spine; he walked his in reverse, from her nape on down.

Both continued the simple caress, the matching expression of the need to be close, to touch, to soothe, to reassure. And then to arouse, slowly at first, as finger-tips pressed harder, rubbing circles that grew wider, until palms slid beneath waistbands to find intimate skin.

Against her cheek, Kinsey felt the beat of Doug's heart, the rapid rise and fall of his chest as his breathing took on a fight-or-flight cadence.

She didn't want him to run, to think she didn't want him here, to go without knowing exactly the ways in which she wanted him. She moved her hands to his chest and one by one released the buttons of his shirt, baring his torso and the silky blond hair that grew low on his belly.

When she moved her hands to the buttons of his jeans, he slid his into her panties and squeezed. He growled and pulled her into his body, trapping her hands between them until she pushed him away.

Backing up to sit again on the sofa's cushy arm, she returned to the business of getting him out of his clothes. He moved his hands to her head, massaged circles at her temples, relaxing her when moments before she'd felt a frantic need to hurry, a panicked sense of losing a last chance.

She slowed, but did not stop. While she freed him from his pants and worked both jeans and boxers down his legs, Doug kicked out of his athletic shoes and shrugged off his shirt.

And then he stood there completely naked, stealing Kinsey's breath away.

She thought of the beauty of Michelangelo's *David*, and knew Doug's shoulders were just as perfectly mus-cled, not overly broad, not underdeveloped or sloped. The perfect frame on which to build the rest of his beautiful body. His hips were lean, his legs thick and long, his abs ridged in perfect symmetry above his groin, where she found her gaze focused.

His erection thrust forward, almost proudly, defiantly full as the head, swollen to the color and dimension of a plum, bobbed upward toward his belly. Beneath, his sac had drawn close around his balls, his arousal causing the tightening of his testicles and the skin covering his penis.

Kinsey felt her body's response in ways she wouldn't have expected. The moisture seeping from her sex to wet her panties was familiar. What she hadn't known was the tingling in her fingertips, the dryness in her mouth, the heavy weight that pulled at her womb, the sharp bite of anticipation that pressed in on the small of her back.

This man completed her; he was her other half, the man with whom she desired to become one.

When he held out his hand, she came to him, standing still as he lifted her pajama top over her head. The breath he drew in whistled sharply. He took his time exhaling, as if each second that passed meant more time for looking at her without having to speak or to breathe.

If he felt half the awe that was sweeping through her... *God, please let him feel what I'm feeling. Please let him want me with this same sense of everything between us being right.*

"Kinsey?"

His whisper brought tears to her eyes. "I'm right here."

"Yeah," he said with a little bit of a laugh. "I see that."

Holding her hand over her head, he twirled her

where she stood, as if showing her off, or taking her in. She wanted to toss back her head and laugh with the pure joy of the moment.

Or at least that's what she wanted until it hit her that she was the only one in love.

When she finally stopped, he pulled her to him. Her breasts flattened against his chest; his erection pulsed against her belly.

And her warring emotions dissipated beneath the thrill of hearing him order, "Let's go to bed."

DOUG KNEW THIS WAS the last night he would ever spend in bed with Kinsey.

After making love with her, he was going to have to make the break, to say goodbye, to go. If he were a better man, he'd get dressed now. He'd leave before making what he feared would be a huge emotional mistake.

But being better meant spending the night alone, and that he just couldn't do. Not tonight, not after having her questions cut so close to a truth he wasn't ready to face.

A truth about who he'd become in the years since his life had taken a turn he'd never expected.

He had yet to convince himself that there was no way he could've seen Gwen's defection coming. So now he ran at the first hint of unwanted change. That much he knew. That much he recognized.

The same way he'd finally come to recognize that the changes facing Neville and Storey as the firm reached into new territory had him on the run. Broadening their boundaries would require his focus on design to lessen even as his corporate responsibilities grew. And pushing a pencil wasn't the reason he'd be-

come an architect. He wanted to build, to hold the blue-
prints, if not the actual hammers and nails, in his hands.

That chance to return to the excitement of his roots
was what he saw when he read Warren Sill's offer. But
for some reason he still hadn't been able to figure out,
he'd started jumping at the hint of change before hearing a noise. And he sure as hell didn't know why restlessness and discontent had settled so deeply into his
bones.

But the biggest question of all was one he didn't
think he could answer. Try as he might, he'd been unable to pinpoint the moment Kinsey Gray had become
so integral to his life.

And now that he'd come to recognize that she had,
why hadn't he told the Warren Sill Group that Houston
was his home?

None of that, however, mattered now—not when he
was climbing into Kinsey's bed with her. She scooted
into the middle, backed up against him once he'd settled into the pillows.

"Doug?"

"Shh." He turned toward her, not wanting to talk
or to listen. He only wanted to act, to take, to devour,
to consume.

Strangely desperate to keep the rest of her questions
at bay, he covered her with his body, climbing above
her and trapping her between his spread legs.

He groaned as his cock slipped down between her
thighs.

"Doug?" she asked again.

This time he stopped her from talking by using his
mouth, first on hers, kissing her with the same intense
pressure that was building and throbbing at the base of

his cock. And then he moved down her body, nuzzling his way from her chin to the hollow of her throat.

She smelled like peaches, tasted like cream, and her plump breasts filled both of his hands like the luscious fruit that she was. He suckled, and she arched up into his mouth, as if she were offering him more than he was taking, as if she wanted him to completely gobble her up.

Back and forth he went, tugging on one nipple, moving to lap at the other, returning to the first and nipping hard enough to make her gasp.

He kneaded the fullness of both breasts, creating a valley between, where he wanted more than anything to shove his aching cock.

He wanted to take her in ways he'd never imagined, to obliterate every question, every doubt he had about himself with this woman's body. No other would offer the relief he needed tonight.

Only the woman he loved.

Heart pounding, he slid down, licking a trail from her breasts to her belly, concentrating on her pleasure so that he didn't have to consider the trouble he was in.

She shuddered beneath him as he circled the tip of his tongue around her navel, and her hands slipped into his hair, feathering through the overly long strands. When he moved lower, she released him. He urged her legs up and farther apart and slipped his arms beneath her raised thighs, lacing his fingers with hers at her hips.

Wanting to do nothing but bring her the satisfaction she'd so often and generously brought him, he opened his mouth and gave her his most intimate kiss. She cried out, lifting her body from the bed and pressing her sex fully against his mouth.

He sucked at her lips, dipped his tongue through her folds, running the tip up one side of her plumped-up pussy and down the other, circling her very center until his cock twitched and the first drops of fluid seeped from the slit in the head.

He wanted her madly, wanted to bury himself as far into her body as she could take him, wanted to feel her contractions grip and squeeze and milk him dry.

But first he wanted to bring her off with his mouth and his fingers. He released her, moving his hands between her legs, sliding his thumbs through her slickness and opening her fully to the thrust of his tongue.

He pushed into her, pulled out, simulating the driving, sliding motion of his cock between his belly and the bedsheet. Sweat broke out on his forehead, and he slid two fingers deep where he'd had his tongue.

With his lips on her clit, he pulled and nibbled and lightly sucked, fingering her with long even strokes. She shoved herself against his hand, matching his rhythm even as he increased to a speed that he feared might tear her apart.

When she came, she sobbed. He thought at first she was crying with delight, but she didn't stop, and he realized she was crying for real. Hiccupping, chest-hitching, throat-tightening spasms that had his own eyes welling.

Shit. This was exactly what he hadn't wanted to happen. And he'd been so stupid to think he could stop it, stop any of it. Not after that incredible night of passion they'd shared on the veranda at Coconut Caye.

He crawled back up her body, soothing her with

softly whispered words of comfort and a long repetitive, ''Shh.''

Holding her close, he tendered tiny kisses into her hair, burying them both deep in the cocoon of her comforter and the shared heat of their skin.

It was all he could do; it was all he could do. It was what he had to do because he loved her.

KINSEY CAME AWAKE hours later, shivers coursing through her, her skin icy and covered with goose bumps. She reached to pull down the nightie she wasn't wearing, then reached for the comforter a very large and warm man had stolen in the night.

She groaned. Ugh. She'd cried, and he'd held her until she'd fallen asleep. What a terribly, horribly, very bad way to spend one of their last few remaining nights together.

He probably couldn't wait to get to Denver, probably regretted having asked her to come along. And then she remembered that he'd asked her again, a second time, here in her house. Cuddling up to the heat of his back, she couldn't help wondering if he'd meant it when he'd said that he meant it.

Or if he'd only been driving home his point that their circumstances allowed them no future.

Funny thing, but her intuition told her he didn't believe that any more than she did. He just wasn't going to be able to come to grips with a relationship lived thousands of miles apart after what had happened with Gwen.

Kinsey understood, truly she did. Life did that to a person—convinced them that solutions were limited, that chances were often too frightening to take when spawned from bad experience.

Kinsey had never in her life considered leaving Houston, living away from her parents, who were aging and would one day need to have her close.

She'd certainly never thought about giving up her career with gIRL-gEAR, or seeing less of the girl-friends who for years had been a daily part of her life.

But now she was thinking about all of that because the alternative was losing Doug.

Closing her eyes, she sighed and snuggled up to his back. He turned toward her, and she lifted her head, settling it in the crook of his shoulder as he held her.

"You done with that crying crap?" he whispered.

She smiled to herself; she loved it that he was such a guy. "For now. I'm sure I have more hormonal displays stored up for the future."

"Humph," he grunted, kissing the top of her head.

She slid her hand to the center of his belly. "I'm sorry. That just sorta came up unexpectedly."

"Good. I'd hate to think you planned it."

"No. I wouldn't sink that low to trap a man."

He was silent for a long moment, during which Kinsey found herself holding her breath. And then he heaved a sigh, the origin of which she couldn't pinpoint.

"Is that what you've been doing here? Trying to trap me?"

Oh, hell. It was a last ditch effort, but why not be truthful. "Honestly? Yes."

"Hmm."

"Has it been working? Because, if you must know, I'm giving it up."

"I see."

She wondered exactly what it was he saw. "It's not

that I don't think my plan is working, it's just that I've come to realize I don't want you trapped.''

He stiffened slightly, the arm around her shoulders tightening, the fingertips stroking her arm growing still. ''You've changed your mind about wanting me?''

Hurriedly, she shook her head, plucking at the hairs growing below his navel. His body was certainly a wonderland. ''Not about wanting you, no. Or about loving you. I do, Doug. I know you told me not to, but my emotions don't take well to being bossed around.''

''Humph.'' He grunted again.

At least he hadn't rolled away. ''I've just changed my mind about going through with any more trapping efforts.''

''You have more up your sleeve?''

''Not at the moment, no. But one never knows when inspiration might strike.''

''Can't argue with that.''

''You can't?''

''Nope. Not when your trapping has been so much fun.''

She pouted just a little bit. ''Are you making fun of me?''

He chuckled, and she felt the rumble vibrate in her palm on his belly and through her breasts crushed to his side. ''Darlin', why would I make fun when you've shown me the best time I've had in years?''

''Sex, you mean.''

He inhaled slowly, deeply, his lungs inflating and his chest expanding. She knew him well enough by now to know he was trying his best for a calm and rational answer.

The fact that he was taking his time rather than resorting to banter or shutting down was a sign he wanted to talk. Kinsey didn't think she'd ever been so frightened.

She was working to steady her breathing pattern when he turned to his side and faced her. ''The sex has been amazing.''

Has been. He'd said ''has been.'' A flush began to burn her skin; her heart began to race.

''But it's not all about the sex.'' He cupped his hand over her cheek, rubbed his thumb across her cheekbone to her ear. ''I've had fun with you. Simple, good-time fun. I haven't slowed down enough to do that for months.''

''But?'' She hated to ask.

''No buts. I just want you to know that when I don't make it back next weekend for the auction, it's not about you. It's about settling things I need to settle in Denver.''

''I understand.''

He kissed her fully on the mouth, a hard, determined kiss. ''I'm telling you the truth, Kinsey. That doesn't mean I expect you to understand.''

''It's okay, Doug. I do understand. I know we don't have a true commitment.'' Dear God, it hurt to say that. ''I went into this with my eyes wide open. So, whatever you have to do, do it. I'll be fine.''

She pressed her lips together for a moment, then declared, ''I'll be peachy-keen fine.''

He waited one heartbeat, two, then said, ''Fine without having me around, you mean?''

''Yes. Exactly,'' she lied, her focus trained on the ceiling.

''Interesting.''

''How so?''

"That's not what I'd expect you to say to the man you want to marry."

She rolled her eyes. "Do we have to go there again?"

"I think we do, and I'll tell you why."

He rolled up onto his elbow and looked down at her, ruining her determination to stare at the ceiling the rest of the night.

"I'm listening," she said, though she cast him only the quickest of glances to avoid being sucked into his spell.

He didn't even ask her permission when he moved his hand and cupped her breast. "It was the bikini that killed me. You and Sydney had been on the beach in front of the house playing Frisbee with Jess and Ray. I watched from the veranda."

"Why didn't you join us?" she asked, ignoring his thumb and forefinger, which had tugged her nipple into a knot.

"I was going to. I was going to finish my beer and do just that. But then you dove to catch Ray's toss. And you rolled right back up to your feet. And I just couldn't take my eyes off your body."

"Sexist pig."

He laughed. "Oh, yeah. The lust I felt was not in my heart. It barely fit in my pants."

Like now, she imagined, feeling the head of his erection brush her bare thigh. He moved his hand to cup the fullness of her breast, then leaned down and sucked the nipple he'd hardened into his mouth.

Before she could do more than gasp and contract her belly, he'd let her go. "That picture stayed with me the rest of the day."

"I did get dressed later, you know."

"Sure. But after dinner, once the moon was up, we all went swimming." He shook his head and slid his palm down her abdomen until his index and middle finger bracketed her clitoris and tugged slightly.

And then he stopped. "Like I said. The bikini killed me. Dry was one thing, but then there you were, head-to-toe wet and dripping everywhere."

Wet and dripping like now, she thought, and shuddered from his touch. "I should've stuck with my one-piece. That bikini was fairly risqué."

"That bikini was perfect."

"Am I ever going to get it back?"

He shook his head, circled the tip of his index finger around the throbbing knot of nerves he'd brought to bear. "Nope. Never."

That was all he said as he urged her legs wider. She clenched overused muscles and braced for his deeper, intimate touch.

A touch that he was obviously in no hurry to deliver, seeing as he'd moved to stroke the crease where her hip met her thigh.

"You'll have to buy me a new one, you know. The top's no good without the bottom half."

"Actually," he began, drawing circles on her inner thigh between her legs, "the idea of you wearing that top and nothing else pretty much revs me up."

She nudged his erection, which pressed into her hip. "You don't say."

"I don't have to say. Erections speak louder than words."

"That was terrible," she said, but couldn't stop the giggle that spilled out.

And then she couldn't stop the gasp that tore from her throat when Doug slipped two fingers into her sex.

"But *that* is wonderful." He moved again; she gasped again. "You like the top? I'll wear the top."

He groaned. "Just thinking about it now is about to do me in. A thong and strings. Barely more than nothing."

"It was obviously a lot more than nothing if you can't get it out of your mind."

"It's you I can't get out of my mind, darlin'. The way you boosted yourself up onto the veranda railing and wrapped your legs around my waist. The way you told me I was the man you wanted to marry."

He was into confessions? Here was her big one.

"Can I tell you something?"

"Anything," he said, pulling his hand from her body and rolling halfway on top of her. His palm rested beneath her left breast; his knee pinned her thighs. But it was his eyes that kept her from sliding out of bed when suddenly she wanted to do nothing but run.

Running would hurt, but staying was going to kill her.

She raised one hand to cup his face. "I've had a crush on you forever. I've probably been in love with you almost as long. That proposal I made? That was the real deal. And I'd say the same thing now if it would make any difference. If it would mean you'd stay here with me and forget about Denver."

There. She'd laid her heart on the line, her soul, her sanity, her self-respect, as well. All she could do was hope that Doug didn't trample what she'd offered him.

His eyes drifted halfway shut; his head bowed. What seemed to be a smile softened his features. But it was hard to tell much in the dark with his gaze directed away.

When he finally moved, it wasn't to speak or to push

free of the hand that now caressed his neck. What he did was shift his weight so that he covered her fully, completely, belly to belly, toes to toes.

And then he kissed her, just a brief exploration of lips and tongue before he pressed his mouth to her jawline, lightly nipping his way down her neck as he slid his body lower over hers.

Sex was not what she wanted; she wanted so very much more, but she loved him, and she didn't have it in her to tell him no.

When he moved between her legs, she opened. He kissed her intimately, though briefly, yet the contact was enough to bring her surging up from the bed.

She cried out, gasped, knowing now this man's touch was the only one that moved her. And move her he did, entering her with one finger, then two, mimicking the rhythm of mated bodies she so wanted to feel.

In only seconds, she knew she'd be finished, and she wasn't ready to come. She wanted him to bury himself inside her, wanted him to take her over the edge, wanted him to feel her contractions around the fullness of his engorged cock.

She told him what she wanted by hooking her feet at his hipbones and urging him to cover her again. He chuckled as he complied, moving up and along her legs, then her torso, sliding farther still until his mouth met hers and he kissed her fully.

She tasted herself on his lips and tongue, and the evidence of her own arousal sent a sharp reckless thrill scuttling down her spine. Her legs came up around his hips, and he shoved himself home.

Buried to the hilt, he stopped, throbbed deep inside where she felt every pulse of blood to the head of his cock. She breathed in short pants, holding on to the edge of her orgasm, wanting to draw out this night.

But she wasn't as strong as she'd thought. The minute Doug began to move, she followed. His strokes were slow and smooth as he leaned a bit to one side and rested his head beside hers on her pillow. She felt his breath, in and out, rough and ragged and hot on her cheek.

Her hands roamed and gripped and clawed and caressed; the tension of sensation drove her mad. How did he manage to stay so controlled when she wanted to thrash and squirm and crawl into his skin? And then he moved a hand between their bodies to cover her breast.

He kneaded and tugged in time to the meter of his thrusts, which steadily grew stronger. She arched against him as much as their position allowed, grinding into him as the fullness of his shaft stretched her open, stimulating her clit until she tingled and ached and burned.

And then she felt it, the deep-seated hunger that surged from her core, releasing even more of her body's slick moisture to ease the ride. Doug began to pant, to lift his hips higher, to slam harder, to pump and thrust and shove himself into her with total abandon and need.

She didn't even attempt to stifle her cries as she met his hammering blows. Her explosion engulfed her in sweeping waves of sensation, shuddering waves, tremors triggered by the warmth of Doug's powerfully breathtaking release.

He slowed but still rocked against her; she rocked in return, reaching for lingering bursts of the electrical charge firing her nerves. One, and then another, and too soon it was over.

Both of them were spent, exhausted, unable to move. Yet they remained joined, neither willing to separate, as if a deeper, elusive completion still remained out of reach.

12

KINSEY PACED the small office-cum-dressing room in Paddington's Ford, her stiletto heels creating a sharp echo on the highly glossed concrete floor. Click, click, click, click, turn. Click, click, click, click, turn.

It didn't matter that Lauren had indeed arranged for gIRL-gEAR's marketing department to work with the agency handling Ryder Falco's publicity, or that the media buzz this last week hyping the diversity of the available bachelorettes had been tremendous. Click, click, click, click, turn.

It didn't matter that the stage out front was worthy of an Oscar nod for set design, and the crowd was seemingly the size of an Oscar audience. Click, click, click, click, turn. It didn't matter that the money raised tonight was for a cause Kinsey fully believed in. Click, click, click, click, turn.

She didn't want to be here. She didn't want to be here at all. She'd rather be undergoing natural childbirth during a colonoscopy while having a root canal; she had zero experience with any of the three, but the combination sounded just torturous enough to cover what she was feeling. Click, click, click, click, turn. Click, click, click, click—

"Would you please sit down?" Poe barked, causing Kinsey's head to whip around, the tone was so totally out of character for the other woman. Poe rubbed at both temples with her fingertips. "You are giving me an insane headache."

"You wouldn't be nervous now, would you, Poe? Maybe over that bet we made?" Oh, but didn't she sound like the tough little bachelorette? Calm, cool and collected indeed. Kinsey felt a diabolical laugh bubbling up

"Of course not." Poe leaned against the corner of the room's single desk, looking serenely at odds with her outburst. She wore the beaded ivory slip, which she'd had altered to show extra leg and extra cleavage while concealing all curves in between. "Your pacing is simply annoying me."

Annoying? Kinsey hadn't even reached annoying yet! She had at least seven layers of irritation yet to explore. "What are we doing here, Poe? Setting ourselves up for absolute ridicule? Who's ever going to take us seriously once they find out this is how we try to find men?"

Poe rolled her eyes at Kinsey's ridiculous question, not even deigning to answer as she examined the pearl polish on her nails. Kinsey started to pace again, checked the urge at the murderous glint in Poe's eye and perched on the opposite corner of the desk instead.

"Ridicule? Have you seen the crowd out there?" Izzy moved away from the crack in the doorway and whistled. "And I am not talking about the crowd here for the book signing. I'm talking about the men."

All Kinsey had seen when arriving earlier was the corner of the bar set up to look like a prison cell, with red-and-blue lighting shining from the four corners and over the eight-foot bars. Supposedly a spotlight had been situated to highlight each of the women during her auction segment.

Oh, yeah. Kinsey could hardly wait. It was bad enough that she looked like a cross between a dominatrix and Madonna in her early years. But having everyone's attention drawn so glaringly to that fact was not her idea of a good time.

Doug, at least, would've been able to see past the sex goddess image and into her heart. Or not. But Doug wasn't here. Doug was in Denver finalizing his plans. Or so she assumed, since that's where he'd told her he'd be.

"I don't want to do this. I can't do this. I'll make a donation to the building project." *To hell with Poe and her murderous glare.* Kinsey got up to pace. Click, click, click, click, turn. "I'll bring hammer and nails and put up the walls myself."

"I know you will," Izzy said, closing the door and leaning back against it. "The site cleanup is finished, and our first building party is next weekend." She pointed a finger at Kinsey. "You will be there, or I'll personally find and kick your ass."

Kinsey stuck out her tongue. "Awfully tough since you started dating that big bad EMT, aren't you?"

"You think I'm tough?" Izzy let out a long, low whistle. "I'll tell you one thing. I feel sorry for whoever ends up buying me tonight should Baron decide he doesn't like the look of the guy."

"Why doesn't Baron buy you himself?" Poe asked.

"Do you know what an EMT brings down in pay?" Izzy asked, brow lifted. "It's a good thing I'm crazy about him, because he certainly couldn't afford me otherwise."

"Assuming any man does bid once he gets a look at you in that getup," Kinsey teased, giving Izzy's yellow camisole and sheer ballet skirt a once-over. Then she cast another look down at her own body, clothed in the ridiculous bustier and tap pants of burgundy and black.

All that was left to do was roll her eyes. "What am I saying? We're doomed, I tell you. Doomed."

"Doomed to bring the room to its knees," Poe said, cutting into Kinsey's pity party. "There won't be a straight man in the place able to keep his wallet or anything else in his pants."

Oh, that was a picture Kinsey so did not need to have painted. "Then can we please get this over with so I can go home and get some sleep?"

"What?" Poe raised a brow. "No all-night, exhausting sexfest with your man?"

"No, Doug's in Denver. Where he's going to be living. And that means he's not my man. All my wicked game-playing, man-trapping schemes failed. Are you happy?"

"Why would that make me happy?" Poe's question was delivered with complete sincerity, giving Kinsey pause. "Ever since our Belize vacation, it's been obvious that you two were in love."

Kinsey's side of the equation may have been obvious. Doug's side was a big fat zero—no matter the wishful sigh Poe's observation caused her to make. "Well, being in love obviously counts for nothing when there's a career ladder calling one's name."

"*Pfft.* Is that all?" Poe waved off Kinsey's doom-and-gloom synopsis. "Except for Chloe and Eric, perhaps, every one of the recent gIRL-gEAR relationships has run into career roadblocks."

"Yeah, but none of their roadblocks were two thousand miles long." Even as she said it, Kinsey was well aware that physical distance had nothing to do with the roadblock keeping her and Doug apart.

Whatever. She was here. He wasn't. And this night wasn't about either one of them, no matter that she'd been making it so. It was about raising funds.

All girls for one and one girl for all. "Since we're stuck, let's do it."

LATE FLYING INTO HOUSTON on Halloween night and even later getting downtown to Paddington's Ford, Doug squeezed his way inside the crowded bar and took up a position in the shadowed corner nearest the door. The stage had been set up across the room, with prison bars and funky red-and-blue lights, he noted, looking around.

He didn't want Kinsey to know he was here. All he wanted to do tonight was watch. That was the only reason he'd come.

He wasn't yet ready to see her again, to talk to her, to explain. He was still working out explanations he owed to himself and to Anton. But he was getting there. He was getting there. And he had a feeling tonight might be a turning point he needed to witness firsthand.

He knew she wanted to help. That's what women did—soothing, easing, consoling. And he loved Kinsey for being the woman she was.

But that was only half of the battle he was waging. The rest was with the restlessness he was on the cusp of resolving—a resolution he had to make if he ever expected to be the sort of man she deserved.

This week away from her had done him good, even though it was the hardest time he'd ever done. But he'd needed the isolation while he worked through a debt he owed—one he owed to himself and had to clear before he changed the direction his life had been headed.

Yeah, he admitted it. Having Gwen walk into Adam's arms had done a number on his confidence as well as on his plans. For some reason, Doug had started using her defection as a gauge of his own worth. And each time he'd had occasion to take his own measure, that had been the yardstick he'd used.

Stupid. Just plain stupid. It had taken Kinsey's constant probing to get him to see he needed a new measuring tool. He allowed himself a private smile and decided a handheld laser meter would be the way to go, screw the yardstick. Up-to-date technology to bring him out of the past.

When the music kicked on with a loud techno beat, he was still in the back of the room, avoiding the biggest crush of the crowd, and still having a hell of a time wrapping his mind around the fact that Kinsey wanted him enough to trap him.

But that reality hadn't hit with half the force of her admission of love.

Or with that of his own admission of being in love with her. And he was. Very much so.

Three spotlights burst on then, moving in one choreographed sweep over the room before coming to a stop and shining down into the "cell." The crowd surge forward, leaving Doug to dodge the press of bodies by backing even farther toward the door.

The "inmates," obviously having entered the stage though Paddington's back door, walked from the rear of the platform to the front, taking hold of the confining bars as if, well, confined.

As the techno soundtrack thumped and blared, Doug

couldn't help but grin. None of the women looked particularly thrilled to be on display—and, whoa! On display was exactly what they were.

He'd seen Kinsey wear less only when she'd been wearing that red bikini. Tonight her costume looked to be basic black with maybe a hint of burgundy: a pair of black short shorts, black stockings and four-inch black heels, and then a bustier out of which she was busting.

His grin became grim and then became a frown. He was just chauvinistic enough, possessive enough, not to like the fact that every inch of her body was being offered to the highest bidder.

Poe and Izzy weren't quite as exposed. Or so he first thought until getting a glimpse straight through Izzy's sheer skirt and a peek at the curve of Poe's bottom when she cocked a hip to the side and her slip of a slip rode up.

Holy spanked monkeys and choked chickens. If he knew men like he knew men, the funds brought in tonight would build a whole block of homes.

"Gentlemen in the house," blared an anonymous voice over the sound system. "Have we got a deal for you. Three gorgeous bachelorettes available for a night—and for a price."

While the audience whooped it up, hooted and hollered like frat boys gone wild, Doug shoved his hands deep in his pockets and tried not to grind his teeth to dust.

A local television celebrity had been tapped as master of ceremonies, and he hopped onto the stage, shaking each woman's hand and sharing a moment of private conversation before turning to the audience to deliver his spiel.

Doug searched the crowd for Anton, finally locating

his partner off to the side of the stage, along with Lauren, Leo and Macy. Then he cast a glance around and located his number one client, Marcus West, not far away.

That taken care of, Doug tuned out the ramblings of the host to concentrate on Kinsey.

He could tell by the set of her shoulders and chin that she was determined to make the most of the night, to do her thing and bring in as much money as she could. He could also tell by the whispered buzz running through the crowd that he wasn't the only man here with a Scandinavian fantasy.

No doubt her bidding would run hot and heavy—even if he was the last man on earth who would experience the reality of her long blond hair, her blue eyes and her legs that went on forever. No one ever said an auction couldn't be rigged, he mused with a self-satisfied smirk.

But, yeah, her eyes gave her away. Definitely bright, but slightly panicky. His gut clenched hard, and he had to fight the urge to push his way through the crowd, sweep her off the stage and out the door. Standing where he was had to be one of the hardest promises he'd ever forced himself to keep.

But going to her now would mean he wouldn't want to leave again in the morning. And he had to leave, had to get back to Denver. He'd just known he'd go insane if he wasn't here in person tonight.

It wasn't as if Anton or Marcus wouldn't phone with the details later; nothing about that had changed. In fact, Doug expected his cell phone to ring before he even made it out the door of Paddington's post show.

But around two o'clock this afternoon, he'd realized this was one event he had to see for himself. He'd headed for the airport without a single thought for the meeting he'd rescheduled.

Here we go, he mused, his mind returning to the present at the sound of the auctioneer's gavel coming down. The lights in the prison cell flashed on and off like crazy, as the cell door, guarded by two costumed rent-a-cops, opened.

Izzy was first on the auction block, twirling in a sheer skirt that floated to her knees but still managed to show off everything underneath. While she did her best to incite the crowd to riot, the host went on about Izzy's work with Doctors Without Borders, as well as her support of local women's shelters and centers for the homeless.

The bidding rose rapidly for several minutes, and then, just as quickly, came to a stop when Joseph Baron stepped forward with a flat four figures that reduced the chatter to silence. At least until the responding cheers rose to the rafters. In fact, the only one in the room not cheering was Izzy herself. Baron's bid had pretty much pissed the lady off.

Oh, yeah. This was going to be a hell of an interesting night, Doug decided, settling in for the show.

IN THE END, Kinsey didn't even mind the spotlight. It kept her from being able to see much of the crowd beyond those gathered near the stage. And, thankfully, they included Lauren and Anton, Leo and Macy.

Friendly faces had never been so welcome. She was doing her best not to pace like a caged animal—a difficult goal to meet when she was trapped behind bars. Sweat tingled beneath her bound breasts. The narrow toes of her shoes pinched; the crotch of her shorts threatened to ride up. The boning of the bustier made it impossible to breathe.

Was this how Doug had felt when she'd tightened her noose? Well, except for the breasts and toes and crotch part. Had he considered bolting for the nearest exit, his only hope for survival?

She couldn't think about that now. All she could focus on was making it through the next few minutes. Izzy had been sold, lucky girl, to Baron, who apparently was working to score points and build her an entire village. Kinsey would love to be a fly on the wall for *that* conversation. Izzy had not appeared overjoyed by the unexpected revelation of Baron's wealth.

Poe was up next and had already taken to strutting her stuff and whipping the crowd into a frenzy with her moves and her you-can-look-but-you-will-never-touch attitude. The woman's mercurial personality never ceased to amaze Kinsey, or inspire equal parts envy and totally heterosexual woman-on-woman lust.

Even though she'd known Poe now for three years, Kinsey still didn't have a handle on what made the other woman tick. And it was much easier to focus on the current bidding war and Poe's reaction to the rapidly climbing amount than to face her own upcoming fall.

And what a fall it would be, flat on her face. Once she got back to her feet, she'd be wearing a big fat capital *L* for loser on her forehead—the very prediction she'd made to Izzy.

Bids for Poe were coming fast and furiously now, and she was egging on the bidders with antics that would've made a stripper proud. The music switched gears to a bump-and-grind rhythm, and Poe never missed a beat.

Suddenly a strange buzz went up, growing louder as the Red Sea of a crowd parted for a bidder making his way to the front of the room. Kinsey watched as the other woman began to stiffen, and she swore she saw Poe break out in a sweat. No wonder.

The bidder causing the room to hum nervously was Patrick Coffey.

And he was paying in cash.

The rest of the bidders backed off and, as Patrick put his money on the table, the auctioneer brought down his gavel with a loud, "Sold." Kinsey jumped at the deafening thud. It was her turn.

Still, it was hard to drag her attention away from the way Patrick was looking at Poe, and the way Poe hadn't yet moved her body from the stage, or her gaze from Patrick's. Oh, my, Kinsey mused. This was the first time she'd ever seen Poe at a loss for words.

When Patrick moved forward and offered her his hand, Poe reached out—only to have him grab her by the waist and lift her bodily from the stage, her hands on his biceps for balance.

They stared at each other for a long, hot moment—Poe in her ivory silk and Patrick in blue jeans, white T-shirt and black bomber jacket, his unruly heathen hair tied back with a brown leather thong—before he took her hand, led her through the crowd to Paddington's front door and out into the night.

And then the host's announcement, "Kinsey Gray!" brought Kinsey and the rest of the audience back to the moment.

She gave a wide smile and waved at the crowd with both hands until her jaw threatened to crumble, her wrists threatened to snap. She gave a little shimmy to the music, and tried not to barf at feeling so *bargain basement.*

So what if she looked as good as the audience loudly insisted? Looking good meant nothing when she couldn't even meet her own gaze in a mirror.

Men. Who needed them? Except more than a few of the screams were decidedly female. It was all Kinsey could do not to jump from the stage and run screaming into the night. Yes, definitely an evening to remember.

The numbers started rising; she had a long way to go before reaching what had to be back-to-back bachelorette sales records set by Izzy and Poe. Who kept such records? Kinsey wondered, pacing back and forth in front of the faux cell, but doing her best to make her walk sexy, beguiling, enticing....

Soon the bidding, just as that for the other women, took on a heightened sense of urgency as one man continued to outbid each other bidder before the auctioneer could get out a single encouraging word.

Kinsey tried not to be obvious as she squinted toward the crowd in an effort to pick out her admirer.... There he was, and wow! Dark hair, dark eyes, piercing green eyes beneath dark lashes and brows. A broad-shouldered hunk of Doug Storey's caliber.

This might be interesting, after all. Or down the road, anyway. In the near future. When she was finished mooning over Doug. Hmm. She wondered if the moneybags hottie would mind putting off their date until she was a free woman, oh, months from now, years maybe. Perhaps she'd ask him to escort her to her retirement party....

"Miss Gray?"

Kinsey looked up to see the host's extended hand as he waited to assist her off the stage and into the arms of her new owner. *Sigh.* She accepted his help and blindly made her way out of the glare of the spotlights, tuning out the rest of the announcements as she approached the man destined to make her forget about Doug.

Or not.

"Hello," Kinsey said, more meekly than she'd intended, definitely more meekly than one would expect from a woman wearing stilettos and velvet lingerie. She held out her hand. "Kinsey Gray."

He waited for an excruciatingly intense moment before he took her hand in his. "Marcus West. It's a pleasure to finally meet you."

She tilted her head, frowned, her heart pitter-pattering. "You're Doug's client."

Marcus nodded, smiled, moved his hands to his waist. The tails of his suit coat flared out behind him like bat wings. She wondered if he'd come to sweep her away to his cave. "I'm also his proxy."

"His what?" she asked, though alarm bells rang in her head and she knew. She knew! Doug might not be here for her, but he'd made damn sure no other man would have her. Did he plan on doing the same thing for the rest of her life?

"I guess I should've padded the bid," Marcus said, stepping closer to block her view of the rest of the crowd. Not a hard feat at all with the shoulders he had. "Made the man suffer for his sins."

"Doug put you up to this?" she asked in a whisper, having lost most of her voice.

"Yes, ma'am."

"Wait. What sins?" she asked, because that accusation was the only thing stuck in her spinning head.

"The sin of even thinking about moving away from Houston and leaving you behind."

13

Izzy PACED THE OFFICE at Paddington's Ford in bare feet, still wearing her auction costume, still denying what had happened out there.

Joseph Baron had bought and paid for her, and done so with a lot of hard-earned money. Exactly how hard he'd had to work to earn it and exactly what that work had entailed was the question that had her hackles raised.

He'd better get his ass back in here fast, and clear up what she prayed was a problem with a simple solution. She refused to be in love with a man who wouldn't come clean.

The thought brought her careening to a stop. She leaned back against the wall and closed her eyes, trying to remember the mechanics of breathing before she passed out flat.

In love? With Joseph Baron? After knowing the man for a month? Oh, not good. Not good at all. How could this be happening? And why now, when she felt so many things in her life finally settling into place?

Oh, wait. Oh, no. She rolled her head back and forth against the wall. She wasn't going to believe it. She couldn't, she wouldn't.

He was not, she repeated, *not* responsible for the satisfaction she'd been experiencing lately. Not at all.

She was too smart, too independent to allow a man's influence to change her ways.

The idea that what she was feeling was due to the time she'd spent with Baron, the conversations they'd had, his insight into her psyche and the way he so calmly, so thoroughly pointed out the forest she couldn't see for the trees, was too frightening to entertain.

No. He couldn't be. He couldn't be. She buried her face in her hands.

A firm knock sounded on the door at the same time it swung inward. "Isabel?"

Her heart beat so hard in her ears it was a wonder she was still able to hear his beautifully deep and rich voice. "In here."

Baron pushed the door open fully and stepped into the small office, stealing half the space and at least that much of her air. She crossed her arms over her chest, holding herself still.

She needed answers and needed them now. Now, before she let go and crossed the room to wrap herself in the strength of his will and his body.

He closed the door, locked it and leaned back, hands behind him, feet crossed at the ankles. His pullover polo shirt was a crisp, sharp black, his stonewashed jeans tight on his thick thighs. His sex was thick, as well—not aroused, but thick, she noted, forcing herself to look elsewhere.

That brought her back to his face, to eyes that were dark and inquisitive, to a mouth that wasn't smiling. She wanted to see him smiling. She wanted to feel his kiss.

But it was best that they get this over with while the

mood between them was as uncertain as her acceptance of her feelings. ''Where did you get the money?''

He stared for a moment, then barked out a laugh, although his eyes remained stern. ''You're kidding me, right? That's the first thing you have to say to me?''

It wasn't the first thing; it was just easier to ask than the question she really wanted answered. ''I know what an EMT makes. You spend that kind of money to buy me, I can't help but wonder what you want in return.''

His dark eyes darkened further. ''What makes you think I want anything?''

''Don't you? Isn't that what this is about?'' She brought up her chin in a challenge and moved away from the wall. ''That was a big donation, Joseph Baron. All I'm asking is if you intended to buy more than my body. If you thought for that price you'd have a say in my life the way everyone in my family thinks they do.''

He pushed himself away from the door and walked toward her. His presence was large and intimidating in the confined space. Izzy didn't know him well enough to say for certain, but she had a feeling he was not always a gentle man.

''You're not indebted to me, Isabel. I'm here because I want to be with you. If I thought I had to pay for that privilege, I wouldn't have come.''

''But you did pay.''

''I made a donation.''

''That was not a donation, Baron. That was—''

''The price of keeping you out of another man's arms. And damn well worth it.''

Shaking her head, she backed up to the edge of the desk. ''The date with the winning bidder wasn't serious. It was all about raising the building funds.''

"I wasn't willing to take that chance." Leaning forward, he planted his hands flat on the desk on either side of her hips. "I'm staking my claim, Isabel."

Her chest heaved mightily as she strove to breathe; her breasts threatened to spill over the top of the camisole. He was so close, so very close. "Your claim?"

It was the only thing she could articulate, what with the way her mind was reeling.

He nodded and moved in closer until his lips were stroking softly along the line of her jaw and her chin. "I want you."

She squeezed her eyes shut and tried to resist the temptation of letting him have his way. "And you're thinking your sizable donation guarantees you can have me?"

"The only thing my donation guarantees is that a house is going to be rebuilt a lot sooner than otherwise," he said, even while he moved his finger, just that one finger, to the edge of her bodice and caressed the swell of both breasts.

Back and forth went his finger, over one firm orb and then the other. His touch was soft, his skin not quite so, his intent hard to ascertain. So she looked down and watched, seeing the contrast of the lemon yellow silk with her skin, which was darker than his.

"I'll tell you what, Isabel. We'll make this easy. I'll go after what I want. If it's something you don't want me to have, then you tell me to stop."

At that, she looked up at his face—only to find his focus drawn to that place where they touched. She wanted to believe him, to believe that he had no interest in directing her choices or decisions, but only in being with her. "You make it sound so simple."

"Why borrow trouble when there's already too

much to be had?'' He dipped his finger beneath the edge of the garment and grazed her hardening nipple. ''I'm here for you. I think we've got something going on that's worth looking into. But if you don't want me here, if you don't agree, tell me and I'll go.''

''How do I know—''

''Faith, Isabel. Trust. Let me earn it…not with donations, but with what I say. And what I do.''

And then he lowered his head and opened his mouth over her camisole-covered breast, sucking her into his mouth, where his tongue swirled and teased.

She watched it all until it became impossible to do more than feel. That was when she tossed her head back and closed her eyes, moving her hands to his shoulders for the support she felt slipping away.

When he freed her, she glanced back in time to brace herself, grabbing his forearms as he took hold of her waist and lifted her to sit on the desk. She spread her legs; he moved between, bunching up her flowing skirt and settling his big bad hands on her bare thighs.

She hissed back a sizzling breath right before his head came down and his mouth covered hers. His kiss was as hard as his body, as fine as the man he was. She circled his neck with both arms, circled his waist with both legs and kissed him back.

His lips were magic, his tongue sweeping into her mouth and sharing his taste, which she loved. Beneath her hands, his neck was thick and strong. Beneath her bare heels, his ass was firm and solid, and suddenly she couldn't stand the barrier of clothing between them. Or what clothing Baron wore, because she certainly had little to get out of the way, as his hands were discovering, having moved up her thighs to the crease of her hip and the elastic leg of her high-cut panties.

She jerked her mouth free and pleaded, "Baron, please, stop."

He eased his head away; his sharp-eyed gaze bored into hers. He'd done as she'd asked, stopped the kiss as well as the seeking caress of his fingers. She had to fix this and quickly.

"Baron?" She locked her legs even tighter around his waist.

"Isabel?" His fingers remained pressed into the crease of her thigh.

"It's hard for me, to let someone new into my life. Someone who doesn't come from the same place that I do."

"You mean someone with my background," he growled.

She hurriedly shook her head. "It's not that. It's just that with my family, I know to expect busybody interference, advice I didn't ask for, don't want and don't need. Mamma and Gramma Fred love me, yes. But I'm tired of fighting their beliefs and their insistence on how I live my life."

She sensed him backing away and knew she had to hurry through her explanation, which suddenly seemed ridiculous when she thought about who it was she was explaining herself to here. "I want to be wanted for who I am, faults and all, not for who I have the potential to be with a nip here and a tuck there."

Baron didn't say a word, but neither did he stop her from going on. As if he knew she had this huge need to get all of these feelings off her chest.

"I respect Mamma and Gramma Fred, and know my ways are not their ways. We're three generations and have seen a lot of change. The clashes we have from time to time are to be expected." She gave herself permission to indulge in a private smile. "You should've heard Gramma Fred when I cut my hair and started working on my dreads."

He smiled then. "Now that I can imagine."

Izzy glanced up into his eyes, laid her palm to his cheek. "It's different, being with a man, a new man, a man I have only started to know, and not being sure—"

He captured her hand in his own. "Are you afraid of me, Isabel?"

Oh, yes. Oh, yes, she was, and she nodded.

"Because you think I'm going to want you to change?"

"Because I don't know. And I'm already so crazy about you that I don't think I can hold myself back."

A broad smile broke over his face. "I wouldn't be here if I wanted you to be anyone other than exactly who you are."

"Are you sure? I mean—"

"Shh." He silenced her with a finger pressed to her lips. "Faith, Isabel. Trust. And, yeah. I know if we hook up here, I'll be seeing a lot of the inside of your uncle Leonard's church."

"And you're okay with that?"

"We can all use a spiritual kick in the pants now and again."

"Leonard delivers a good one."

His smile widened, and he moved his hand to rub a thumb along her cheekbone before he cupped the back of her neck and held her still. "You better now?"

She nodded. "I think so. And I'm sorry for spoiling the mood."

"Ah, Isabel. You didn't spoil a damn thing," he said before he brought his mouth back down to hers.

His kiss was solid and hard, and he filled her mouth with the taste of his tongue and that of her freedom. He swept her away until she knew nothing more than the feel of his hands roaming her body and the need to shed her clothes.

Instead of reaching up to cup her hands around his face, or to wrap her arms around his neck, or to hold him by his broad shoulders and pull him close, she grabbed the hem of her camisole and pulled it over her head.

Her breasts bounced; her nipples tightened in the cool air and beneath the heat of his gaze. Then they tightened further as he began to suck, his hands making their way beneath her skirt again until he managed to slip one long finger under the elastic of her panties and into the wet and swollen folds of her sex.

She tossed back her head and cried out, leaning her weight on her palms first, and then her elbows as she lowered herself to the desk. Her legs remained wrapped around Baron's waist—at least until he moved back and away and held them braced against his thick thighs.

He stared down at her, his chest heaving. She met his gaze fully, her breathing no less labored. And then he slid his hands from her feet to her ankles, her calves, stopping just short of her knees.

"Are you sure about this, Isabel?" he asked, his fingers circling behind her knees, tickling there just below her thighs.

She blew out a steadying breath before she shifted her weight to one elbow, her free hand tugging her skirt to her waist, exposing her panties and the sweet gift beneath she was giving him.

His eyes smoldering, his jaw taut, he dug into his pocket for a condom, tossed his leather wallet to the desk and reached for the button of his jeans. He did it all without saying another word.

Anticipation had Izzy wanting to lick her lips; her feet against his thighs already knew the fullness behind his fly. When he shoved his jeans and briefs down his hips and his erection sprang free, it was all she could do not to sit up and take him into her hands.

She wanted to know the smooth velvet feel of that ripely swollen head, the hardness, the firmness of his long, thick shaft. But she didn't want to feel all of that with her hands the way she wanted to know him buried in her body.

So she spread her legs wide.

Baron rolled on his condom, then moved into the welcoming V of her legs, stopping only long enough to test her wetness with the slow slide of one long finger. While she was shuddering and shivering and coming undone, he tore her panties away and took hold of her hips.

His eyes never left hers as he drove himself home, filling her, stretching her, opening her in ways she'd never experienced, never known.

She settled her weight on her elbows, her hands flat on the desk at her hips. Baron braced himself similarly, lacing his fingers with hers, while his palms bore the brunt of his weight. And then he began to rock, to pump, to shove himself into her body with a rhythm and a speed that spoke of needs and desperation she matched with each of her upward thrusts.

Neither spoke; both barely managed to breathe with their gazes locked and their bodies engaged and their hearts exposed and on the line. The tension in the room simmered. The tension in their bodies tightened. The tension in their mated gazes reached a breaking point, and Izzy felt the same burn of tears she saw reddening Baron's eyes.

Holding back was no longer an option. Letting go was a necessity as powerful as the rush of blood through her veins. She cried out, consumed, and Joseph continued to watch, loving her to completion, waiting until she took a deep breath and grabbed for one last convulsion before he allowed himself the same pleasure.

The tempo of his thrusts steadily rose, as did the power behind them. He was strong and he was hard and he wasn't a man who held back. She hooked her heels in the small of his back and took all that he had to give.

A long minute later he groaned, and then grunted and came with a low guttural cry. She tightened her fingers in response to his hard grip and gave him her body and her heart.

When he finally slowed and shuddered and reached a place where he was able to stop, his grip loosened, as did the tautness in his body. She pushed herself up slowly, keeping their bodies joined, needing that connection as much as she needed to wrap her arms around his neck, to press her face to his chest and absorb his heat and his heartbeat.

He held her close, his arms around her back, his penis still hard and throbbing and solid inside of her. And she knew in that moment that she'd never been so close to a man.

Or so close to falling in love for the rest of her life.

ROLLING OUT OF BED at six o'clock Saturday morning, Kinsey decided that tomorrow would be the first day of the rest of her life.

Today was more about finishing details of her old existence still left undone.

The gIRL-gEAR partners, along with their significant others, boy toys and, in Lauren's case, husband, were spending today in an all-out Habitat for Humanity buildathon.

Today's plan was to get the structure erected, enclosed and wired so that the finishers could start on the interior tomorrow.

What with the partners, their men and the original crew from Leonard's congregation, not to mention newly recruited family and friends—many brought in by the auction—the goal was definitely attainable.

Kinsey didn't know how much help she'd actually be, but she would haul and deliver and run errands with a vengeance. All girls for one and one girl for all.

The auction money had been collected immediately and added to the donations that had been pouring in since the fire. This past week, according to Izzy's reports, supplies had been purchased and plans organized for the weekend buildathon.

Kinsey was still recovering from and digesting the bizarre way the auction had gone down. The fact that Baron had paid for Izzy wasn't that much of a surprise. The surprise had been the news of his money coming via a legacy from the doctor who'd taken him in as a teen.

Now, the fact that Patrick had bought Poe was quite the event, even more so than the amount he'd paid. Still, thanks to Patrick, the Habitat for Humanity project would not run short of money for a long time to come.

But it was Doug's orders to Marcus West, instructing him to see that no other man got his hands on Kinsey, that still had her reeling. Why would he have bothered to assign Marcus his proxy, considering that he'd made his lack of intentions toward her perfectly clear?

Or perfectly muddy, depending on whether one took the optimistic or pessimistic approach.

Doug could hardly shadow her forever and pay off future dates. If she had future dates. Right now, hanging with her girlfriends pretty much covered her social calendar.

Really, though. How much grief could she possibly have to put up with being the last single partner, since, judging by Poe's strange behavior and silence this last week, Patrick was obviously getting his money's worth?

Pulling her SUV in behind Jacob Faulkner's black Sport Trac, Kinsey glanced around the site. The sun was just breaking over the horizon, casting a cool bluish pink glow over the concrete slab.

She grabbed her worn University of Texas sweatshirt and tugged it on over her faded Queensryche concert T-shirt and her oldest pair of jeans with a working zipper. The morning's cool air stole her breath, but the zip in the breeze energized her. She caught site of Lauren and Izzy distributing supplies, and headed in that direction.

"So, what can I do to help?" she asked, shading her eyes as the sun rose higher and brighter. The constant strikes of hammers on wood echoed in the still morning air.

"Are you sure you're up to doing anything? You've been fairly cranky this past week," Lauren said, pulling the knotted sleeves of her sweatshirt tighter around her waist.

Kinsey rubbed at her forehead. "It's just been a

rough week, getting used to Doug being gone. But it's over with and I'll be fine.''

Lauren and Izzy exchanged a strangely knowing look, Lauren finally asking, ''Are you sure about that?''

''About it being over with or about being fine?''

Izzy gave a little shrug. ''Either one. Both.''

Emphatically, Kinsey nodded. ''Yep. I've already decided that tomorrow will be the first day of the rest of my life.''

''I don't know, girl.'' Izzy glanced from Kinsey to Lauren and grinned. ''You might want to consider making that happen today.'' She nodded toward the frame structure.

Frowning, Kinsey turned. It took her a minute to scan the site, the house's frame, which was already taking shape due to the corp of volunteers with power saws and nail guns and simple claw hammers.

And then she saw him. In that very moment her focus narrowed until everything around her faded away and nothing existed but for the man braced against the roof's triangular frame.

He wore blue jeans and work boots; she could see every detail even from this distance. A blue bandanna around his forehead kept his hair from falling in his face. Wraparound Oakleys kept the glare of the rising sun from his eyes. And the white T-shirt he wore revealed muscles she'd never known he had.

She'd spent hours naked with this man, yet in all that time of learning her way around his body, she'd never seen him like this. Swinging a hammer instead of reading a blueprint; working with his body, by the sweat of his brow, instead of relying solely on his brilliant mind.

She took her first step toward the structure, a slow step while she continued to shade her eyes and stare. Straddling one board, he held the end of another with one hand, striking a nail repeatedly with strong sharp blows of his hammer. He grabbed a second nail from his mouth, where he held a third, and went through the motions until he'd secured the board in place.

Then he straightened, smiling at the man on the other end of the board and laughing with a visible joy Kinsey hadn't seen on his face in ages. Perhaps since last summer's vacation on Coconut Caye, when he'd spent days in a marathon game of beach Frisbee.

She cupped both hands to her mouth because she was afraid to let go and cry. Her eyes welled with tears of happiness at seeing him again; when he'd left, she'd wondered if she ever would. His being here, his working alongside the rest of the usual crew had to mean something.

He'd come back. He'd come home.

But had he come home to her?

He caught sight of her then, and his smile froze. Kinsey's stomach tumbled into a pit. Surely he'd known he'd see her here today. So why did he look as if her appearance hadn't even crossed his mind?

Or maybe that was only what she was reading into it from this distance—a distance he was rapidly closing as he hooked his hammer into the tool belt at his waist and made his way across the roofing beams toward the closest ladder.

She wanted a mirror, a hairbrush, time to prepare a statement in response to whatever he was on his way to say. Her hands were twisted into knots she wasn't sure she'd be able to unravel by the time he reached her. She finally pulled herself together enough to give him a smile.

"This is a surprise."

"What? You didn't think I had it in me to do manual labor?"

His grin totally unnerved her, and she remembered how much she loved his dimples. "No, silly. I didn't think you'd be back to Houston so soon."

His hands went to his hips, and he glanced at the concrete slab for a moment before his gaze returned to hers. "I'm not exactly back."

"Well, yeah. I knew that." She checked her ponytail to have something to do with her hands. "I just meant—"

"No." He shook his head. "I'm not back because I never left."

"What?" Butterflies swarmed inside her.

"Well, I left just long enough to wrap up my few Denver loose ends." He shrugged. "But that was all."

That was all? What did he mean, that was all? "Loose ends? So, you'll be staying here for a while then?"

He nodded, raising hopes she thought she'd trained to lie low. "C'mere," he said, and turned away.

She glanced back at her girlfriends, who were both waving her on, before she scurried after him. Doug led her off the property and down the row of parked cars until they reached his 350Z. She expected him to open the door, climb in and drive away.

Instead, he simply leaned against the rear panel, hands in his pockets and ankles crossed. She stopped before she was close enough to touch him, should her inability to keep her hands to herself strike.

The silence around them wasn't the least bit uncomfortable, though she couldn't say the same about her stomach. So she prompted him with a breezy, "Well?"

"I have something for you."

His face remained completely straight, but she still couldn't help but think he'd brought her here to tease her. "Not my bikini bottoms."

He grimaced.

She rolled her eyes. "Please tell me no."

"Honestly? I never made it off the island with them. I hid them under my mattress." His mouth twisted in a wry grin. "They're probably still there."

"You dog!" She moved toward him, raised a hand to sock him one, but he caught her by the wrist, spun her around and tumbled her into his arms.

"Yes. It's true. I cannot tell a lie."

"Ha! You've told plenty the last couple of months, teasing me about that suit." When he moved to wrap his arms around her waist, she let him. She didn't know why. It was as if nothing between them had changed, when that wasn't the case at all.

Everything had changed, because she'd fallen in love. And she wasn't going to play any more of their wicked games.

She leaned back against his chest. "You said you have something to give me?"

"Yeah." He dug into one of his pockets for what looked like a uselessly bent and twisted nail. "I figured I'd see you today, so I made this when I got here this morning."

She stepped out of his embrace and turned to face him, giving him her best evil eye because she had no idea what was going on. He was quiet, his expression peaceful, and his smile, when he looked at her, was one she felt to her toes.

"Doug?"

He took hold of her left hand. "Kinsey, I've been a total shit to you lately. Hell, I've been a shit to a lot of people, but you're the only one who matters."

"You haven't been—"

"Yes, I have. Now let me finish."

"Fine. Finish." He had no idea how out of control her heart was racing right now.

"I've been restless for a very long time. And I've been looking for something to settle me down. I was pretty sure I'd found it at Warren Sill. Being wooed by the big boys?" He sighed, shook his head. "That was heady stuff, darlin'. Heady. But it didn't do anything but hose me up even worse."

She frowned. "I don't understand—"

"And you never will if you don't stop cutting me off."

She glared up at him. "Are you being a shit again?"

At that, he grinned. "Just being me, and trying to tell you how much I love you while I'm still able to talk here."

"You love me?" Her heart throbbed; her eyes watered. "You love me?"

"Darlin', I love you so much that it's about to kill me." Doug's eyes grew red-rimmed and misty. "You were what I was looking for, and you were right here all the time."

"Yeah. I was," she managed to whisper.

"I'm hoping you'll stay for a while."

"I'm not going anywhere."

"Neither am I. In fact…" He lifted a shoulder and rubbed it over one eye. And then he took the twisted nail and slid it like a ring over the third finger of her left hand. "In fact, I was sorta hoping we could stay here a while together. You and me. But you and me as a couple.''

''A couple?'' She wasn't sure she still knew how to breathe. ''You and me?''

''You did say you wanted to marry me,'' he said, holding her hand as if he feared she'd bolt. ''I don't really care whether or not you were drunk. I accept your proposal.''

''Doug?'' Kinsey looked from the ring on her finger to his face. His smile was crooked, but his eyes were sincere. She couldn't find her voice to save her life.

''I'm actually flying to Tulsa tomorrow to see my folks for the day. I'd really like it if you went with me.''

Her answer remained lost in the back of her throat, caught by the suction of the emotional whirlwind sweeping her along.

''Thing is, I'd need to know whether or not to introduce you to my parents as friend or fiancée.'' His expression grew uncertain, and she knew he was waiting for her answer. ''We can have as long an engagement as you'd like. Or we can go to Vegas.''

God, but she loved this man. Her grin broke out, widening until her face began to ache. ''We don't have to go to Vegas.''

''What do you mean?'' he asked with a frown.

''We can go back to the building site and find Leonard. He is an ordained minister, you know.''

It took a moment, a moment during which Kinsey felt doubts fall away like the last five pounds she'd never managed to shed.

But once Doug realized what she'd said, he grabbed her up and swung her around and around until the giddy dizziness threatened her with a return visit from the coffee she'd gulped down on the drive over.

"Stop, please."

He set her down. "I take it that was a yes?"

"Hey, I was the one who proposed, remember?" Unable to keep the smile from her face and not caring that, as wide as it was, she must resemble a clown, she placed her hand on Doug's face. "I love you, Doug Storey. I've loved you for so very long."

"Ah, darlin'. I've probably loved you even longer." He laid his palm over her hand, looking down into her eyes before he grabbed her and pulled her into a hug. "And I promise to buy you a real ring ASAP."

"I kinda like this one." She eased around so that she remained in his arms, but was able to admire her ten-penny ring. "The nail that secured our relationship. Very symbolic. And sentimental."

"And clunky and heavy and dangerous."

She nestled her head beneath his chin. "Afraid I'll stab you in the middle of the night?"

"I'll be doing the middle-of-the-night stabbing, if you don't mind."

She couldn't hold in her grin. "I really do need at least seven or eight hours of sleep, you know."

He gave a shrug and wrapped her back up in his arms. "Hey, the more time in bed, the better."

Engulfed by a rush of amazing joy, Kinsey didn't even punch him for his sex joke or try to hide her tears. "I love you, Doug."

"You damn well better, darlin'." He brushed the dampness from her cheeks. "Now, how about we go find ourselves a preacher?"

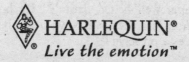

If you enjoyed what you just read,
then we've got an offer you can't resist!

Take 2 bestselling
love stories FREE!
Plus get a FREE surprise gift!

Clip this page and mail it to Harlequin Reader Service®

IN U.S.A.
3010 Walden Ave.
P.O. Box 1867
Buffalo, N.Y. 14240-1867

IN CANADA
P.O. Box 609
Fort Erie, Ontario
L2A 5X3

YES! Please send me 2 free Blaze™ novels and my free surprise gift. After receiving them, if I don't wish to receive anymore, I can return the shipping statement marked cancel. If I don't cancel, I will receive 4 brand-new novels each month, before they're available in stores! In the U.S.A., bill me at the bargain price of $3.80 plus 25¢ shipping and handling per book and applicable sales tax, if any*. In Canada, bill me at the bargain price of $4.21 plus 25¢ shipping and handling per book and applicable taxes**. That's the complete price and a savings of at least 10% off the cover prices—what a great deal! I understand that accepting the 2 free books and gift places me under no obligation ever to buy any books. I can always return a shipment and cancel at any time. Even if I never buy another book from Harlequin, the 2 free books and gift are mine to keep forever.

150 HDN DNWD
350 HDN DNWE

Name	(PLEASE PRINT)	
Address	Apt.#	
City	State/Prov.	Zip/Postal Code

* Terms and prices subject to change without notice. Sales tax applicable in N.Y.
** Canadian residents will be charged applicable provincial taxes and GST.
   All orders subject to approval. Offer limited to one per household and not valid to
   current Blaze™ subscribers.
   ® are registered trademarks of Harlequin Enterprises Limited.

BLZ02-R

An offer you can't afford to refuse!

High-valued coupons for upcoming books

A sneak peek at Harlequin's newest line— Harlequin Flipside™

Send away for a hardcover by *New York Times* bestselling author Debbie Macomber

How can you get all this?

Buy four Harlequin or Silhouette books during October–December 2003, fill out the form below and send the form and four proofs of purchase (cash register receipts) to the address below.

I accept this amazing offer!
Send me a coupon booklet:

Name (PLEASE PRINT)

Address   Apt. #

City   State/Prov.   Zip/Postal Code
                                                                                            098 KIN DXHT

Please send this form, along with your cash register receipts
as proofs of purchase, to:

In the U.S.:
Harlequin Coupon Booklet Offer, P.O. Box 9071, Buffalo, NY 14269-9071

In Canada:
Harlequin Coupon Booklet Offer, P.O. Box 609, Fort Erie, Ontario L2A 5X3

Allow 4–6 weeks for delivery. Offer expires December 31, 2003.
Offer good only while quantities last.

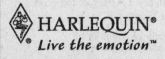

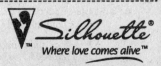

Visit us at www.eHarlequin.com

Q42003

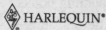

HARLEQUIN® *Blaze*™

HARLEQUIN® *Temptation*®

Single in South Beach

Nightlife on the Strip just got a little hotter!

Join author Joanne Rock as she takes you to Miami Beach
and its hottest new singles playground. Club Paradise
has opened for business and the women in charge are
determined to succeed at all costs. So what will they
do with the sexy men who show up at the club?

SEX & THE SINGLE GIRL
Harlequin Blaze #104
September 2003

GIRL'S GUIDE TO HUNTING & KISSING
Harlequin Blaze #108
October 2003

ONE NAUGHTY NIGHT
Harlequin Temptation #951
November 2003

Don't miss these red-hot stories from Joanne Rock!
Watch for the sizzling nightlife to continue in spring 2004.

Look for these books at your favorite retail outlet.

Visit us at www.eHarlequin.com

HBSSB

COMING NEXT MONTH

#109 FLAVOR OF THE MONTH Tori Carrington
Kiss & Tell, Bk. 2

Four friends. Countless secrets… Pastry shop owner Reilly Cudowski
has spent most of her life squelching her secret cravings. But when delicious
Benjamin Kane shows up, she can't help indulging a little.
Only, the more she has Ben, the more she wants. So what else can
Reilly do but convince him that a lifetime of desserts can be even sweet-
er…?

#110 OVER THE EDGE Jeanie London

After ten years of patient planning, Mallory Hunt finally has Jake Trinity
right where she wants him. He's contracted her security expertise, and
while she's at it, she'll push *his* sensual edges. Their long-ago first meeting—
and its steamy kiss—changed her life, and now it's time
for payback. But Mallory doesn't count on the intense heat between
them or the fact she doesn't *want* this to end!

#111 YOURS TO SEDUCE Karen Anders
Women Who Dare, Bk. 2

When firefighter Lana Dempsey finally tackles fellow firefighter
Sean O'Neill in the…showers, it's a five-alarm blaze. Stripped of their uni-
forms, it's what Lana's always wanted. Having had a crush on Sean since
forever, she'd never been brave enough to do anything about it. Until the
bet she'd made with her girlfriends gives her the courage
to finally squelch that burning desire for Sean!

#112 ANYTHING GOES… Debbi Rawlins

Seven days of sun, sand and sex, sex, sex! That's exactly what
Carly Saunders needs—anonymous sex…and lots of it. She has
one week of sin before she heads home to a teaching job—and her
place as the pastor's daughter. So she's going to make this week count.
Only, she never dreams she'll meet Rick, her best friend growing up.
Or that he'll have the same agenda…

Visit us at www.eHarlequin.com